The charge was
MURDER!

Heading toward Colonel North was a small,
scowling Thai officer with a large
businesslike gun at his hip. The small man
raised himself to the top of his
five-foot-one height and asked in a
piping voice, "Misser Chahss Boyden, pliss?"

North's disguise left him no
choice. "That's me—I'm Charles Boyden."

"I Cappain Pilanung Pokh, Bangkok Imperial
Troop. You under arrest, pliss."

"Arrest! On what charge?"

The Thai's brown eyes bored up
into the Colonel's. "You under arrest
for murder, pliss!"

Secret Mission to Bangkok, one of
Colonel North's most dangerous assignments, was
originally published by Doubleday & Company, Inc.,
at $3.95.

Other books by Van Wyck Mason

*Published by Pocket Books, Inc., in a CARDINAL edition.

†Published by Pocket Books, Inc., in a POCKET BOOK edition.

**Published by Pocket Books, Inc., in a GIANT CARDINAL edition.

VAN WYCK MASON

SECRET MISSION TO Bangkok

POCKET
BOOKS,
INC.,
NEW YORK

SECRET MISSION TO BANGKOK

Doubleday edition published January, 1960

POCKET BOOK edition published May, 1961
1st printing.......................March, 1961

L

POCKET BOOK editions are distributed in the U.S. by Affiliated Publishers, Inc., 630 Fifth Avenue, New York 20, N.Y.

SECRET MISSION TO BANGKOK

CHAPTER 1

1.

THAI AIRLINES FLIGHT 184, Hong Kong to
Bangkok, had a full load that day. There were thirty-four
names on the passenger list besides that of Mr. Charles Boyden, New York, N. Y.

"Charles Boyden" actually was Colonel Hugh North of
the U. S. Army's Intelligence Division, G-2, and Hugh was
not in his usual agreeable frame of mind. He did not object
to travel but he privately deemed it a damned shame that
G-2 had practically had to drop everything to safeguard an
old man who was recklessly chasing after a young and beautiful runaway wife.

Besides "Boyden," the passenger list included these names
that were branded in Hugh's memory by the events that followed:

      MISS LITA NALINE, HOLLYWOOD, CALIF.

      MR. ANTON CARSS, HOLLYWOOD, CALIF.

      MR. JOHN WALLEN, DITTO.

      MR. LEX ROSS, DITTO.

      MR. CHU HOONG, HONG KONG.

      M. GEORGES MARCHET, CHOLON, SOUTH VIETNAM.

      FRAULEIN MARY HOLLBERG, WEST BERLIN, GERMANY.

      MR. BORIS SALENKOV, MOSCOW, U.S.S.R.

      MR. HENRY BARROWS, WASHINGTON, D.C.

This "Mr. Henry Barrows" was the old man with the errant
wife, the one responsible for Hugh North being aboard the

1

Thai airliner. Stripped of his pseudonym, he was Dr. Hans Bracht, the world's foremost authority on space travel, the intercontinental ballistics missile genius the Reds would give the spire of the Kremlin to lay hands on.

2.

Colonel North settled himself in his seat beside Mary Hollberg aboard the Bangkok plane and cast one fleeting glance across the aisle and down one space before he turned his eyes to look past Fräulein Hollberg's well-carved profile to watch the departure bustle outside on Hong Kong's Kaitak Airport.

His man was where he was supposed to be, in Seat 4, cater-cornered from Hugh's Seat 5, from which he could be best covered against all possible eventualities.

Bracht should have been protected by a platoon of security guards. Instead, there was only Hugh North presently standing between the doctor and possible kidnaping or even assassination, and Hugh would have been the first to admit that this was not good.

North had never complained about too much of a job being loaded on his broad shoulders but if he ever had, this assignment certainly would have been the one to evoke the protest. It was bad enough that the man most wanted by the enemies of the free world should be guarded by a lone G-2 operative but it was worse that this agent must, above all, keep Dr. Bracht from suspecting that he was being protected at all!

Add to this weird setup the fact that Bracht apparently was blindly pursuing a runaway wife young enough to be his daughter, certainly, and possibly his granddaughter, entirely oblivious to the danger he invited, and it could be understood why Hugh North felt the new gray hairs being added to the patches at his temples.

And if that wasn't enough, aboard this plane was an assortment of characters guaranteed to out-Wonderland Lewis Carroll. There was Lita Naline, the sloe-eyed, slope-hipped motion-picture star with the spectacular reputation for man grabbing. There was the fabulously temperamental director-producer, Anton Carss, and a couple of the biggest names among male movie stars, Lex Ross and John Wallen. There was Chu Hoong, the multimillionaire maker of that boon to mankind, Dragon's Tooth Elixir. There was this pretty, curvaceous Mary Hollberg, who sat beside North, and there was Comrade Boris Salenkov, who needed only a little more fullness to his walrus mustache to be the perfect image of his obvious hero, Joseph Vissarionovich Stalin.

All we need to make it complete, Hugh told himself, *is the four Marx Brothers chasing the stewardess up and down the aisle.*

It was about at this time that Hugh North became aware of the fact that Fräulein Mary Hollberg was on the make. Quite definitely. She could have been wriggling to make herself more comfortable in the plane seat, but if she was she must have decided that Hugh's place on the aisle was the one she must have, the way she pressed closer to the G-2 colonel with each move.

North sighed inwardly. Why was it that each time a beauty made a pass in his direction (or almost every time) he was on a job that would require his full attention? If he was bound for home, say, at the end of a job, his seatmate would almost certainly be a scrawny missionary-type female or a fat man who snored; when he was on a mission like this there was very apt to be a luscious doll like Fräulein Mary Hollberg at hand. Or at least at hip.

Still, a man had to be polite, G-2 operative or not. Hugh turned his best smile on the girl. "These seats are not too wide, are they, Fräulein?" he asked in perfect German.

Mary had china-blue eyes, a complexion such as the ads often promise but seldom deliver, a smile that was slow and wide and very, very guileless.

"You speak German very well, *mein Herr,*" she offered. "Is it perhaps that you are of my country?"

"No, but I have spent many hours in Germany, some pleasant, some not so pleasant."

The blue, blue eyes clouded for an instant. "Ah, the war,"

3

Mary Hollberg mourned. Then she brightened. "But that is far behind us now, *nicht wahr?* Now we are friends, allies, you Americans and we of West Berlin—allies against such pigs as that Russian monster who sits behind us, that Salenkov."

Hugh used his smile for an answer. Mary Hollberg, encouraged, continued. "But one day the Russians will be gone. One day there will be no more East or West Berlin and everything will be as it once was."

"Before Hitler," Hugh could not help adding.

The blue eyes clouded again momentarily, then Mary shrugged. "My family were never Nazis," she recited. "I was but a little girl, but I remember my father cursing the Nazis, even though he was not interested in politics. He was an artist, such as I am in my modest way."

"Artist?" Hugh murmured.

"I am a pianist," Mary Hollberg explained. "I am making a concert tour of the Asian cities." She waved a shapely hand, and a large emerald winked. "There is not much money, but one sees the world, eh?"

"So you're a pianist," North breathed in awe, and to himself he said: *In a pig's eye.*

For the hand that Mary Hollberg had waved so expressively was tipped by long, sharp-pointed carmine nails. Hugh North admittedly knew little about classical music, but he knew enough to know that those fingernails would have been anathema to any concert pianist even if they had been strong enough to survive the first chord, *pianissimo.*

So Mary Hollberg was not what she said she was. Which meant that she was what? An East German, perhaps, a beautiful Commie agent who was on this plane because Hans Bracht was aboard, who was making her hip-wriggle approach to him because she suspected or even knew that he, Colonel Hugh North, G-2, was the man she must get out of the way to get to Hans Bracht?

The warning gong sounded in Hugh's brain. *Watch it, lad!*

Outside, the boarding stage was being wheeled away and

4

the first of the Thai airliner's four engines spluttered into life. The take-off from Kaitak was already twenty minutes late and most of those twenty minutes had been consumed by a swift and thorough search of every piece of baggage loaded aboard the plane. Some delicate points of law might have been bruised in the use of skeleton keys on the passengers' luggage but the British authorities at Hong Kong had agreed with North that the niceties could be overlooked when the alternative might well be the planting of a bomb intended to blow Dr. Hans Bracht—and incidentally everybody else on the plane—into eternity.

The ancient city of Bangkok, according to the coded information furnished Hugh by G-2 headquarters, would be the place where, if all went well and the people who wanted so desperately to capture or kill him were frustrated, Dr. Hans Bracht would find Tao Muong, be reconciled with her, and—pray heaven—take her back to the United States to resume his position as head of the Army's Project Galaxy, the most ambitious intercontinental space ballistics program ever attempted. Now the airliner began trundling toward the end of the runway, destination Bangkok, last stop on a wild, reckless journey that had carried Bracht halfway around the world, an exposed target for the forces of evil who would capture or kill him.

From Hong Kong's Kaitak Airport to Cape Canaveral, Florida, is more than a walk around the corner for a pack of cigarettes, but it is necessary to go back to the Cape because it all started there.

At 11:04 of a bright, hot Florida morning, to be exact. That was when Hans Bracht had toppled off a high stool in his laboratory and landed on the floor with a crash that the guards outside the door later said must have been heard in Cocoa Beach, eight miles away.

The guards' first thought was that the enemy had somehow gotten to Dr. Bracht. Their fear was a natural one; nobody had any illusions about the lengths to which the Reds would go to get this man.

"I hit the big alarm first thing," one guard told his su-

5

periors later, "and then I got out my gun. We kicked open the door and went in ready for anything. We knew the place didn't have any windows, no way in except past us, but for a second when we saw Doc lyin' there I guess we all thought the same thing; jeez, now the Commies had invisible suits or something and they came past everybody without anybody seein' 'em!"

It proved to be nothing quite so Buck Rogers. In fact the alarm bells, the sirens, the Signal Red Alert, the roadblocks, the readying of the Nikes and other ground-to-air missiles, the whining take-off of the jet umbrella squadron were all followed by an embarrassed All Clear, False Alarm.

Dr. Hans Bracht, it developed, had merely fainted.

Because of that giddy spell Colonel Hugh North, G-2, was now headed for Bangkok, riding herd on the most difficult ward it had ever been his misfortune to be assigned to keep alive and out of the hands of the cleverest, most ruthless agents world communism could mobilize.

From where he sat, Hugh got a three-quarter view of the man he must protect. Bracht had shaved off the beard that had been his chief distinguishing feature and although the scientist must have thought that this constituted a baffling disguise, North was sure he must scream his identity to everybody who looked at him.

There was no disguising the hooded eyes behind the spectacles, the beaked nose, the domed, bald forehead, the frizzy side and back hair that identified the Big Brain. Hans Bracht's photograph had appeared on a thousand front pages; his name was synonymous with rockets, intercontinental missiles, space travel, a story-book career.

The man had a fantastic background. Born an Alsatian, he had been one of Hitler's top rocket men in the early days of World War II. Midway in the war he had dared defect from the Nazis and—almost unbelievably—he had escaped Germany. After the war, and long after he had been given up for dead by both the Gestapo who hunted him and the Allied Intelligence men who sought him as tirelessly, he had reap-

6

peared in Bangkok of all places, complete with a tiny Annamite or Siamese bride, Tao Muong.

Bracht's first announcement after his emergence from limbo was that he wanted to become an American citizen and work for the free world against the disciples of totalitarianism. There was a terrific hassle, but even in 1945 there had been enough farsighted men in high circles who knew the potential value of the missile man to override the fierce objections. Hans Bracht was admitted to the United States and given citizenship; after a probationary period he had been allowed more and more authority until now he was head of the Army's Project Galaxy.

Tao Muong had become an American citizen, too, and surely one of the most delightful ever to be naturalized. Tiny, with a fragile oriental beauty that contrasted so directly with her husband's bearded, hawk-beaked, bald-headed ruggedness, Tao Muong had been hailed with delight by Bracht's colleagues as a welcome contrast to the usual females found at physicists' functions. Perhaps the hailing had been too joyful because Bracht, after the first few public affairs, had withdrawn his little beauty from the public view.

Hans Bracht was jealous and perhaps he had reason to be. He was somewhere in his tough, leathery sixties while Tao Muong was—well, it was anybody's guess as to just how old she was, but it could not be half her husband's age. She was as friendly as a kitten with everybody. That included some promising young scientists, assistants of Dr. Bracht, who had not yet let the complexities of logarithms blind them to the pursuit of more obvious pleasures.

So, North mused as he pretended to read a magazine, the elderly husband had tried to hold his young wife a prisoner and the wife had finally rebelled. From what G-2 had been able to learn, working with a secrecy usually reserved for more world-shaking problems, Tao Muong had run away from her Cape Canaveral apartment sometime during a weekend during which her husband had been tied to his laboratory with a test launching. Hans Bracht had kept his wife's disappearance a secret for at least a week, hoping she would come back, and then the strain had been too much. He had

7

collapsed with the crash that had alerted the Cape in the aforementioned Signal Red.

The best doctors the Army, Navy, and Air Force could muster had worked over Bracht and had found the genius close to complete nervous exhaustion. A grateful government was prepared to do anything to help its top missile man's recovery, but even so the Pentagon and the White House boggled at Bracht's demands:

"I must go away for a while. Nobody can follow me; I will not have a single security guard trailing after me. If you do not do this I won't work on Project Galaxy another day."

There had been nothing to do but agree, not with the nation's space and missile programs depending so heavily on the man who demanded these concessions. Bracht was given a free hand to travel where he would despite the staggering risk. The Kremlin wanted Bracht as a captive scientist; the Reds' alternative goal might well be to have him killed, thus removing the free world's greatest genius in his field. Yet Hans Bracht must be permitted to wander only God knew where, alone and unguarded by the forces of civilization that needed him so desperately.

Well, not entirely unguarded. The Army's G-2, a body of men about whom Bracht knew nothing and with whom the scientist had had no previous contact (at least none that *he* knew about) was put on the job of keeping Bracht alive and out of Communist hands. It was a calculated risk and a big one. Let Bracht discover he was being tailed and the unpredictable genius might do almost anything—go on a sit-down strike, even turn on his adopted country and defect to communism; there was no telling.

A G-2 agent was aboard the plane that took Bracht from Florida to San Francisco. Another flew with him to Hawaii, a third to Manila. That was where Hugh North took over with orders to carry on to Hong Kong and Bangkok, where it was assumed little Tao Muong had gone to ground.

North sighed again. The Army's immense Project Galaxy, a program intended to eclipse even the most feverish speculations of the wildest science-fiction pulp-magazine writer, was being sabotaged by a family quarrel. But no usual mister and missus spat, this. It was doubtful that ever before had a wife fled halfway around the world to go home to Mother. It was just as doubtful that a man with so many brains ever before had deliberately put his life and freedom in such jeopardy as Bracht had in blundering into a country where a Red agent could be found behind every third banyan tree.

"By now," the G-2 colonel told himself darkly, "they must be elbowing for ambush space in Bangkok, no matter how well Washington thinks it's kept the whole lousy deal a secret. And Little Miss Paderewski here may well have beaten them all to a front seat."

When North had taken over his assignment in Manila he had hoped to strike up a conversation (with luck an acquaintance) with Bracht before the plane reached Hong Kong. In this he had failed miserably; his few attempts to start even the most casual fellow-traveler chat had been brusquely, scowlingly rejected by the space scientist. Then, after the brief stopover at Hong Kong, any chance he might have had to break down Bracht's cold reserve had gone glimmering. That was when the *Tiger, Tiger!* company had come bustling, chattering, laughing, shrieking, aboard the Thai Airlines plane.

The *Tiger, Tiger!* company, all who understood English were immediately informed, was on its way to Thailand, where the superepic to end all superepics was to be filmed under the direction of the great Anton Carss himself. The company had been marooned for several days in Hong Kong (although "marooned" is hardly the word, not for one kept in that exciting city) by a quirk of Carss's renowned temperament; the director for reasons known only to himself had refused to move on to Siam on schedule. But now the dark mood was broken, the *Tiger, Tiger!* company was on its way, and move over, everybody—make way for the gods and goddesses of the silver screen!

If Hans Bracht had been in a shell before that, he was down in that shell's cyclone cellar now. Hugh North had given up his idea of wangling his way into the older man's confidence during the air journey to Bangkok. He would have to play it at a distance and rely on the luck that had smiled

9

on him so often during his long career—and which had turned its back as often when it had been desperately needed.

"Ah, look," said Fräulein Hollberg, with still another wriggle. "Is the setting sun not beautiful on the water? Here, lean over me and look down, *mein Herr*—you cannot see it from where you sit."

Hugh obliged. After all, it was improbable that this girl would slug him behind the ear at this stage of the game, and it was very nice to relax a moment against all that soft loveliness, so invitingly proffered. Mary Hollberg wore a piquant perfume, too, and as she maneuvered herself to give North a better view of the beautiful sunset the scent came up in a wave from her young body.

"Wonderful," Hugh muttered as he straightened. And, brief as it had been, it was.

The G-2 colonel had barely gotten his pulse back in order when up the aisle past him came a man in a wrinkled linen suit, the man identified by the passenger list as Georges Marchet of Cholon, South Vietnam. North had marked Marchet well, as he had marked all the people boarding the plane at Hong Kong. He was the obvious French planter, rice or rubber, with the Indochina planter's gauntness, the malaria-yellowed complexion, the too-bright eyes that bespoke a resort to drugs, opium, or something stronger.

When North had first scanned Marchet he had been struck by the thought that the man was perhaps a bit *too* obviously the French planter in Indochina, on the smoke. It was almost as though he had dressed for the part and acted a role down to the finest nuance, the dirty-nailed, frayed-collared look of a man who had succumbed to dope in the heat and the loneliness.

And if he was acting—ahh, North had sighed, they might all be acting, the French planter, the Chinese patent-medicine king or even the American movie star. Any of them could be a Red agent, a Commie killer.

As Marchet walked past him on his way forward, North moved imperceptibly. When the Frenchman stopped beside Bracht's seat the G-2 colonel's hand was on the snub-nosed

.38 he wore at his armpit. It would be unusual for a Red agent to walk up and murder a man so deliberately and amateurishly, but one could never be sure in this business. Let Marchet make one move toward any of his pockets and the .38 would be out and ready to speak.

Georges Marchet did not reach for a weapon. Instead, he put a hand on the back of the scientist's seat and leaned down toward the missile expert.

"Your pardon, monsieur," the Frenchman said—seemed to bellow—in heavily accented English, "but do I not recognize you as one I knew well in Indochina during the war?"

3.

"Oh-oh," Hugh said inwardly. "Already we've got old chums."

The airliner was a pressurized job, which meant the engine noises did not penetrate this cabin enough to drown out Marchet's voice. Everybody on the plane must have heard what Marchet had said; everybody would hear what Marchet would say if he were permitted to keep talking and that might well be the identification of "Mr. Henry Barrows" as Dr. Hans Bracht.

The colonel saw Bracht jerk erect in his seat as he swung his face about to meet Marchet's stare. The physicist's face was the color of putty, his jaw sagged, and fear stared out of his dark eyes behind the spectacles. Still, he made an awkward effort to cling to his incognito once the shock of Marchet's greeting faded.

"You must be mistaken," he managed. "I don't know you, sir. My name's Barrows—Henry Barrows."

The planter shook his head, his too-brilliant eyes pinned on the man in the seat. "I did not know you by that name," he said. "But you used many names, did you not? It has been a long time and my memory is not what it once was, but let me think what you told me your real name was, *mon ami.*"

The man in the wrinkled white suit brushed a long hand down

the side of his face uncertainly. "Let me think—ah yes, I remember now. You told me you were—"

Hugh North was out of his seat by that time and across the aisle, moving around Marchet and getting halfway between the Frenchman and the scientist as the planter bent closer, recognition lighting his face. At Hugh's interruption, Marchet drew back, his dawning smile fading to be replaced by a frown.

"What is the meaning of this, monsieur?" he demanded with a grasp at dignity that was almost ludicrous in a man so shopworn. "I am conversing with my friend, the good Doctor—"

"This gentleman has told you that you've mistaken him for someone else," North said in low-pitched, penetrating French. "You'll have the kindness to return to your seat quietly, monsieur, and avoid unpleasantness."

Marchet took a backward step, drawing himself up to his full angular height. "What do you mean?" he cried in his native tongue. "Is it a crime to address an old friend, one with whom I have shared wartime adventures? Who are you to interfere here, monsieur?" With which, incongruously, the Frenchman put a hand to his face to sneeze.

Hugh North was sure now that Marchet was a drug addict. The planter bore all the signs, the dilated pupils, the sniffs that punctuated his speech, the uncertain facial muscles, and, most of all, that sneeze, the almost inevitable telltale sign of a drug addict under stress.

The Intelligence colonel had been well taught by experience to work fast with the tools at hand. He leaned closer to Marchet, lowered his voice another notch. "Come, come, Monsieur Marchet," he barely muttered, still in French, "we have been very lenient with you, we of the International Department. Do not force us to deal with you as a disorderly addict who must be hospitalized, his drugs cut off. Return to your seat at once, sir, and stop annoying this gentleman. Quickly, quickly!"

It worked, as North had been almost sure it would. Hugh had no idea what "International Department" would be interested in a seedy, down-at-the-heel planter who was on the smoke or the needle, but he had banked on Marchet's fear of any authority that might threaten his precious drug dreams. The official air in which the G-2 colonel had couched his warning was enough; Marchet did not tarry to find out just which "International Department" North represented or to offer any denial that he was an addict. The Frenchman gaped at Hugh, his quivering jaw sagging, then turned and blindly scurried down the aisle to his seat near the tail of the plane.

"Hey," Hugh North heard Lita Naline exclaim. "What gives here, anyway? Why's the big bully scarin' the skinny guy?"

"Be quiet, Lita," said Anton Carss, his voice heavy and faintly accented. "Do not get us all involved in something that does not concern us. We have work to do and I'll not have us delayed further by . . ."

His voice dropped away to a murmur. Glancing back toward the movie party, Hugh saw that the squat, dark-faced director had dropped an arm about Lita's shoulders and was murmuring in her ear. The movie star's luminous dark eyes rose to meet North's squarely, then slid away.

"Okay, okay," the G-2 colonel heard her tell Carss. "I'll be good, Anton. Lita will be a good little girl for her poopsy."

Repressing a wince at the description of Anton Carss as anybody's poopsy, North switched his glance to the Russian, Salenkov. The man from Moscow had his thick-lensed glasses pointed at Bracht, but it was impossible for the colonel to read any expression in the Russian's face. The man's walrus mustache, his boarish features made him a hard man to make out, and Hugh gained nothing from that passing glance before he turned to go back to his seat beside Mary Hollberg.

He started across the aisle when there was the touch of a hand at his wrist.

"Sit down," said the greatest ballistics missile genius the world had ever known. "Sit down beside me."

And, as North slid down into the seat, Bracht added in a voice barely above a whisper: "I suppose you're from Security and I told them—but I may need you, after all."

13

4.

Hugh grimaced inwardly at the thought of what G-2 head-quarters would say when it learned that its top operative, Hugh North, had been forced to disclose himself to Hans Bracht as a bodyguard within hours of taking over the assignment of protecting "Mr. Henry Barrows."

That damned Marchet! Why did a man whom Bracht must have known during those silent years in Southeast Asia have to be on this plane? From his looks, the Frenchman could not afford many plane trips; why, oh why, did he have to come aboard this Hong Kong-Bangkok airliner?

One fairly obvious thing had come out of the brief encounter; Georges Marchet was no Red agent, whatever else he might be. Even the clumsiest MVD man (and Hugh had met up with some incredibly heavy-footed specimens) would have handled his mission better than that. Yes, Georges Marchet could be put down for what he was, a French planter with a drug habit, dangerous only because he had recognized Hans Bracht and might tell others who "Mr. Henry Barrows" really was.

Not that any Soviet agent on this plane would be likely to need the introduction. No, if Mary Hollberg or Boris Salenkov were on Bracht's tail, waiting for the chance to put the snatch on the scientist, they would have been fully briefed, they would know their man from the moment they caught sight of him. But if Salenkov and Hollberg were not Red agents, if the Commies had not yet caught up with Bracht, Marchet's blabbing could be disastrous. Nobody was more untrustworthy than a drug addict; in Bangkok, where there almost certainly must be Soviet agents waiting, Marchet could give his identification of Bracht in places where it could cause real trouble.

"You are from Security, aren't you?" Hans Bracht murmured in an undertone.

"I can't talk now," the G-2 colonel said swiftly. "I'll explain when we get to Bangkok. But I *am* your friend."

The missile genius turned his large, bespectacled eyes on

14

the colonel, suspicion replacing the fear that had been there. "How do I know?" he asked bluntly. "Who can I trust?"

Hugh repressed the anger that stirred faintly. This tall, balding man with the faint accent certainly switched from fears to surliness in a hurry. A couple of seconds before he had looked panic-stricken; now he was demanding assurances from the one who had rescued him from Marchet, in a manner of speaking.

Remember, this man's under a strain, Hugh told himself. *His wife's disappearance has cracked him up.*

"I'm afraid you'll just have to take me on faith for the time being," he told Bracht, and accompanied the remark with a brilliant smile for the benefit of any eyes that might be watching them. "I'll show you my credentials in Bangkok. Right now I'd better get back to my seat. Much safer for both of us."

For a second Bracht seemed on the verge of asking North to stay with him but then the scientist's lip curled and he turned toward the window.

"Go ahead, *policeman,*" he grunted. "I don't care what you do."

Hugh kept his smile intact as he got up, nodded cheerily at the back of Bracht's head, and returned to his seat beside Mary Hollberg. He had expected no effusive thanks from the missile genius, having heard of Bracht's reputation for rudeness, but there had been a note of something approaching contempt in the other man's tone that did not sit well with North, however he might hide his resentment. A nice, personable guy, this Hans Bracht.

"What was it that he called you?" Mary Hollberg asked. "A *policeman?*"

"Uh-uh." Hugh grinned. "Anything but that. He said something about calling a policeman if that fellow bothered him in Bangkok."

It was pretty lame but it would have to do, even though North knew Mary Hollberg was not convinced in the least. The German girl eyed him speculatively for a moment before she turned to the window again. North pretended to doze while from beneath his lids he saw the woman beside him revolve the ring with the big emerald around and around a slender finger with the give-away long nail. Fräulein Hollberg, then, was doing some heavy thinking. She might even be wondering if she had gotten away with that concert pianist gag. *If* Mary really was an MVD agent, Moscow must be slipping; in the old days the Reds would have gotten hold of a real concert pianist for the role, thrown the person she held dearest into the clink, and told the pianist that she would do this job for them or the loved one would die, very slowly, very painfully. They wouldn't have sent out a wriggle-butt girl who fell flat on her face the first time she tried to put over her story.

There was a new crowd in Russian Intelligence these days, Hugh reminded himself; perhaps the latest occupants of the seats once held by Beria & Company had new methods that entailed the use of such agents as Mary Hollberg for reasons yet to be analyzed. Maybe, too, that was why such an obvious Russky as Boris Salenkov was on this job, a downright caricature of what the world thought a Communist commissar looked like. They'd both bear watching, Mary Hollberg and Boris Salenkov.

As though she knew North was speculating on her real role aboard this Bangkok plane, Fräulein Hollberg stirred in her seat, half rose. "Pardon me, *mein Herr,*" she murmured, and slid past Hugh—with what seemed more than necessary pressure of her leg against his knees—and went down the aisle to the Ladies'. Hugh did not turn but he would have liked to watch her pass Boris Salenkov. Did she signal the Russian? Did Boris change that stolid expression one iota when his eyes caught hers?

The G-2 colonel had little time to wonder about this. Hardly had Mary left when Lita Naline arrived, preceded by a wave of some kind of expensive perfume that was overpowering and aphrodisiac.

"I'm sure I've met you somewhere," the movie star said, and with no more preface than that moved past North's knees to drop into Hollberg's place beside Hugh.

Oh hell! This was getting to be ridiculous. How did a man, even G-2's most accomplished agent, tell one of the screen's

16

loveliest stars to move her famed fanny back where it had come from? Answer: he didn't. Hugh North acted the role of the overwhelmed male and beamed fatuously upon Miss Lita Naline.

She was quite something to beam upon, was Lita. According to her publicity, she was an East Indian, strongly hinted but never baldly claimed as being the natural daughter of a maharajah. Not too long before, this glamorous story had been disputed by a scandal rag which claimed she had been born Lily Novotny in Danbury, Connecticut, but Lita apparently had not let the exposure cramp her style. She affected turban headgears featured by a blazing ruby the size of a hen's egg and clanking jewelry of Hindu design. She did not, however, go so far as to wear a sari. At present she was clad in satin that might have been a coat of paint and which left nothing of her statistical excellence to Hugh's imagination.

As she pressed a warm hip against North (the second warm hip to have impressed itself against North's since this trip began) she gave him her famous long, lazy smile, dropped her heavily fringed eyes, and murmured: "I know I'm shameless to be so bold but I *had* to talk to you."

"Pleasure, I'm sure," Hugh gargled in approved style.

"I'm Lita Naline."

"I know, I know." North gave a snorted giggle. "Guess any man in the world would recognize *you*, Miss Naline. Uh —you going back home, are you?"

"Home?" Lita's eyebrows shot upward toward the rim of her cloth-of-gold turban. "Oh, you mean India? Well, no. No, we're on our way to Thailand"—she pronounced it Thay-land—"to make an epic, *Tiger, Tiger!* Anton and dear Jack and Lex, the four of us, and of course the minor roles and technicians. The crew's in Bangkok and on location already, some of them, and Anton—that's my fabulous Anton Carss back there, you know—Anton says this is going to be his best effort. His very best. He promised me. Dear Poopsy."

She leaned a fraction of an inch closer to Hugh and one of her much publicized statistics burned into his arm. "Did you see *The Fleshly and the Doomed?*" she asked.

"No—uh—no, I'm afraid I missed that one," Hugh confessed. (As a matter of fact, North's duties seldom gave him a chance to see a movie that was not at least ten years old and garnished with native language subtitles screamed at the top of the translator's voice. Hugh always said that the struggle between an antiquated English sound track and a native translator in full cry was one of the most unnerving experiences known to man.)

"A great pity," Lita murmured. "They say it was Anton's best effort since *Scum,* the one he did in Italy. It was the first time he ever directed me, you know. In *Fleshly,* I mean. That perfectly silly Italian girl, what's-her-name, was in *Scum.* And, boy, did she louse it up!"

"Uh-huh," Hugh nodded solemnly. "I know."

"And you—why are you going to Bangkok?"

North spread his hands, hunched his shoulders. "Business," he explained apologetically.

"Oh? What kind of business?"

Hugh shrugged again. "Nothing that would interest you, I'm afraid," he said. "Nothing like being a movie star." He paused and tagged on a heavy gallantry. "The greatest star on the screen today, I might add."

The heavy lashes dropped again. "Why, thank you," the woman chirruped softly. "But I'm afraid you're an awful flatterer, Mr.—"

"Boyden, Charley Boyden," Hugh supplied. "And I'm not flattering you at all, Miss Naline. Everybody says there never was a star like you." Which, considering Lita's record, marital, extra-marital, escapadic, and otherwise, was not stretching the truth far, if at all.

The girl laid a sharp-nailed hand on his arm and pressed it gently. "You're nice," she said simply (*and what happened to the big bully?*). "I knew you'd be nice to talk to when I saw you rescue that poor old gentleman"—with a nod of the turban toward Bracht—"from that perfectly horrible man in the crummy white suit. What was that all about, anyway?"

Hugh resorted to his shrug. "The old fellow was being bothered," he said. "Maybe the other guy's drunk."

Lita sniffed. "He certainly acted like he was drunk or on

18

some kind of a kick." She paused and asked with immense casualness: "What's the old gent's name, d'you know?"

"Barrows, I think."

"I've heard the name before," the movie star said thoughtfully. "Barrows, Barrows—wasn't there a producer by that name over at Gargantua before they cleaned house?" She was off again on her favorite subject. "Not that they shouldn't have done it years before—cleaned house at Gargantua, I mean. Stupendous loaned me to them for a picture once and, my God, it was terrible, but terrible! The critics were very kind to me but they all said the script and the direction stunk up the joint. I remember I said to the director—Landow, his name was—I said, Landow, if you don't—"

"Lita," a gentle voice interrupted. North swiveled his head to look into the smiling eyes of a man who must have been spectacularly handsome once and who still retained the quiet, courtly good looks that helped make him one of the highest-priced specialists in motion pictures. This was Lex Ross, once juvenile and leading man to silent screen stars, later a headliner in his own right and, more recently, a smooth, sinister "heavy" who had perfected the art of make-up disguise to a degree never attained since the days of Lon Chaney.

At his soft-voiced greeting Lita Naline jumped as though stuck with a pin. She half rose from her seat, the stenographer caught taking a too long coffee break, and then remembered that she was the star of this little caravan and sank back, closer if anything to the G-2 colonel.

"Well, what do you want, Lex?" she demanded imperiously.

Lex Ross smiled. "Nothing at all, personally, dear Lita, but our guiding genius, the man who's going to win Oscars for all of us, sent me to tell you to come back to him."

"Him!" Lita snorted, and almost tossed her turbaned head.

"Yes, him." Lex Ross nodded. "He happens to be a very temperamental Joe and a very jealous one. Come on, be a good girl and hurry back to Anton before he pops a blood vessel."

Lita hesitated but not for long. "Oh, all right," she said finally, and surged out of her seat past Hugh. "Honestly," she complained, "anybody would think he was my *husband,* the way he orders me around."

She was gone in a swirl of that expensive and titillating perfume. Ross stepped back to let her pass, then followed her, but not before he cast Hugh North one wry, tilted-eyebrow glance.

North permitted himself a chuckle. He did not know much about motion pictures but he had the idea that life was not going to be an idyllic dream in that Siamese location camp, wherever the superepic *Tiger, Tiger!* was going to be filmed. He could imagine Lita in the jungle, reaching for everything in pants while her "fabulous"—and jealous—producer-director-lover stewed in something more than the heat. He was glad his duty consisted of merely protecting an invaluable missile genius from the Reds and did not include having to join that little ménage somewhere in Thailand.

His thoughts returned to Hans Bracht. Speaking of temperament, he had on his hands a genius who could rival Anton Carss in that department. Bracht had long been noted for his ability to hurt, frustrate, and infuriate everybody who had tried to work with him. His associates in the field of nuclear physics and electronics admitted that he was the greatest among them, but none too privately they named him the scientific equivalent of an ornery sonofabitch.

He possessed a terrific ego, which, North conceded, he might have a right to own. He was ruthless in his demands for perfection in his subordinates, and many a young scientist had been utterly demolished while trying to work with Bracht. The missile genius had no friends and quite obviously wanted none; his background was dominated by the fact that all his life Bracht had been a lone wolf by preference.

Except in the case of Tao Muong, and Hugh dwelt on the runaway wife for a moment.

The information with which G-2 headquarters had supplied him said that little was known of Tao Muong beyond the fact that the girl was very beautiful, even for a Siamese woman, long noted for their adorable doll-like qualities. It was thought possible that Muong might be a Eurasian or an Annamite, a native of Indochina; her features were not quite so oriental

20

as the average Thai's. Where Bracht had found her, even where and when they had been married, was not known. The strange alliance was part of the blank period in Bracht's life which the scientist guarded as his own secret.

It was a secret that the best brains of the State Department's Counter-Intelligence, plus the investigation agencies of practically every other nation in the world, had failed to crack. Conjectures might be a dime a dozen, but not one provable fact was on the books as to where Hans Bracht had been or what he had done between the time he had disappeared from Hitler's rocket laboratories until the day he had emerged from hiding in Bangkok.

Upon his disclosure of his identity authorities had been so incredulous that at first the bearded man was considered a crack-brained impostor. Bracht had soon banished all doubts by his work, the touch of the master in all things having to do with ballistics missiles. But how he had escaped from Germany, how he had survived, how and why he had made his way to Siam—these were questions that never had come close to being answered.

Hugh told himself now that aside from being a fascinating subject the hiatus in Bracht's life, per se, was none of his concern. His job was to see that the genius got to Bangkok alive and free, that Bracht was reunited with his runaway bride, and that man and wife—or at least Bracht—was delivered home again safe and sound. North considered this a big enough order without trying to crack the secret of those hidden years in Bracht's life.

"Still," the G-2 agent murmured under his breath as he stared sightlessly at the pages of his magazine, "it looks as though those mysterious years are mixed up in this case already—as witness Monsieur Marchet."

CHAPTER 2

1.

THE AIRLINER dipped a wing and began a long turn. Hugh looked at the lights that wheeled below. Down there was Bangkok's Don Muang Airport, one of the busiest air terminals in the world.

Down there, too, was danger to Dr. Hans Bracht, who, since he could mean success or failure to America's intercontinental ballistics missile plans, was not just the elderly husband panting after the beautiful runaway wife.

Hugh had long since concluded that Bracht would be dangerously vulnerable during the landing at Don Muang. It was night, there would be an inevitable confusion at the busy airport, and any enemy agent awaiting Bracht's arrival could find it relatively easy to do his work. Second, there was a longish trip from Don Muang to the city of Bangkok itself, a trip that had made North shudder. If the Reds knew of Bracht's arrival they would have plenty of chances to stage an ambush.

When he got Bracht into Bangkok the danger would be lessened but not by much. G-2 headquarters had learned that Bracht would stay at the Imperial (and had arranged for an adjoining room for North), and while the Imperial was a beautiful luxury hotel it never had been built with an eye toward permitting an Intelligence agent easy coverage of his man. There were a dozen entrances to the big building, some of them leading into the living quarters of the hotel without going near the lobby. Many of the upper rooms and suites were connected by balconies which in effect provided second hallways for persons who might want to prowl the place

22

unseen. There was the usual profusion of servants found in every oriental hotel, operating on a system that required a separate "boy" for almost every duty, heightening the possibility that the Reds might slip one or more Asian agents in among them. The hotel proposed enough problems to give a splitting headache to the person who had to know what his ward or quarry was doing at any given moment—that, Hugh North had found out by personal experience years before.

Then there were the Thai law-enforcement agencies. Hugh would have been among the first to acknowledge that since World War II the little country of Thailand had come far in modernizing herself in nearly every way, but the question was whether the Siamese had improved their old, venal, inefficient police system enough to be of any real help in protecting Hans Bracht from the agents of the Kremlin, if called upon. One factor in favor of this possibility was the location of the Southeast Asia Treaty Organization's headquarters in Bangkok; certainly the Thai police must have been reorganized, modernized, to some extent to safeguard the important personages who attended the SEATO sessions.

The Pentagon had informed North that a General Genung was chief of the Bangkok Imperial Troops, a unit which actually was a city army, apart from but co-ordinated with the regular Thai Army. Hugh's instructions had been to avoid calling on Genung for assistance if at all possible (the preservation of Bracht's incognito again) but to be assured of friendly aid *to the limit of the troops' capability* if an emergency required a call. G-2 headquarters did not say so, but the inference was there: don't expect too much.

North shrugged mentally as the plane began its descent. He would have to play it by ear and trust to luck—that, and hope that Bracht was so uncharacteristically scared, as he had appeared to be for that moment when Marchet had confronted him, that he would co-operate. Not much; just enough to possibly save his own life.

"You have been in Bangkok before, *mein Herr?*" Mary Hollberg asked as the airliner began sloping down toward Don Muang.

"A few times," North said briefly. "Have you?"

23

"No." The girl shook her head, her eyes appealingly wide. "No, I have never been in Siam and I confess I am frightened. Is it a—a jungle country, Herr Boyden? Will I be trampled by elephants, attacked by tigers?"

"Not in Bangkok," Hugh laughed. "Is someone meeting you?"

Another headshake. "No, I will be all alone unless some kind gentleman rescues me." There was the invitation: *I'm all yours to tuck under your wing.*

"But surely the people who arranged your concert must be going to have somebody meet you," North could not resist saying.

Mary recognized the slip and attempted to recover. "Oh, them I have forgotten," she acknowledged. "Yes, probably they will have somebody to meet me."

"By the way, where are you appearing in Bangkok?" North continued.

A shrug. "That I leave up to the people who arrange the performance. I do not bother with such things. They have told me, of course, but I forget."

"No doubt the Prajadhapok," Hugh suggested. "All the better artists give their concerts there."

Fräulein Hollberg studied the G-2 colonel with a long glance that told North he had gone too far. Now Mary knew that *he* knew she was no concert pianist because Mary Hollberg had been in Bangkok before and realized there was no Prajadhapok Theater. If Mary Hollberg had made a slip, Hugh North had made one too.

He waited, his face reflecting none of the cursing he was giving himself for overplaying his hand. And Mary Hollberg, whoever she really was, proved equal to the occasion.

"I do not think that is the name of the place," she said dubiously, "but it may be. All these strange names out here confuse me so. But I do know that I will stay at the Hotel Imperial. You too?"

North nodded, and the girl gave a tiny crow of delight. "Then I shall have a friend in Bangkok after all," she exulted. "You must come visit me in my room and I will give you a drink." She put a hand to her mouth in winsome dismay. "But that would be indiscreet, *nicht wahr?* What is the custom of this country—does the gentleman call on the lady in her room or does she call on him in his?"

"I'm not sure that either is strictly proper"—North smiled —"but in the case of a concert pianist I'm sure the Imperial will stretch the rules."

"Then it is a date," Mary Hollberg said gleefully. "You will phone me at the Imperial and we shall get to know each other better. Much better."

"I'll do my very best," North promised solemnly. And meant every word of it.

The night landing at Don Muang brought with it a chaos provided by Lita Naline's presence.

Lita's publicity men apparently worked under the threat that if Lita should ever arrive anywhere or leave anyplace without the greeting or farewell of a screaming mob of fans, heads would roll. At Hong Kong, Hugh had watched Lita wave good-by to a seething caldron of humanity which shouted ecstatic godspeeds in English, Mandarin Chinese, and Cantonese. Here at Don Muang was an identical mob with an identical enthusiasm, although here the shouts were in Siamese, with a sprinkling of Chinese and a few words cried in broken English. This swirling mass broke past the barriers at the edge of the field and descended on Lita's plane in a howling avalanche while airport officials cursed, yelled pleas and threats, and finally announced in French, English, and the native language (of which North knew barely a smattering) that Miss Naline would remain aboard the airplane until all persons not authorized on the field were back behind the fence, even if the waiting took all night.

Aboard the plane, Miss Naline expressed energetic disapproval of this ultimatum.

"These dear, dear people have come here to see me and what right has some lousy Bangkok jerk to deny them the privilege?" she cried in rich, throaty tones. "Anton, make them open that door and let me meet my public!"

Anton Carss moved his bulging self up beside Naline and took one of her hands between his. "But what if this—ah—

25

demonstration of affection should get out of hand?" he asked. "What if you were injured? Imagine an unlucky accident, a broken nose—"

"Jesus!" squealed Miss Lita Naline. "Me get my face messed up? Not on your life!"

"Of course not," Carss said soothingly. "For then there would be no epic, no world recognition of my Lita as the greatest actress Carss has ever directed, no chance for Lita to show the Italian that she is far greater—"

"Somebody do something," Lita said hoarsely. "Get those goddamn maniacs off the field."

"Go out and sing to them, sweetheart," John Wallen, Lita's leading man, sniggered. "That'll drive 'em to cover fast enough."

Hugh, standing in the aisle to block any approach to the silent, unmoving Bracht, almost laughed aloud at Lita's expression. The siren with the jeweled turban faced "dear Jack" with a glare gone ashen with fury. Wallen sneered back at her, his too-handsome, aquiline features a mask of jealous contempt.

"Listen, you . . ." the self-publicized maharajah's daughter began, and proceeded to tell John Wallen what he could do with his suggestion, plus a few recommendations for further activities along strange lines. She used terms that made Hugh North wince and Mary Hollberg gasp. Anton Carss stepped in again.

"Let me go out and—ah—see if I can find somebody who has control over this crowd," he said. "The fans won't molest me." A dramatically pathetic shrug. "They won't even know me."

"Sure, Anton." Wallen laughed. "Find the bright boy who staged this and tell him to pay off the hired cheering section and send 'em home."

Miss Naline had a few more words to say to Mr. Wallen for daring to suggest that this was not a spontaneous tribute. While she was so engaged, Carss spoke to the stewardess urgently and was allowed to leave the plane. North bent to look out a window. He saw the pudgy director plunge into the crowd and wedge his way to the rear of the throng where two white men who looked like Americans stood. There was an earnest conversation during which Carss waved his hands.

Out of the knot of irked, impatient, or amused passengers came a small round man who approached North, smiling. It was the goateed patent-medicine king, Chu Hoong, concocter of that cure-all of unequaled potency, Dragon's Tooth Elixir.

"Excuse me," he said to North, "but does it happen that you understand Siamese? You have the look of one who has traveled much and I must find someone to share my amusement."

Hugh went on guard instinctively. It might possibly be true that this multimillionaire Chinese had wedged his way the length of the plane merely to share a joke with somebody he had astonishingly picked out of that crowd as a world traveler, but it was not probable. Brother Chu had something on his mind besides seeking companionship for a laugh. North edged himself a bit to the left to shield Hans Bracht's chair more completely.

"I'm very weak in Siamese," he told Chu. "What's the joke?"

The Chinese tilted his head to one side, listening, and then shook it regretfully. "Ah, they have closed the door again and you cannot distinguish the words," he said sorrowfully. "While it was open I heard enough to decide that joyous excitement must have unhinged that crowd outside. What they were shouting was, liberally translated: *Let the shameless foreign bitch show herself so we can get our pay.*"

He appeared to realize suddenly that Mary Hollberg was within hearing distance and turned toward the German "pianist," his hands folded on his chest, his head bowed. "Ah, try to forgive this unworthy one's shocking language, honorable lady," he begged. "I did not see you standing so close by."

The pretty blonde *Fräulein* curved her mouth in a smile that revealed a dimple. "You're forgiven," she told Chu. "Perhaps I, too, wish Miss Naline would show herself to the crowd so they'd go away and we could get out of here."

"The lady is too kind. I am ashamed to—"

Chu Hoong's voice was cut off as though a needle had

27

been lifted from a phonograph record. Hugh North saw the Chinese patent-medicine king gape at a point just beyond him, his jaw dropping, his eyes reflecting a surprise that was entirely out of keeping with the cultured Oriental's unshakable composure.

Hugh turned and saw the reason for this startling change. Behind him, Hans Bracht had risen from his seat and had moved so that Chu Hoong had come face to face with him.

Bracht had reacted almost as violently as had Chu. The tall, balding scientist staggered back a step against the seat in front of his and put out a long, bony hand to steady himself. He opened his mouth to speak, but the Chinese beat him to it with just one word: *"You!"*

So saying, and before Bracht could have spoken if he would, Chu Hoong turned and wedged his way back down the aisle toward the rear of the plane. Only once did he venture a look over his shoulder, and when he did, Hugh North saw fear reflected in the multimillionaire's slanted almond eyes.

2.

Now, what the hell?

The G-2 colonel might have noticed nothing, for all his expression would have told an onlooker, but his brain was clicking off conclusions, questions, conjectures.

First, these two men, the world's greatest space-travel authority and a Chinese patent-medicine magnate, knew each other and feared each other.

Second, Chu had not come to the front of the plane to see Bracht; his surprise had been as complete as the doctor's when the scientist had risen from his seat and faced the Chinese. That meant that Chu Hoong had offered his conversational gambit about the crowd's antics in an attempt to get closer to him, Hugh North the person, and not Bracht's bodyguard.

Hugh had never seen Chu before in his life until this flight. Then why would the Chinese want to talk to him if not because of Bracht? Possible answer: it had something to do with North's tangle with Georges Marchet.

And how about Miss Concert Pianist? She had been aft, passing the place where Chu had been sitting; could she have arranged something?

Fräulein Hollberg was edging past him, down the aisle. "The crowd outside is breaking up," she told North. "Don't forget to call me at the Imperial." And she was gone after Chu.

Hans Bracht had sat down again and was staring bleakly out his window at the floodlighted field. Unbidden, the G-2 colonel sat down beside him and looked past the scientist to see that the two Americans to whom Carss had appealed apparently had told their charges that payoff time was at hand. A couple of Pied Pipers in Western business suits, the publicity men led the Bangkok branch of the Lita Naline Fan Club off the field. The passengers aboard the Thai airliner moved toward the exit, the siege lifted at last.

Hugh saw that Georges Marchet was the first to disembark, pushing past Lita, who was preening herself for the flash bulbs that waited to flicker. The planter hurried down the steps, through the knot of newsmen gathered to welcome Naline, and plunged off, head bent, toward the customs shed.

Miss Naline came next and posed prettily on the landing stage while the flash bulbs popped. She was followed by Wallen and Ross, who stood with her for a single shot (arms entwined and smiling chummily, three dear friends off on a lark) before the trio moved toward customs. Then followed the Russian, Boris Salenkov, Chu Hoong, and, at the very end of the line behind the least important underling of the *Tiger, Tiger!* company, Mary Hollberg.

As he watched, Hugh saw the German girl turn and glance back at the big aircraft, her eyes seeking the window through which Dr. Bracht peered gloomily. The G-2 colonel wondered again what game Fräulein Hollberg was playing. Could she be some new type of Russian agent or—and North nearly laughed aloud as the ridiculously obvious explanation came to him—was she merely an international trollop using the airlines as her beat and doing very well off the proceeds of cus-

29

tomers she might pick up on the continent-spanning planes? Surely she had been forward enough with her invitations, and what better role to travel under than that of a concert pianist?

This last theory would explain Mary's interest in that overheard word of Bracht's, *policeman!* If she was a high-flying *fille de joie* it was probable that there had been some incidents in her past that would make the word *policeman* an unwelcome one.

You're starting to see Russian bogeymen under the bed when you mistake a high-class chippy for a Red agent, the Intelligence officer warned himself.

He checked the airfield again and saw that the immediate vicinity was deserted except for the airliner's crew, unloading luggage and mail. All the men were intent on their jobs; there were no loiterers.

"I think it's all right to leave the plane now, sir," he told Bracht. "If you'll please keep close to me and let me handle—"

Any hopes of co-operation went glimmering when Bracht cut in. "You will please go away and leave me alone," the scientist rasped. "I was promised that no security men would bother me on this trip and I don't intend—"

It was North's turn to break in. "Listen, Doctor," he said evenly, "that wasn't a security man bothering you a few minutes ago. It was a Frenchman named Georges Marchet who recognized you without your beard and was ready to blat your name to everybody within earshot. Marchet's probably in customs now, and if I'm not with you he might smash this incognito of yours all to hell. I'm pretty sure the man's a drug addict and—"

"He is," Bracht grunted. *"Ach, Gott,* how I hate that tribe, all of them!"

"If you know anything about addicts you know how undependable they are," Hugh went on. "Think about the importance of keeping your identity secret, sir. If it got out that Hans Bracht was in Bangkok"—*not that the odds aren't ten to one that the Reds already know it,* he added silently— "there'd almost surely be trouble. You're getting close to your

30

wife—don't ruin everything now by refusing to co-operate with me."

It worked. Bracht lost his sneer, his contemptuous disdain. Suddenly the scientist's fear showed in his long face again as plainly as before and again Hugh wondered. How could a man of Bracht's toughness, a man capable of risking death by torture as he had when he had escaped from under Hitler's nose, be so shaken now?

"All right, all right," the missile expert mumbled as his eyes dropped. "I'll—co-operate."

"Good," Hugh said briskly. "Now follow me and keep close."

Bracht nodded, rose from his seat, and came down the aisle behind North. The two men had just reached the ground at the foot of the landing stage and North was replying to the stewardess's good-by when a figure stepped out of the shadow cast by the plane's tail assembly.

"Doctah Bracht!" a voice rapped out. "Hol' it, pliss!"

Hugh whirled himself in front of Bracht. The B-2 colonel caught a glimpse of a man raising something, aiming something. Hugh's gun was in his hand, his finger tightening, when he realized what was happening. He held the shot that would have drilled the accoster's head and then there was a blinding flash of light.

3.

Hugh cursed under his breath as his gun flowed back into its shoulder holster. Somebody leaving the airliner had told one of the news photographers assembled to greet Lita Naline that Dr. Hans Bracht was aboard the plane. Marchet!

"Gott im Himmel!" Bracht exclaimed, beside Hugh.

"It's okay," the colonel said tersely. "A photographer. Let me handle it."

"The stupid dog!" Bracht blazed. "Just let me get my hands on him and I'll—"

"I said I'd handle it!" North crackled. He advanced toward the photographer, who was reversing the plateholder. The cameraman who had come so close to being killed proved to

31

be a youngster, a Eurasian by his looks in this uncertain light, who now wore an aggrieved frown.

"You spoil picture," he complained. "I pay Frenchman one hundedd bahts for tip famous scientist on plane and you spoil picture."

"If you paid anybody a hundred bahts for a bum steer, that's your lookout." North smiled. "The gentleman with me is Mr. Henry Barrows."

"No savvy bum steer," the cameraman scowled. He began trying to edge around North for another shot at Bracht. Hugh blocked the little man's view again.

"I wouldn't take any more pictures if I were you," he said. "General Genung wouldn't like it. You savvy General Genung?"

The cameraman savvied, all right. At mention of the general's name the little fellow abruptly abandoned his flanking movement, lowered his camera. Astonishingly, he emptied his old Graphic of the plateholder and proffered the oblong to Hugh.

"Here you are, gentleman," he twittered. "You see I do nothing General Genung don' like. You tell General Genung I most pleasant, agreeable man, oh yes. Good-by, pliss."

He was off, gone in the shadows, leaving North with the plateholder that contained a negative which must show a tall, wide-shouldered G-2 colonel bearing down with a .38 pistol.

North laughed as he slid the slides out of the plateholder, exposing both films, and then replaced them. He deposited the wooden-framed oblong on the cement apron in the event the most pleasant, agreeable photographer dared return for his property and rejoined Bracht. The scientist regarded him with murky eyes. "You should have given him a swift kick in the *Schwanz*," he grumbled.

"News photographers are strange people," North replied easily. "They don't like being kicked in the tail. When somebody kicks them or otherwise roughs them up they usually get even the best way they know how. I don't imagine you'd want to be dogged by a passel of Siamese cameramen during your stay here, and that's what would have happened if I'd followed your suggestion. The word would have gone out that we were tough guys when it came to having our picture taken, and cameramen—I don't care whether they're Siamese or Siberian—always have to prove that nobody's too tough to be photographed."

Bracht grunted, "How did you get that little worm to run off like that?"

"I mentioned a name—what appears to be a magic name in Thailand." North smiled. "And, believe me, I'm glad to know it wields such authority. We may have to use that name on somebody more important than an enterprising cameraman. This way, please."

Bracht grunted again but he trudged along beside North. He kept his silence almost to the customs shed and then he asked: "Was that photographer one of Lita's publicity crowd?"

Hugh hid his surprise at Bracht's mention of the star's first name. "I don't think so," he said. "He acted more like a news cameraman." He laughed in an attempt to improve the dour relations that existed between him and the man he had been detailed to guard. "Quite a performance Lita put on back there in the plane, wasn't it?" he asked. "One minute she was ready to swan-dive into that mob and then she was yelling for somebody to get those maniacs off the field."

Again Hans Bracht did the unexpected; he defended the volatile Miss Naline. "What Anton Carss told her made sense," he said somberly. "Suppose there had been an accident and her beauty was ruined." He looked at North, his face haggard. "Can you imagine how a beautiful woman would feel to be disfigured, even accidentally? Could there be anything more terrible for her?"

Colonel North's face did not change. There was not the slightest indication that within him there was a sudden, surging, silent cry:

So that's it!

4.

Hugh and Hans Bracht went through customs without a hitch, North at the scientist's side, his eyes always roving, his right hand always free and never far from the butt of that hidden .38. The reason North had chosen "Boyden" as a pseudonym was to be as close as possible to Bracht-"Barrows" in all such situations where an alphabetical grouping might occur, and if one could take the lack of any untoward incident as proof, the foresight had been a wise one. Both missile genius and G-2 colonel were shot through a cursory customs inspection without delay at the "B" counter.

But if their move through customs was smooth, Lita Naline's wasn't, to judge by the uproar that arose from down the line under the big letter "N." Lita was in full cry when Bracht and North entered the customs shed and she was still going strong when they moved out onto the platform where the taxis waited.

"A little temperamental, eh?" North laughed with a jerk of his head toward the sound and the fury behind them. "I pity Anton Carss when they're in the jungle making that picture."

"Oh, Carss will handle her," Bracht said. "He's done wonders directing more difficult stars than Lita."

This time Hugh could not hide his surprise as he glanced at the scientist. "Don't tell me you're a movie fan," he grinned.

The greatest space-travel authority in the world answered in a grating voice that lacked any hint of apology or embarrassment. "Not me, my wife," he explained. "She—she has eye trouble, so I must read the movie columns and the fan magazines to her." He paused and then added in a soft voice North had not heard him use before: "Poor little thing, the movies are about all the pleasure she gets out of life."

He caught himself and added hastily: "Her eyes, you see."

"Tough," North sympathized. He got the picture of this world-famous figure, this top man of all space scientists, sitting at home patiently reading aloud from the frothy movie magazines his beautiful young wife, Tao Muong, could not translate if, indeed, she could read her own language. Hans Bracht had done this in the hope of keeping her contented, and to Hugh the incongruous picture was a sad one.

"Here's our cab," the colonel offered into the brief silence that had fallen.

Bracht preceded Hugh into the rickety vehicle that slumped,

34

fourth in the taxi line. The scientist had no complaints to make about North's choice of a cab, the shabbiest of the lot, and if he had Hugh could hardly have explained that he was merely following a G-2 agent's pattern, laid down by experience. Never take the first cab in line; *They* might have provided it. Don't take the second, either, because They might expect you to pass up the first and have two waiting. They might even have three cabs in a line but hardly more than three. The fourth was as safe as any, as far as being a planted cab was concerned, but to confuse anybody who might be following the agent's choice of cabs over a space of time, the rule was to mix them up, sometimes taking the fifth, sometimes the seventh, sometimes (but not often because it was too easily appended to a waiting cab line in quick switch) the last cab in the lot.

This taxi Hugh chose at the Don Muang Airport was a real veteran, a British Panhard of prewar vintage with fenders that seemed to flap even before the machine moved.

"Imperial Hotel," the G-2 officer told the driver, and they were off in a clatter of fouled sparkplugs, carbon-choked cylinders, and cricket-chorusing squeaks.

Don Muang Airport lay several miles upriver on the Menam Chao Phya, and because it was night, with none of the gorgeous scenery to distract his ward, Hugh North hoped to use the trip to gain Hans Bracht's confidence, if possible. The driver of the antiquated cab probably had his accelerator down to the floor in the clear stretches, but even then his wheezy cab could only limp along and the clear stretches were few and far between. The Siamese quite obviously had shed the superstitions that once had kept them indoors after nightfall out of fear of demons; the Don Muang-Bangkok road was cluttered with traffic even at this time of night. Oxcarts, automobiles, lumbering trucks, and an occasional ponderous elephant moved up and down the highway with a total disregard of the rules of the road. North's driver kept his horn squawking almost continuously, not that anyone, human, bovine, or elephantine, paid him the least mind, and the taxi more or less inched its way toward Bangkok.

Hugh realized it was the perfect setup for an ambush, the

35

snatching of Hans Bracht out of his cab during one of the innumerable traffic jams or a shot out of the night to dispose of Hans Bracht's one bodyguard. Under such conditions it was impossible to guard against such a possibility; North had to ride out this trip wheel turn by wheel turn and hope he could meet and parry the stab in the dark when and if it came.

"Can't we go faster?" Bracht fretted. "I've got to get to the hotel before midnight. Somebody might call." His eyes met North's squarely. "I won't tell you who," he added defiantly.

"That's up to you," Hugh said lightly.

"And just who are you?" the scientist demanded. "You said aboard the plane you'd tell me when we landed."

Hugh nodded. It was time to tell Bracht who he was. His orders had been to keep the doctor from knowing he was being covered, but those orders, like all instructions given undercover agents, were open to change to meet urgencies and exigencies. North had always been given a great deal of latitude in his operations and seldom, if ever, had his decision to strike off at a tangent opposite to the strict letter of his orders brought him a chewing-out from higher headquarters. He hoped he was right this time too.

The noise outside the cab was tumultuous, helped along in no little measure by the horn of their own cab. Still, the colonel pitched his voice low, at the exact level that could be heard by Bracht and not by the taxi driver, no matter how rabbit-eared or what kind of English linguist that worthy might be.

"Colonel Hugh North, Army Intelligence," he told his ward. "Assigned as your companion, Dr. Bracht, until you're safely back in the States."

"They promised me there'd be no guards," Bracht muttered.

North sighed. Bracht ought to be getting tired of the tune he fiddled on that one string. "If you'll remember," he said, "your demands were that no *security* guards be put on your tail. You'll probably call it splitting hairs, but that was the promise they gave you—no security guards. I'm not from Security. I'm Army G-2. The Army has a big stake in you,

36

Doctor, just as the country and for that matter the whole free world has. You're head of Army's Project Galaxy. We don't want anything to happen to you." And could not resist adding: "At least not until Project Galaxy is a success."

"And after that?" Bracht grunted.

Hugh was reaching for his cigarettes. "Seems to me we've got enough to do without looking that far ahead."

The scientist fell silent on the cracked leather seat beside North, staring ahead moodily, oblivious to the sights, the sounds, the smells that surrounded him. A full minute passed before he asked: "You do not like me, eh, Colonel?"

North shrugged. "In my business a man can seldom afford personal likes and dislikes. Until I get you back to the States I'm going to try to stick closer than a brother, so it would be easier on both of us if we could get along amiably, if not cordially."

He considered his next statement and decided on it against certain qualms. "It might help if you'd remember that just as you're an expert in your field I'm pretty experienced in mine. Let me be the expert until you're back in your laboratory. Let me do the masterminding for both of us. And, above all, level with me, Doctor."

"Level with you?"

"Be honest. Don't try to play it your way. Don't go it alone. Confide in me. If you knew me better you'd know I never broke a confidence in my life. I couldn't afford to. Let it get out that North broke his word and my career wouldn't be worth a plugged nickel—not to speak of my neck."

Bracht looked down at his big hands twisting in his lap. "Words are cheap," he grumbled.

"My word isn't," Hugh rapped out. He paused and when he spoke again he used German, a double precaution against some incredibly sharp-eared, English-speaking taxi driver.

"Or do you prefer to take the word of the people who kidnaped your wife?" he asked calmly.

The results were electric. Hans Bracht's long, lean body was transfixed by shock. He stared at the G-2 colonel, his

37

protuberant eyes wide behind their glasses, his thin-lipped mouth agape.

"You know?" he gasped finally. "You know they stole Tao Muong?" He turned in his seat, and his spatulate hands shot out to grasp North's arm, his fingers biting. "How?" he demanded fiercely. "How did you find out? Was it something I said? They warned me that if I breathed a word they'd maim her, torture her, kill her!"

"Easy," North counseled. "Take it easy."

Bracht flung himself away and crumpled in his corner, the unnerved ruin of a man. "Take it easy," he half sobbed. "It's fine for you to tell me that, but those devils have my wife. Unless I do what they say, Muong will—" He choked, staring down at his trembling hands, surrendered to his fear again.

Fear, Hugh knew now, for Tao Muong, never for Hans Bracht. Now the G-2 agent knew why Bracht had crumpled before Marchet's question, Chu Hoong's recognition; the missile genius had been terrified that Marchet's appearance, and Chu Hoong's, might wreck his deal with Muong's kidnapers. Regardless of what lay behind the Chinese multimillionaire's own fear, Bracht had been panicked only by the thought that these unlucky meetings (if that was what they had been) would be witnessed by a tail, the snatchers would suspect some kind of double cross, and Muong would be mutilated. Hugh told himself that this poor devil, Hans Bracht, must always be seeing his wife in the kidnaper's hands; his imagination must paint scenes that stripped him of his inherent rock-hard courage.

There was genuine sympathy in the colonel's voice when he spoke. "Doctor, believe me when I say that until you get your wife back I'll do my best to keep hands off any deals you've made with the kidnapers. That's a promise."

The scientist's bald, friz-fringed head swung around slowly. "Can I really believe that?" he asked. He chewed his lower lip for a moment and then added: "What do you mean exactly —you'll *do your best* to keep hands off?"

North winced inwardly at the second question. It might be the cardinal rule of all law-enforcement officers, from the pre-

cinct cop up to the FBI, to let kidnapers operate with a free
hand until the ransom was paid or the snatch victim found,
dead or alive, but international secret agents were not bound
by that rule. G-2 and comparable agencies sometimes—indeed
usually—played for higher stakes than the life of one person.
Tao Muong might be an adorable young woman and Hugh
North might pity her fate at the hands of angered or scared
kidnapers, but against the life of the world's greatest intercontinental ballistics missile genius the life of a little Siamese
girl was an inconsequential thing, actually.

"Put it this way," he said finally. "My first job is to keep
you alive and out of the hands of our enemies, to get you
back to Project Galaxy as soon as possible. If a fast deal with
the kidnapers will expedite that, it stands to reason I'll help
in any way I can to arrange the ransom payoff and get your
wife returned."

But this is no ordinary snatch, he added silently, bitterly.
*The ransom they want is Hans Bracht. And when they try to
collect I may have to forget there ever was such a person as
Tao Muong.*

Bracht was pondering what North had told him and, as
the taxi jolted ahead in a sudden, miraculous spurt, he
nodded slowly. "That makes sense," he said in a low voice.
The doubt flowed back into his lean face.

"But they'll know!" he exclaimed. "They told me they'd
watch every move I made. They'll know you're from this—
this Army Intelligence or whatever it is. They said not to
talk to *anybody.*"

"I'd say no to any kidnaper knowing who I am," Hugh
offered reassuringly. "My work has been with the Army.
This is a special case and I'm on it only because you're working on an Army missile project. If I were so well known that
a kidnap gang would recognize me I wouldn't be of much use
to the Army, would I? No, Doctor, kidnapers will be looking
for police, not Army G-2."

If they're just kidnapers, that is, he told himself. *If they're
bigger game they might be looking out for somebody like
me, but that's a chance we'll have to take.*

"Suppose the kidnapers did have somebody on that plane,"

he went on to Bracht. "He saw Marchet's approach. He saw me interfere, the nearest passenger and the logical man to step in. What could be more understandable than that I struck up a conversation with you after the incident?"

It was hard going, but Hugh got through to the missile genius beside him. By this time the G-2 colonel had decided that Hans Bracht desperately wanted a friend, an ally, in his terrible predicament. He might be a Prussian drillmaster in his laboratory, but in the outside world that he had always shunned (except for that mysterious hiatus), and tormented as he was by fears for his wife, he must have welcomed the offer of help that came from North, even against all his doubts and misgivings. He inclined his long head in a nod once more, so grudgingly that Hugh almost expected to hear a creak.

"All right," he said heavily. "All right, Colonel North, I'll—"

"First, you'll call me Charley Boyden," North interposed. "That was my name back on the plane, the name any tail will expect."

Bracht grimaced. "I hope I remember. I am no good at this."

You must have been once, when you were getting out of Hitler's Germany. Aloud, Hugh said easily: "Don't worry about me. I said I intended to stick closer than a brother and I will, but that doesn't mean I'll be underfoot. This possibly is the last time we'll be seen together in public"— he looked at the roof of the shabby cab, the back of the driver's head, and grinned—"if this can be called public. When we get to the Imperial I'll fade into the background as much as possible. I'll contact you and I'll keep an eye on you but I won't clutter up the picture—not if I work it right."

The cab rattled and banged its way over the bridges of innumerable canals into the outskirts of Bangkok's Samsen district, an area featured by vast parks and the imposing Parliament Building, a huge dark pile of masonry at this hour. The street traffic was still thick and now the pedestrian flow grew more turbulent. An occasional street lamp cast a wan glow that showed Hugh the polyglot dress worn by these people of

Thailand. Some were clad in the native garb of short loose trousers or sarong, with sleeveless jackets for the men and diaper-type pantaloons for the women. Others wore Western clothes of the outmoded, garish type. A few were smartly dressed in the latest Western fashion, but these were greatly outnumbered by the men and women in native costume.

The taxi edged past a couple of tramcars which seemed to be making no better progress than was permitted by the occasional elephant that invariably ambled down the middle of the tracks, its mahout seeming to dare the bell-clanging, cursing streetcar motorman to do anything more than make a lot of useless noise. Despite Thailand's progress within recent years it was evident that the elephant had lost none of its honorable position in Siam; the people still revered the great beast as an emblem of authority, a symbol of their religion, and, incongruously, as still the greatest source of locomotive power, all hydroelectric projects, turbine engines, and gasoline motors notwithstanding.

Hugh North always marveled at the constant refutation of Kipling's "Never the twain shall meet" in these little Southeast Asian countries which had taken such tremendous strides toward modernity in the past decade. East certainly did meet West in Bangkok, as it did in Singapore, Karachi, Saigon, and other like cities that Hugh had visited in the pursuit of his duties.

The intermingling of the two opposite cultures went deeper than in such things as dress and machines; it was the G-2 colonel's opinion that the old maxim about the East's inscrutability was being made more passé every day. The Siamese, like the Vietnamese, the Cambodians, and their oriental cousins, had too long let the world mistake ignorance, superstition, and oppression by their rulers for inscrutability. Now they were tasting freedom, progress, opportunity, and they were reacting to these new-found delights as typically as any European or American.

The colonel wrenched himself from these ruminations and turned his attention back to his ward. "We haven't got much more time alone. I've got a couple of questions. First, who is Georges Marchet and where did he know you?"

Bracht's lower lip pushed out obstinately. "I won't tell you."

North held his temper in check. "Then where did you meet Chu Hoong? Why is he afraid of you?"

"I never met anybody named Chu Hoong in my life."

"I asked you to be honest with me," the colonel reminded the scientist.

"I am being honest. If you mean that Chinese, if I ever knew him it wasn't under the name of Chu Hoong. As for Marchet, he has nothing to do with the kidnaping, not that drug-sodden worm."

"Let me decide whether or not he's important to us. Who is he and where did you know him?"

North watched the space-travel genius wrestle with his doubts, his natural reticence, the old determination to keep the secret he had preserved for so many years. "Marchet would not have the courage to be mixed up with anything even so cowardly as the kidnaping of a little girl," he said finally. "He has been a *Raucher,* a smoker, for years and by now he has probably gone down the scale to worse drugs —if such nasty things can be graded."

"And you knew him when you were out here?" Hugh prodded. "During the war, after you left Germany?"

The long head inclined in the barest suggestion of a nod. "In Siam?"

This time there was a grudging negative headshake. "No, Marchet was in French Indochina, now Vietnam," the doctor said. "I—I was passing through and—"

Hugh North flung both arms around Hans Bracht and bore him down off the seat onto the littered floor of the cab. The next second there was a rending, ripping, grinding bedlam as a big black Citroën that had come out of nowhere sideswiped the taxi and sent it careening over the curb, across the sidewalk, and up against a tree in a park that bordered the street.

42

CHAPTER 3

1.

HUGH'S FIRST THOUGHT was that whoever had arranged the ramming had chosen the spot well. While he had been trying to drag explanations out of Hans Bracht the cab had turned off the crowded main thoroughfare onto a dark, empty side street that skirted a black stretch of park, and the driver of the Citroën had not wasted a second when he saw the coast was clear.

The taxi driver? Had They outwitted him and planted an agent at the wheel of this rickety cab, outguessed him by stationing the stooge in the fourth position of the taxi rank at Don Muang Airport? If the cab driver was a Red agent he had been double-crossed, too; the tree trunk the cab had smashed into had crushed the driver's head and now the threadbare little man sagged over the wheel, dead.

The collision's impact had sent the door on Bracht's side flying off its hinges as the cab slewed around. The scientist's way lay open, then, when Hugh released his grip and shoved himself upright, his hand darting beneath his jacket to emerge with his gun. Hans Bracht did not hesitate. The missile expert scrambled through the gaping doorway on hands and knees and dropped to the grass with an agility that belied his years.

"Hold it!" North barked. "Don't panic now!"

The scientist got to his feet and stared about wildly. The crash, coming on top of everything else, seemed likely to snap the tenuous hold Bracht had on himself, and North lunged at his man to grab him and shield him from whatever might be about to follow.

43

He might have made it had it not been for one of the crowd which appeared as miraculously as though a throng had been waiting amidst the trees to pop out at the instant of the crash. What had been a deserted side street immediately became a millrace of humanity as from all directions streamed chattering onlookers, avid for a glimpse of disaster.

One of these diminutive Siamese appointed himself upholder of the law. He had seen Bracht scurry away and now there was another Westerner trying to escape the scene of this accident, and with the taxi driver so obviously dead. No, this never-to-be-named hero would not permit it! He wrapped his arms about North's middle and began screaming in shrill Thai to send for the police; this foreigner was trying to leave the scene of a fatal accident as every good subject of the King knew was against the law.

Cursing savagely, North fought himself free of the little man's clutch and found himself surrounded by a close-packed crowd that pressed closer to enjoy the excitement. The G-2 colonel caught a glimpse of Bracht's bald head bucking the tide of people who swarmed toward the wreck from ahead. Hugh tried to give chase but it was hopeless; the throng about the smashed cab, the drunkenly tilted Citroën, simply refused to give way for him. The spectators, all Siamese, stood in a blank-faced wall that ringed the two wrecks, and before North had managed to shove his big frame through the first couple of ranks, Bracht was long gone.

Hugh turned back to the cab. Perhaps the car could be made to run and he could chase Bracht down. One look at the decrepit veteran and its dead driver stoppered that hope, and the black car was in not much better shape, its front stove in, water and oil leaking in a widening pool on the glass-littered pavement.

Well, then, perhaps Bracht had actually done the smart thing by getting out of there. If he could make the hotel and that telephone call he was so anxious about, he would be safer than in the midst of this mob. Nobody had been chasing Bracht when North had glimpsed him. If this had been a deliberate ramming (and Hugh had little doubt that it was) those who had staged it might have been caught in the same

44

human whirlpool that held North and from which Bracht had escaped before it was fully formed. The doctor should be able to get a cab or a tram (unless he had flipped entirely) and make his way to the Imperial safely. At least that was a hope Hugh tried to cling to.

And now for the driver of the Citroën; had he gotten away or did he need dealing wth?

He needed dealing wth. He came at North, a large, loud-mouthed man in dirty Western clothes, a Manchu Chinese by the cast of his features and a strange one to be driving such a big car unless he was a chauffeur for some owner who did not mind a sloppy uniform—or, more probably, a hired assassin who had been furnished transportation.

He advanced on Hugh, chattering high-pitched imprecations in Chinese. Close to the colonel he stopped and pointed a long-nailed, very dirty finger at North. He used the Cantonese dialect, which Hugh could understand.

"First he murders the poor taxicab driver, this foreign devil, and now he threatens me with his gun," he bawled.

"Which will blow a hole in your guts unless you tell me who hired you," North rapped back in Cantonese. "Quick, my gun is impatient."

The big Manchu hesitated, his eyes sliding away too obviously. Hugh half turned to meet the threat from the rear that the big man's eyes had warned him of.

It was the little interferer, the self-appointed guardian of the law again. The undersized Siamese grabbed North's gun hand with both of his and recklessly tussled for possession of the .38. The G-2 agent knew a dozen tricks that would have sent this little fellow flying twenty feet, a crippled wreck, but he could not bring himself to use any one of them. This busybody was only a misguided bystander, after all; despite his disastrous interference he did not deserve the treatment an out-and-out enemy would have gotten.

Hugh tore himself free from the Thai's clutch with relative ease, but in so doing and in trying not to hurt the gad-fly, he lost effective use of his pistol. He still had the gun when he broke loose, but the hold-breaking maneuver re-

45

quired him to twist the .38 so that he was holding the weapon by its barrel as he turned to meet the Manchu.

It was then that the Chinese giant leaped, a knife glimmering in his right fist.

The G-2 colonel acted by instinct; there was no time to think. He dropped the gun (he needed both hands now) and twisted sideways, lurched in toward the oncoming knife wielder, under the upflung arm that brought down the blade. Even as he reached for his hold, braced himself for the throw, Hugh's brain automatically registered the thought that the Chinese never learned; they *always* made a flourishing downward sweep with a knife, never the short, ugly, almost undefensible upward stab at the lower belly and groin.

His hands found their place. The colonel turned a fraction of an inch farther so that when he dropped one knee to the pavement the Manchu was crouched awkwardly over his back, the knife hand hauled rigidly forward by Hugh's double grip. The Intelligence officer's shoulders seemed merely to twitch—but the cutthroat went pinwheeling through the air, screaming with the pain of a broken arm.

The big man's parabola scattered the crowd in a frenzied rush. The horde of onlookers disappeared as if by magic. Hardly had the knife clanged down on the pavement, the would-be assassin smashed to the roadway with a sickening thud, when North found himself the only man on his feet within a considerable radius.

The G-2 colonel stooped and recovered his gun, trained it on the motionless cutthroat, but it was an unnecessary move. The Manchu's fall had knocked him out and now he lay sprawled beside his Citroën, totally unavailable for questioning.

Hugh knelt beside the unconscious man, ran through his pockets swiftly. There was a sizable wad of Thai bank notes in the would-be assassin's pants—his pay for the job, no doubt—but nothing else of value, materially or information-wise. North straightened, chewing his underlip. Much as he wanted to give this big hulk a going-over, grind out of the man the name of his boss (and he had ways and means

46

of making the most uncommunicative talk, if given time), he had to get out of here. The crowd would be back as soon as its instinctive fear of involvement faded, and with them would doubtless come the police; there would be a thousand explanations to make under time-wasting circumstances, possibly a journey to headquarters to find somebody who understood English, and Hugh North just did not have the time. He had to locate Hans Bracht as soon as possible or, failing that, get in touch with General Genung.

Getting away from this place without attaching to his wake a column of jibbering, murder-crying Siamese was not going to be simple. Already heads were beginning to peer around the trunks of trees in the park behind him and the bolder of the scattered mob were beginning to inch toward him, ready to set up their holler again. Hugh had no idea of how to get to the Imperial from this street; to hail a cab while a Greek chorus of denunciatory Siamese howled their imprecations was an impossibility. Better make a run for it now and try to shake this bunch somehow.

He turned to sprint in the general direction the taxi had been taking at the time of the crash when, from behind him, came the mellow bleat of a horn that could be part of nothing but the most expensive car. Glancing over his shoulder, North saw a gleaming Rolls limousine curve around the Citroën and head for him, its tires heedlessly crushing the glass shards strewn on the pavement. As the big car approached, Hugh could make out a head and arm protruding from the rear window, the hand beckoning urgently.

The G-2 colonel had his pistol in his hand again as he paused to let the limousine come alongside.

"Quick," Chu Hoong hissed from the depths of the Rolls. "Get in, please. These people can be nasty when they get aroused."

A door was flung open and North hesitated only a second before he accepted the pressing invitation. He knew that Chu was involved somehow in Bracht's past, he was suspicious of the Chinese millionaire's place in the picture, but he could not afford to be too finicky at this moment. There were only Chu Hoong and the chauffeur to deal with immediately in case the Chinese was planning surprises, and if it was Chu's intention to liquidate him, why hadn't he gunned him down from the car?

It was a risk, certainly, but the alternative was even less inviting. North sank onto the deep cushions beside the round little millionaire and said: "Thanks. There was an accident and that crowd—"

"I know how these people behave, Mr. Boyden," Chu nodded quietly. "They are good people, but excitable. And they are not especially fond of foreigners or even we Chinese, who have built their country for them. It was fortunate that my driver took this way to the Imperial."

He beamed on North, his almond eyes closed to slits as he grinned. "You can thank your beautiful countrywoman, Miss Naline, for this," he went on. "We would have used another, more traveled, street if it had not been for her motorcade. I had no idea that her artistry had gained her such world-wide fame—the police have roped off the main avenue, even herded the elephants onto detours, so that Miss Lita Naline might stream into the city unhindered, preceded by motorcycles, various city and national dignitaries, and, one presumes, a brass band. I suppose that's why your taxi driver took such an ill-lighted route to the hotel, resulting in the unfortunate accident, eh?"

"I suppose so," North said tersely. "You're going to the Imperial, you say?"

"Yes." Chu nodded. "I maintain a suite at the Imperial." He glanced at North, the suggestion of a twinkle in his slanted eyes. "As a matter of fact," he added, "I own it."

Oof! This was going to be just dandy, keeping watch over Hans Bracht, the temperamental, non-co-operative missile genius who didn't want any watch kept over him, in a many-exit hotel owned and thus controlled down to the lowliest kitchen slavey by a man who was known and feared by this same Hans Bracht.

"And I may say in all humility," Chu Hoong said softly, "that the Imperial is the best hotel in Bangkok. I am not boasting when I say this; the staff maintains its excellence. I'm sure you will enjoy your stay there, Mr. Boyden."

I'll move Bracht to another hotel, North vowed silently, and instantly contradicted himself. *No good; the people who have Tao Muong have told Bracht to stay at the Imperial and I'm committed to keep hands off the kidnap deal.*

"I'm sure I shall," he replied evenly. His hand brought out a pack of cigarettes and he shook one out toward the Chinese. Chu Hoong hesitated and then accepted the cigarette, eyed it dubiously. "I'm afraid I'm not too well acquainted with these American filters," he murmured. "Is there any special procedure involved in smoking this?"

North repressed his anxiety over Hans Bracht enough to summon a chuckle. "No," he replied. "Just treat it as you would a common ordinary cigarette made of tobacco."

Chu Hoong laughed appreciatively and bent forward to the flame of North's lighter. His first puff brought a fleeting frown of disappointment to his round, goateed face, but his expression smoothed immediately. "Delicious," he said politely.

"They take some getting used to," North admitted.

The Rolls stopped for a traffic signal (one completely ignored by a large bull elephant that swaggered cater-cornered across the intersection, nearly crushing a tiny Renault in the process) and from somewhere came the whine of a siren, quavering above the noise of the bustling city.

"That will be your Miss Naline," Chu Hoong observed. And after a pause: "Or possibly the police rushing to the scene of your recent lamentable accident. I forgot to inquire —was anybody injured?"

As if you didn't see that cab driver and the Manchu when you drove past. "I'm afraid the taxi driver was hurt pretty badly. The other driver seemed to be slightly banged up too."

"Ah well, they will drive like madmen in this city, so what can they expect?" Chu sighed. "I stay off the streets as much as possible when I'm in Bangkok, Mr. Boyden. I'd advise you to do the same, if I don't appear to be officious in saying that. A man can very easily be hurt or even killed in Bangkok by reckless motorists—and other things."

49

"Such as?"

The Chinese multimillionaire shrugged. "Oh, there are many hazards here for the person who is not very careful. Footpads, misguided patriots who still consider all white men as exploiters of Southeast Asia—there are many, many dangers to the unwary man."

He turned a bland face toward Hugh. "If I do not presume, what brings you to Bangkok, Mr. Boyden?" he asked. "I am rude enough to ask because I have a certain influence in this city and it may be that I can be of assistance to you. Sometimes, unless he has entree to the right people, a Westerner can find it very frustrating to try to do business in Thailand."

"I know," North returned. "I've been here before, Mr. Chu."

"Oh? Then perhaps my warnings were presumptuous. No doubt you know this country better than this miserably vain person."

"I doubt that," North said. "From what I've heard and read about you, this whole section of Southeast Asia is very well known, indeed, to you and your organization, Mr. Chu."

"What you read and heard must have been gross flattery," the Chinese demurred. "Actually, I am only a modestly successful businessman trying to spend my few remaining years acquiring a modicum of peace of mind."

North repressed a snort. This little fat man who glibly recited his denial of importance was a person who, the G-2 colonel knew, could have spoken with the authority of firsthand knowledge of many things about which the U. S. State Department, the Southeast Asia Treaty Organization, the British Foreign Office, and, doubtless, the police of half a dozen countries would like very much to be informed.

Chu Hoong was more than a millionaire who had amassed a great fortune by selling a potion eagerly lapped up in every part of the Orient. Regardless of how he effaced himself, men with North's knowledge of the Far East knew that Chu had his fingers in a whole bakery of pies, shipping, textiles, tea, rubber, rice, tin, and—although there never had

50

been the slightest shred of proof nailed to the little fat man
—opium.

As far as the G-2 colonel had ever heard, Chu Hoong had
never become involved in politics on any large scale. His system seemed to be to support with liberal donations about
every political party that dunned him, operating on the theory that no matter who won the ever-mounting struggle for
power, Chu Hoong would be in solid. For that reason, Hugh
could not quite sell himself on the idea that Chu could be
a Red agent involved in the case of Dr. Hans Bracht.

Still, there had been a reaction when Chu had faced Bracht,
violent on both sides, and the multimillionaire thereby had
joined the list of people to be watched. But a Red agent?
It was almost inconceivable that Chu would so far desert
his many sharply angled principles as to act as either agent
or tool of the Reds. He didn't need to for money reasons;
his political philosophy—or cynicism—forbade it.

Still, the arm of the MVD was long and its hand reached
into strange places to come up with agents, coerced into
obedience or victims of their own idealism. Under these circumstances no man, least of all Hugh North, was safe in
positively writing off Chu Hoong as a possible tool of
Moscow.

"Mr. Boyden," the Chinese was saying smoothly, "I am
going to do the unforgivable and ask you again why you are
in Bangkok. You have every right to be outraged at this
invasion of your privacy but, believe me, I have my reasons
for asking."

"And I have my reasons for declining to answer," Hugh
replied, as smoothly. "Let's just say it's a business deal that
hasn't been completed yet. Until it is signed, sealed, and
delivered I can't talk about it, I'm sorry."

Chu Hoong took the rebuff without a change of expression. "I understand," he murmured. "Then may I ask you
this: has this business deal anything to do with a certain
teak lumber cartel I may have heard rumors of?"

"God damn it!" North exploded furiously, and then caught
himself. "I'm sorry, Mr. Chu, but the office—I mean—no,
of course not. It has nothing to do with teak. Hell, I couldn't

51

tell a stick of sapwood from heartwood if my life depended on it. No sir, Mr. Chu, it has nothing to do with teak, believe me!"

He watched Chu's eyes as he launched forth with this fierce and senseless protestation, and when he was through he knew he had to put it down as a good try but no score. The little devil, Chu, hadn't had the slightest thought that he really was connected with any teak cartel—a hundred to one there wasn't any such thing in the making—and North's "off-guard" explosion had done nothing more than confirm in the multimillionaire's mind the idea that Hugh North, "Mr. Boyden," was in Thailand for reasons other than commercial.

"I am relieved to hear that." Chu smiled after a tiny pause. "You see, Mr. Boyden, I am interested in lumber, among other things. If you had been an agent for—shall we say the opposition?—you would necessarily have to be considered my enemy and I would not like that. No, I am basically a friendly person, Mr. Boyden, and it's always unpleasant to me when a situation requires my action against another man. It has happened quite often, I'm sorry to say, and I've always felt sad at what I've been forced to do to these *business* enemies. I am so happy that you are not a member of the—ah—opposition."

"I'm glad too," Hugh said simply. "Because, like you, I've had to deal directly with certain *business* enemies and sometimes it's been a pretty messy business. I'm so glad we won't have to butt heads, as the saying goes."

"A very expressive way of putting it," Chu Hoong beamed. "And here we are at the Imperial. May your stay with us be happy, Mr. Boyden, and feel free to call on me for anything you wish. Anything."

Including a knife in the back? Hugh asked, but silently, while he smiled his thanks.

Inside the luxurious lobby (Chu Hoong having had himself driven around to a private entrance after dropping the G-2 colonel) North looked about for signs of his missing ward, Dr. Hans Bracht.

He caught no glimpse of Bracht, but Lita Naline had arrived; there was no mistaking that. When Hugh had last seen her at Don Muang Airport she had been complaining loudly and she still was. Trying to soothe her and keep her voice from shattering glass were a covey of hotel minions, some underlings from the *Tiger, Tiger!* company, and her lover-director, Anton Carss.

"I don't care what time it is," the lovely Lita was declaiming, "I want a masseur and a hairdresser right now, before I even go up and look at the lousy suite. I know I'm a fright. All those hours cooped up in that stinking plane and then that Cook's Tour of Bangkok in the middle of the night—what jerk thought that up?"

"A fright?" Anton Carss asked, aghast. "Why, you never were lovelier, dear Lita."

"Ha, I'll bet! And if it was that Italian, what's-her-name, you'd probably have a masseur and a hairdresser and God knows what waiting for her."

"Perhaps." Carss nodded.

"What?" Stark outrage.

"I said perhaps we would have those things for her because for her there would be a need. For you, no, darling."

Lita melted. "Oh, Anton," she sighed, "you say such nice things. No wonder I love you more than anybody."

"And now," offered the manager of the Imperial, a large, over-dressed Greek, presently completely wilted, "will the lady be gracious enough to look over her suite to make sure it is as she wants it?

"Except," he added hastily, "for the masseur and the hairdresser, who will be here first thing in the morning, I personally promise you."

Lita Naline, her famous show smile recovered, reached out to touch the manager's cheek with a light pat. "You're a doll," she told him.

Despite his concern for Dr. Bracht, Hugh automatically registered the black shadow that flitted across Anton Carss's face. A damned jealous man, there, North told himself, if he got upset over a meaningless kittenish tap like that.

The G-2 colonel was passing the little curio shop that

apparently had stayed open late to lure the moneyed arrivals when Lita hailed him from across the lobby. "Hoo-hoo," she squealed. "Mr. Boylan or whatever it is. Hey, you in the gray suit!"

Hugh bit back what he wanted to say and turned, his Boyden smile in place. Lita descended upon him, trailed by *Tiger, Tiger!* sycophants, Carss at her side.

"We found your boy friend," Lita said with a dazzling smile.

"Boy friend?" the colonel asked.

"Oh, the old man on the plane, the one you protected from that perfectly foul person in the wrinkled white suit. He said he was with you in a cab and you had an accident."

North repressed his sigh of relief. "Oh, Mr. Barrows," was the best he could offer at the moment.

"My God, what happened?" Lita wanted to know. "Anton and I found the guy wandering around in a perfect *daze,* didn't we, Anton? Mumbled something about kidnapers and dope fiends being after him and all that sort of jazz, didn't he, Anton?"

2.

"*Dope fiends?*" The question was jerked out of the G-2 colonel by his surprise. What in the name of heaven had Hans Bracht told this loose-mouthed woman in the shock of his experience?

"That's what he said." Lita nodded vociferously. "He said the two of you—"

It was Anton Carss who came to North's rescue to prevent Lita Naline from broadcasting Bracht's words in a voice that surely must have carried to Klong Toi, twelve miles down the Menam Chao Phya.

"Now, Lita," he said gently, but with a hint of iron beneath the velvety voice, "we mustn't let the whole world know about the accident and perhaps involve that nice old

54

gentleman, with the police. A little less volume, please, darling."

Lita lowered her voice dramatically, came so close to Hugh that her celebrated bosom twin-branded his chest. "It's a fact," she breathed. "It was positively weird. I thought I saw the guy leave the airport with you, you see, and then I happened to look over—I was sitting on the back of this open car, you understand—and there he was, sort of stumbling along the sidewalk and—and—" She ran out of breath and inhaled, swelling the magnificence that outjutted all her sisters' claims to dramatic talent. "We were just in time, too, weren't we, Anton?"

"Lita darling, don't you think—"

"Just as we drove past and I recognized him—we had a police escort, of course—this mugger came up behind him. I screamed and the cops with us— Well, there was a lot of excitement and Anton grabbed Mr. Barrows and hauled him into our car and—well, I guess he was all shook up, but anyway he said—"

"Lita," Carss rumbled with another steel core to his furry voice, "you must not excite yourself. You have that official reception early tomorrow and you know you're never at your best if you don't get your sleep."

"Omigawd," the self-styled maharajah's daughter cried. "A big do like that and I'll look like a hag! Come on, Anton; what're we hanging around here for?"

She was gone, Carss trotting after her. Hugh North mentally drew a shaking hand across his brow. Thank his lucky stars for favors received. If Lita Naline's cavalcade had not passed a certain street corner at exactly the right minute, Dr. Hans Bracht doubtless would be in the hands of the Reds right now. Instead, by the way Lita spoke, he was safe in this hotel—if he hadn't taken it into his logarithm-packed head to take off for parts unknown again.

He headed for the desk where the Greek manager of the Imperial stood, breathing heavily and mopping his forehead with a large silk handkerchief, exhausted by his set-to with the fair Lita.

55

"I'd like to inquire about a Mr. Barrows," Hugh began. "Is he—"

The manager's face assumed a piteous expression. "Please, kind gentleman," he begged. "Let us not have any more unpleasantness over the mistake that was made. I am deeply ashamed at the stupidity of my clerk, but such things will happen. They do happen to me, I assure you. Mr. Barrows gave me to understand that he was completely satisfied and now you— Oh, I implore you not to add to my troubles now."

"Wait a minute," Hugh said. "Just what happened?"

"The desk clerk should have known that merely because Mr. Barrows arrived at the hotel in Miss Naline's company did not mean that he was Mr. Wallen. No, that fool, that brainless sonofabitch, should have known that an elderly gentleman such as Mr. Barrows could not be the motion-picture star, Mr. Wallen. You would have known it, sir, and so would I, but that goat, that toad of a clerk, has never shed the scales from his eyes and that is why he put Mr. Barrows in Mr. Wallen's suite. I assure you, sir, there was no intent to embarrass Mr. Wallen or Mr. Barrows, even though Mr. Wallen seemed to consider the whole affair as a personal affront. And now you, I suppose, wish to add to Mr. Wallen's complaint and—"

"Not at all," Hugh broke in to stop the manager's impending tears. "I only wanted to check on what room Mr. Barrows is in now."

"Room 439, sir, the room he had reserved," the manager said, seeing a reason to live again. "As I said, he assured me he was quite comfortable in Room 439. It is a nice room; no suite like Mr. Wallen's but a very comfortable room. All the rooms at the Imperial are comfortable, all very modern. You will see." He remembered his obligations as an innkeeper and gave North a beautiful bow. "Welcome to the Imperial, sir. We hope your stay will be very pleasant. Guided tours of the city may be arranged at the travel bureau in the lobby, opening at nine o'clock sharp tomorrow morning. Good evening, sir."

Then, as though fearing that to linger further would invite

some new catastrophe, the manager headed for his office, stepped inside, and closed the door after him. Hugh North could hear a bolt being forcibly shoved home.

The G-2 colonel went to the bank of house phones and asked for Room 439. There was the click-click of the connection and more clicks as the operator pressed the key that rang Bracht's phone. Alarm was rising within North again when the receiver at the other end was finally lifted.

"What is it?" Hans Bracht asked harshly.

"This is Boyden," North said. "I just wanted to make sure—"

"Stay away from me!" the missile genius shouted. "You're going to ruin everything by your meddling."

"Mr. Barrows," Hugh began, "listen to me a minute."

"I listened to you once against my better judgment and you know what happened. They nearly killed me for disobeying orders. No, I'm not going to have anything more to do with you, Boyden or North or whatever your name is. I'm going to play it my way!"

The phone was slammed down with a crash that made Hugh's head ring. The colonel hung up slowly, wincing at the prospects. To be honest, he could hardly blame the missile genius in Room 439 for being less than enthusiastic about his services so far, but that did not alter the fact that re-enlisting Bracht's co-operation was going to be a tough assignment. Fear that Marchet's appearance, and possibly Chu Hoong's, might mess up the ransom negotiations for Tao Muong's release had forced Bracht into a reluctant agreement to work with North; now the same fear had driven Bracht right back to the un-co-operative side of the fence again.

The colonel sighed. How winsome could a hard-bitten G-2 agent get in trying to win back a cantankerous old fool who— But hold it! North told himself to remember that this man was half crazy from worry for his missing wife; he could be excused a lot of wrong thinking.

North went to the desk and registered, got his key. Yes, he had the room adjacent to Bracht's, 437. His bags had arrived from the airport and would be sent up immediately. The clerk who gave these assurances bore the look of a man just released from the rack; apparently the Greek manager had chided him more than mildly for the Wallen-Barrows mix-up.

Now for something to eat, North told himself. Bracht was reasonably safe, shut up in his room, still unstrung from the cab crash and hardly likely to go sightseeing. Or was he? In any case, a man had to eat, and the airline sandwich had been too long ago.

He found one of the hotel's many dining rooms still open, serving a scattering of late airline arrivals plus some Orientals who may have been SEATO officials. North chose a table which gave him a good view of the doorway and ordered up an omelet as a safe test of the Imperial's kitchen.

He was waiting for his supper, sipping a delicious cup of tea, when the slender, beautifully tailored figure of Lita Naline's colleague, Lex Ross, entered the dining room, looked about him as though searching for someone, spotted North, and beelined across the room to the G-2 colonel's table.

"Mind if I join you?" he asked. There was plenty of charm in the actor's voice but something more than that, a kind of urgency that forestalled Hugh's intended brush-off.

"Glad to have you," North said pleasantly. "It's Mr. Ross, isn't it?"

"That's right, Lex Ross, and your name's Boyden." The gray-templed actor smiled. "And I trust you have our famous friend safely tucked in bed?"

A chill struck the pit of Hugh North's stomach and slowly widened. His face did not change, nor his voice, but he recognized danger in those fluid words, spoken with the actor's professional timbre.

"Famous friend?" the Intelligence agent asked, half-mooning his eyebrows. "Come again?"

Ross hunched his shoulders, slipped into the chair opposite North, leaned over, and spoke in a voice barely above a murmur. "Afraid I'm sticking my nose in," he said. "You see, I knew that was Hans Bracht the minute he stepped aboard the plane in Hong Kong."

3.

Oh, fine! First Marchet and now this movie actor, Lex Ross, of all people. Not to speak of Chu Hoong if the Dragon's Tooth Elixir maker actually did know Bracht. Shout it in the streets; put it on the front page! This was just dandy.

North's long training forbade him to inject even a note of wariness in his voice when he spoke. "Hans Bracht?" he asked. "I'm still out in left field, Mr. Ross."

The actor made an impatient gesture with a long, artistic hand. "Oh, come now," he said. "You're quite safe in having me know the man. I'd never tell—"

He shut off his words as Hugh's waiter approached the table with the omelet. Ross ordered a pot of tea and some cakes and, as the mess-jacketed waiter retired, gave Hugh an on-camera smile.

"As I was saying, the secret's perfectly safe with me, Boyden. But I do know it's Hans Bracht. Had the pleasure of attending one of the three public lectures he made before he retired into the great silence, and he's got a face that's not easy to forget, especially for somebody in my business."

He paused, but the G-2 colonel was busy with the omelet he suddenly did not want.

"You see," Ross went on after a wait, "I make a specialty of disguise. I've become a bit too long in the tooth to play dashing young leading men, and since I enjoy my work and want to stay in it as long as I can I've specialized in something that doesn't require a Rock Hudson face. I'm a menace with emphasis on the art of make-up disguise."

As North stirred restlessly the other man held up a hand. "I'm telling you this so you'll understand how I recognized Bracht on sight, even without his beard. To the master of make-up, as to the art student, bone structure means everything, and even a full beard such as Bracht wore couldn't hide the nose, the eyes, the cranial structure, and— But I didn't mean to get technical."

"Very interesting, I'm sure," Hugh murmured, "but why tell me all this?"

"Because," said Lex Ross coolly, "you're quite obviously the man assigned to protect Dr. Bracht while he's traveling. It figures. Here we have the world's greatest space-travel authority going halfway around the world, not only incognito but in disguise, if you can call it that. Would Washington let him travel alone? Of course not. When that Frenchman approached him you were right there—oh, very smoothly and professionally—to keep your man out of harm's way."

Hugh North laid down his fork deliberately, touched his napkin to his lips.

"Mr. Ross," he said, "I don't know what you're aiming at but I remember reading something in the Victoria paper in Hong Kong that said Hans Bracht was at Cape Canaveral, putting the finishing touches on some kind of missile deal, a Mars shoot or something like that. Now how could the man be in Florida, back in the States, and still be riding the Bangkok plane, will you tell me?"

"Oh, that." Ross shrugged. "They could put that out easily enough to protect Bracht's incognito."

North laughed, sipped his tea, and pushed back his chair. "Excuse me, Ross," he said, his voice half nettled, half amused, "but I've had a long day and I'm going to have another one tomorrow, closing a business deal, I hope. I'd like to spend more time listening to your story about incognitos and bone structure and stuff but I'm afraid—"

He stopped, his eyes fixed on the doorway. The Bangkok police or the Imperial Troop, whichever was represented here, were not the Keystone Kops he had thought they might be. For heading toward him was a small, scowling Thai officer with a large businesslike gun at his hip. There was not a doubt in the world that he was there to put the hand on Colonel Hugh North.

The G-2 agent waited while the small man drew up in front of him, raised himself to the top of his five-feet-one height, and asked in a piping voice: "Misser Chahss Boyden?"

North nodded. "That's me."

"Cappain Pilanung Pokh, Bangkok Imperial Troop. You under arrest, pliss."

Lex Ross spoke up before North could reply. "Arrest? Why, officer, this man's—"

Pokh whirled on the handsome actor seated at the table. "Quiet, pliss," he rapped out. "You keep still like good gentleman or maybe I arrest you too on same charge."

"Which is?" Hugh North asked.

The Thai's brown eyes came back to bore up into the colonel's.

"Murder," said Captain Pilanung Pokh of the Bangkok Imperial Troop.

Hugh heard Ross's gasp, sensed the consternation of the nearest diners who had overheard Pokh's blunt word, and at the same time the G-2 agent's brain clicked into high gear. Murder, and even the Thai police would know better than to think the cab driver had been killed in anything but the smashup. That probably meant that whoever had sicked the cops on him, the ones who had arranged the whole auto-smash ambush, had disposed of that Manchu knife wielder sometime after North had been picked up by Chu. Somehow, somebody in the crowd that had hired the Chinese cutthroat had added to that broken arm North had given him and had notified the police that an American named Boyden, staying at the Imperial, was responsible for the complete job.

They worked fast, these boys, and they played for keeps.

But why pin a murder frame on him; what was their objective? Simple; they wanted him out of the way, thrown into the Bangkok clink, so they would have a clear way to Dr. Hans Bracht.

Hugh wordlessly started for the dining-room door, Pokh trotting at his side. "Do not try getaway," the little Siamese twittered. "I best shot in whole country."

The captain uttered these words just as North was passing the table occupied by the bulky Russian textile commissar, Boris Salenkov. And did the Red fail to hide a smirking smile as he looked up at the colonel from behind his steel-framed glasses; was the light in his eyes triumphant?

North kept on, not slowing his pace until both men were

61

outside the gawking dining room and down a corridor to the door of one of the small, seldom-used parlors affected by all such big hotels. Unbidden, Hugh turned into this dimly lit room and turned to face Captain Pokh.

"No tricks," the little Thai warned. "We go to headquarters quick-like."

"Listen, Captain," Hugh said tersely, "I've got to get in touch with General Genung right away. Where do I telephone him?"

Pokh stared up in amazement. "You crazy man?" he asked. "You want to call General Genung in middle of the night? He chop you up in little pieces. Most angry fellow when annoyed after office hours, General Genung."

"I'll take my chances on that," North grunted. "I don't think he'll be annoyed when I tell him what I have to say. This murder charge is a frame, Captain, a—a—" He reached for a simpler word to give Pokh.

"Oh, I know what frame is," the diminutive officer chirped. "Know all American police words. But this no frame. Have word of most honorable witness that you killed poor Chinese auto driver because you mad he hit your taxicab."

"I didn't kill him; I only broke his arm when he came at me with a knife," North protested. "He was knocked out when he—er—when he fell. There were a hundred people—"

He checked himself. Which one of that crowd would step forward to support his story, even if one of that mob actually did not believe he had killed the Manchu with that judo toss? They were wasting time arguing the point; he had to get to Bracht. He walked to the door of the parlor, looked up and down the corridor to make sure it was empty, turned back to Pokh, who was fingering his revolver butt again.

"Captain," he said in a voice barely above a whisper, "my name isn't Charles Boyden. It's North, Hugh North, and I'm with the United States Army, Intelligence Division."

Little Pokh's face wrinkled in a disdainful grin. "Ho, this is new one," he crowed. "I have arrested men who said they were boss in SEATO and would have me thrown out of Imperial Troop. Once I got a pickpocket who said he one of royal family, but I never got Intelligence officer of the

62

U. S. A. Army before." He shook his head, his toupee wagging decisively. "No good, Misser Boyden. We go headquarters and—"

"But I can't leave the hotel," North said urgently. "The ones who fixed the frame want to get me away from here so they— Can't you call General Genung? Just mention the name Hugh North to him; I'm sure he'll tell you to cooperate with me."

Pokh had had enough of this. The time had come, he obviously decided, to get tough with this big American and his silly story about calling General Genung in the middle of the night, and the general enjoying the new wife he had married only a week before. The little man resumed his official scowl and tapped the ponderous revolver at his side.

"No more foolishment," he barked. "We go headquarters. And no tricks, Misser Boyden. Must tell you I am whatyousay fast on draw, shoot you dead before you wink your eye if you try tricks."

"I'm not so slow with a gun myself," North said grimly. "See?"

And Captain Pilanung Pokh looked into the O of a .38-caliber revolver's muzzle, one inch from his button nose.

The Thai captain gave a squawk of outraged amazement and then, crazily, suicidally, went for his own gun. North moved with camera-shutter speed, and when Pokh recovered his balance (he never knew whether he had been pushed or pulled or both, and why had his knees suddenly buckled?) his heavy pistol was in the colonel's left hand, its muzzle making the second of a deadly pair of eyes.

There was a moment's stark silence before Hugh smiled gently. "Always remember to give a murder suspect a frisk, Captain," he said. "Now, do we telephone General Genung?"

Pokh spluttered in Thai, undoubtedly blasphemously, before he got his linguistic gears into English. "Why you no shoot—I mean, give me my gun. Is bad trick to take my gun away like that."

"Admitted." North nodded. "But I had to show you I'm no murderer. If I were I'd put a round through that second tunic button or at least let you have a gun barrel over the

63

head, wouldn't I? Instead, I'm asking you to call General Genung."

Captain Pokh considered. It was a bad moment for Hugh. If this little man's "face" had been too badly shaken he could prove a mortal enemy, an obstacle to all Hugh would have to do while in Bangkok. The captain had fancied himself as an oriental Wyatt Earp, and to have had his gun taken from him as easily as a lollipop lifted from a mewling infant must have been a crushing blow to his ego. Now the question was whether Pokh would be so insulted that he would refuse to reason, and if his shame and anger made him positively balk at calling Genung, what would be North's next move?

Then Hugh relaxed. A beautiful grin overspread Pokh's face and North knew that here was a walking miracle, a Far Eastern official with a Western sense of humor, able to laugh at himself.

"Okay," the little captain said wryly. "You win. But I make whatyousay proposition. You don't tell General Genung about taking my gun and I'll call him, get him right out of new number-five wife's arms. Is deal?"

"Is deal," said North promptly. He debated his next step quickly, decided it was a risk worth taking, seeing that he wanted to make a good friend of all Bangkok police authorities, starting with Captain Pokh. He reversed the heavy, badly balanced revolver he had taken from the Thai and offered Pokh the butt of his gun. "Here you are," he said. "I never had it."

Pokh beamed, bowed. "You are real gentleman, Misser North," he said, and slid the great weapon into its holster. "We go call General Genung from lobby, hey?"

North rubbed a thumb along his jaw. "Just how safe is the hotel switchboard?" he asked.

The captain shrugged. "Sorry to say all telephones in Thailand not good for secrets. Is pretty new here. Everybody like to listen, tell everybody else what he hear. General Genung speak English, though." He looked about to make sure his general had not rolled into the parlor. "Not good like

64

me, but he pretty good. Eavesfaller don't understand you if you speak English to him."

But Chu Hoong would. Or Mary Hollberg. Or quite possibly Comrade Boris Salenkov.

"We'll take a chance on calling from my room," he decided. "Maybe I can get over to the general without saying too much."

The two men, tiny police captain and strapping G-2 agent, crossed the deserted lobby to the elevators, entered the only one in operation at this hour, and ascended to the fourth floor. If Chu Hoong had built this luxurious pile he had saved money on the elevators; it seemed to North to take forever to gain the fourth floor. Room 437 was next to the last door on a corridor stretching to the left from the elevator bank; Room 439 was at the end of the hall, an outside corner room.

Hugh noted the fact and frowned. People in Bracht's position should never be given outside corner rooms; it made it too easy for the Opposition. Unwelcome strangers could be lowered from the room above from two directions and then, too, an outside corner room with its windows gave long-distance snipers two angles from which to peer through telescopic sights.

He unlocked his door, entered, snapping on the overhead lights, and crossed directly to the connecting door to 439. He checked it, found it locked, and rattled his knuckles against the panel. The response was immediate.

"Who is it?" Hans Bracht asked sleepily. "What do you want?"

Good; Bracht was a light sleeper. Or had he been lying there, fighting to stay awake, waiting for that phone call from the kidnapers that he had mentioned on the way in from Don Muang?

"It's Boyden," North said into the crack between door and frame. "Just checking to make sure you're all right."

There was a snort from the scientist. "Leave me alone," Bracht growled. "Let a man sleep."

"Did you get your call?"

"No, I— Leave me alone, can't you?" Hugh could hear the faint pad of Bracht's bare feet leaving the connecting door and then there came the creak of springs, the rustle of bedclothes.

The Intelligence officer turned back from the door, reassured. They had not made their follow-up move after the framed arrest; it was possible that They knew he had stayed out of jail and had canceled their plans or postponed them.

Captain Pokh was politely engaged in studying a hideous chromo that hung on the wall, his ears almost but not quite vibrating visibly. Hugh walked to the cowhide portmanteau that had been set on the luggage rack, opened the case, and drew out a bottle of Dewar's White Label.

"Would it be a terrible breach of regulations for you to have a small drink before we talk to General Genung?" he asked the captain.

Pokh looked horrified. "On duty?" he asked. "Good heaven, General Genung chop me in pieces." He studied his wrist watch and beamed beatifically. "I off duty in eighteen minutes," he added. "You go ahead; I join you later."

North nodded, splashed a generous dollop of scotch into a bathroom glass, and added a light dusting of tap water. He swallowed the drink in two gulps, grateful for the invigorating warmth that spread through his bone-weary body. Since he had picked up Bracht at Manila he had had about four hours' sleep, and this mission, with all its weird peculiarities, looked as though it was not going to give him much leisure time for rest and relaxation. North would have been the first to agree that scotch was a poor substitute for sleep, but there were times when one was impossible and the other came in mighty handy.

Then, while Pokh watched wonderingly, the G-2 colonel made a tour of the room, tilting the awful chromo and the mirror on the other wall, running his fingers on the underside of bed, bureau, and desk, unscrewing the base of the telephone with a pocket-knife screw driver and examining the wires therein, reversing all the rugs, standing on a chair to feel along the top of the window. At length he quit his search and went back to the phone, dusting his hands.

"I don't think they've bugged me but I haven't time for a real look," he told Captain Pokh. "I want to talk to the general. What's his phone number?"

4.

Five minutes later, North hung up the telephone and heard a marveling Captain Pokh exclaim: "Is a wonder! I get General Genung out of warm bed and when he begin to scream and curse you take telephone and say one-two words and lo, General Genung is like father with ugly daughter talking to nearsighted suitor. What you say to him, Colonel North? I don't understand those words."

"Let's hope whoever may have been listening in didn't understand, either." Hugh grimaced. "How about that drink now?"

Pokh looked at his wrist watch earnestly. "Has been running very slow lately," he said finally. "Is surely time up now, thank you."

North mixed a strong drink for Pokh, a milder one for himself, handed the little captain his highball, and took his own to the bed, where he lounged while he talked.

"I gave your general a couple of code identification words that my crowd sent him when this job began," he explained to the awe-struck Thai. "I'd hoped I wouldn't have to involve you boys in this case, but when They put that murder frame on me I could see trouble ahead unless I cleared myself with you."

"You are here on big mission, hey?" Pokh murmured. He jerked his head toward the connecting door. "Is about him?"

"There are a lot of things involved," North said vaguely. "Tell me about the tip that I murdered the Manchu—any idea where it came from?"

Pokh shook his head. "Came to me from headquarters on radio. Was close to hotel anyway, and radio says Misser Chahss Boyden wanted for murder of poor Chinese in Samsen district. First went to murder—*accident* scene. Everybody

67

there say big American run away after Chinese fall down dead. Come back to hotel; clerk say you in dining room and tell me what you look like—large, pretty man with brown eyes, curly hair, white teeth—oh, real pretty man!"

"Never mind that, damn it," North growled. "You say you were close to the hotel when the call came from headquarters, so it couldn't have taken you long to do all this. That means whoever phoned headquarters must have put in the call right after the fight."

"Did not take long," Pokh agreed. "I was leaving hotel after escorting Miss Movie Star Lita Naline, beautiful woman, from airport to hotel. Was fine parade. Blew siren like hell alla way. Oh, very fine, noisy procession."

North sat bolt upright. "You were in that parade? Then you must have seen the commotion when Miss Naline's car stopped and she took a man into her car—a man who'd been walking along the street."

Pokh nodded placidly. "Oh yes. Man name of Barrows. American like you. Got lost in Bangkok and was very fortunate we come by. Badman in crowd was going to"—he searched among his "American police words" and found what he was after—"going to *mug* him, by goodness. Miss Naline screamed, badman fled."

He stopped long enough to take a mighty swig of his highball and then regarded North pridefully. "But he not get away," he announced. "Is caught by Sergeant Lagynan two-three blocks from scene of attempted crime."

North bounced to his feet, his glass slopping. "What? You mean you got the guy?"

Another placid nod. "Of course. *Nobody* get away from Imperial Troop. You know about Bangkok Imperial Troop, Colonel? Is private army suppose to only guard King but is *real* police force in Bangkok, better than stupid city policemen, so got authority anywhere in country if we want it. Was organized in—"

"Yes, yes," North broke in. "What about this man you caught?"

"Oh, is miserable Macanese who calls himself Aloysius

68

Robinson, real name unknown but something low, have no doubt."

"Macanese—you mean this Robinson is from Macao? A traveler? What do you know about him?"

Pokh's button nose wrinkled in disgust. "Nothing good. He is no traveler, just whatyousay hoodlum that goes from one place to another, anywhere he can make mischief. He should be kept out of Thailand, but strange shh-shh influences let him in and protect him, too. Lock him up for anything, bothering little girls, picking pockets, getting drunk and beating people, and strange shh-shh influences get him out of jail quick-like. Is so that we don't bother to arrest him any more. Give him kick in"—he used a Thai word— "and tell him begone."

"But this time you must have locked him up."

Pokh nodded. "Oh yes," he said unenthusiastically, "but is dollahs to"—he searched again and came up with a near miss—"dollnuts he is out by now. Make five thousand bahts bail pssst, like that, and goes out again, scotch-free." He looked at his empty glass as he said the word "scotch."

"Can you find out if he's in or out while I mix you another drink?" Hugh asked.

"Oh sure." Pokh smiled. "This time no water, pliss." He spoke over the phone in Siamese while the colonel poured a staggering jolt, and when he hung up the captain shrugged his narrow shoulders. "Is like I said," he told North. "Bail at headquarters almost before Sargent Lagynan get him there."

"Who is this Robinson? What do you know about him?"

Another grimace. "Is young whatyousay *hood*, twenty-one-two years old. Nobody knows what he does except make trouble. Always plenty money. Clothes full of loud colors. Was in U.S.A. plenty times, last time two-three months ago. Talks American dialect, bop. You know bop, Colonel?"

"Not enough to want to learn more," North grunted. "Has this Robinson ever been hooked up with the Communists, Captain?"

Pokh gave a brief laugh. "Aloysius Robinson? Even Communists tell him begone if he try to join them. This man *very*

69

dumb-stupid, Colonel. Makes trouble for everybody who try to— Whassa mattah?"

Colonel North had slapped a forefinger to his lips in the midst of Pokh's recitation. He had been intent on what the little captain had been telling him, but his long years of experience in this work had developed some part of his hearing mechanism to send out constant radar waves, if they could be called that, to pick up any sounds that needed explaining.

And there had been something, a click of metal against metal, a furtive scraping of a key in a lock or a latch being slipped, that did need explaining. Hugh moved silently to the door of his room, the snub-snouted .38 out and ready. Pokh started to speak, stopped at North's headshake, and then, seeing the colonel's gun, unholstered his own big pistol.

The scraping noise had stopped. North put his ear to the door, heard nothing for the space of about thirty seconds, and then the stealthy scratching clink began again.

Whoever was at work was operating on the door to Hans Bracht's adjacent room, and Hugh could tell from the sounds that he was no expert keyman. Himself an adept at picking locks when necessary, North knew that the types of locks installed in the Imperial's doors would take even a fair key-man only a few seconds to open, the night latches not much longer, and yet this prowler was making a First National Bank job out of it.

Noiselessly the G-2 agent slipped open the night latch of his own door. He hefted his gun, seized the knob, and flung open the door, moving into the hall with a fluid motion that put him next to the crouched prowler in a single step, his .38 boring into the man's neck.

"Hold it," he hissed.

The figure under his gun stiffened, dropped the key he had been using. Colonel North grabbed the man's right arm and twisted it up and behind the prowler's back, jerked him upright, and whirled him around and through the door into Room 437 in a single motion.

"By goodness," Captain Pokh cried excitedly. "We just talking about no-good Aloysius Robinson and here he is!"

5.

Aloysius Robinson of Macao proved to be a narrow-shouldered, dark-visaged young man with an effluvious crop of greasy black hair and a nasty snarl that revealed bad teeth.

But it was not his face that made Hugh North stare as he twisted the hood away from him, still pinioned, to get a look; it was the clothes the man wore. It was a warm, humid night in Bangkok, and yet Robinson wore a heavy flannel sports coat of horse-blanket plaid, the predominant color a bilious yellow-green; a pair of mauve, almost purple slacks; the only pair of pointed saddle shoes North had ever seen in his life; a multicolored Hawaiian sports shirt, and, unbelievably, a blue-and-white-striped Guards tie. On the aforementioned oily hair, Robinson had perched a ridiculous red beret, the bopster's uniform helmet.

Aloysius was drunk. His breath and every pore of his unwashed body exuded the stink of stale whisky.

"Lemmo go," he burbled moistly as he glared back at North. "Got no ri' to do this."

Keeping a firm grip on the young man's wrist from behind, the G-2 colonel gave Robinson a quick, thorough frisk. He came up with an evil-looking switchblade knife but no gun. Hugh shoved the Macanese away, turning him so that the back of his knees caught the edge of the bed, dumping Robinson onto the coverlet.

"Stay right there," North warned.

Instead, Aloysius tried to struggle to his feet. He had barely started when North's hand prodded his shoulder and sent him back again.

"Goddamn you, you lousy—"

The colonel's hand whipcracked across the young man's mouth with a stinging slap. The jolt sent a shock of the greasy hair flopping down over Robinson's eyes, and Aloysius took quite a time to brush it back, his wavering stare trying to fix itself on North.

"You'll pay plenty f'r that," he managed finally, and drew the back of his hand across his mouth, looked down for

71

signs of blood that were not there. He looked back up at the colonel. "When I get through with you, Daddy-o, you'll wish you never—"

"Shut up!" Hugh North crackled. "Who are you working for?"

A sneer overspread the dark features. "Whaddaya mean, man, who'm I workin' for? Only squares work, didn't you know that? Me, I just lay back and let things transpire. Dig that, copper, that transpire bit?"

"Is most strange dialect, the bop," Pokh murmured. "Very confusing to Thai police."

"Oh, Strong Man here digs it, don't you?" Robinson jeered. "Strong Man here knows everything about everything but what's real. Reet, Strong Man?"

Hugh North clamped his jaws tightly to keep his words from spilling out. He counted himself as tolerant as the next man, but an accidental and brief acquaintance with some members of the beat generation during a recent trip back to the States had given him nothing but pain. If being the opposite to one of those people was to be a square, Hugh hoped all his corners were sharp.

Aloysius Robinson was trying to get to his feet again. Hugh shoved the young man back on the bed and leaned over him, breathing through his mouth to escape those liquor fumes.

"Listen, Robinson," he grated, "you can turn off the bop talk long enough to answer a couple of questions. Who sent you after that man on the street tonight, that Mr. Barrows? Who sent you up here to get into his room? You'd better talk, son, because I'm going to get some answers one way or another and there'll be nobody coming here to bail you out of this room till I do, I promise you."

"Big Man," Robinson gibed. "You scare me, Pops—you scare me to death."

North's hand reached down to bunch the gaudy sports jacket at the lapels. He pulled Robinson up toward him and grunted his words into the brown, pitted face. "You'd better scare, Robinson, because I get real mean when I'm sore and I'm sore now. Maybe you were there to see what

72

I did to that guy who came at me with a knife after that taxi smashup. That was just a broken arm until you boys finished the job, but it was real neat, don't you think? How'd you like one, or maybe a broken leg? Or a flattened nose? Because, believe me, I'd like to show you how neat I can be."

"You—you wouldn't dare," Aloysius faltered.

"Try me. Just keep on with this bop crap or giving me any other kind of lip and you'll see. Now, who sent you up here after Barrows?"

The black eyes slid away, roamed about the room. North's grip tightened and his left hand rose from his side, slowly, significantly. Robinson blurted his words: "I tellya nobody sent me nowhere," he protested. "I was just tryin' to get in my own room when you jumped me, is all."

"You've got to do better than that," North said grimly.

"I tellya that's the truth," Robinson squalled. "Lookit my key. It's for next door, Room 539. Lookit the key, wise guy, and you'll see I'm tellin' the truth."

Hugh jerked his head toward the door. "The key's on the floor just outside the door to 439, Captain," he said. Pokh slipped out and was back in a couple of seconds.

"This is the key to 539, Colonel," he said regretfully. "It is as this—this *ponk* says."

"Colonel?" Aloysius asked, his eyes widening. "What's with this colonel jazz, huh? If you're a colonel why ain't you wearin' a doorman suit with the sword, with the spurs, with the gold lace ricky-ticky? Why ain't you—"

"Oh, shut up," North said coldly. The number on the key tag meant nothing at all. Any half-smart group behind a move on Hans Bracht would have figured on a possible misfire enough to have an alibi ready for their man; a tag with a similar room number on it could be put on a skeleton key easily enough—didn't Chu Hoong own this hotel and wasn't he somehow linked with the Opposition?

"How about that business on the street when you tried to jump Barrows?" he demanded. "I suppose you made an honest mistake there, too."

Robinson slumped back, resting on an elbow. "Jeez, what

73

a blister," he complained. "A guy tries to do a guy a favor and first the cops throw him in the can and then this colonel character makes with the fierce questions."

He sat up again. "Look, Pops," he said, "all I know is what I told them down to the main place; I saw this guy, an old cat with the frantic look, walkin' along like he was lost, but I mean real lost, in orbit. Now Bangkok ain't a good place for an old gent with the vague look and maybe here is a chance to pick up a stray baht or six bein' a guide to this guy from Quaintsville. So I step up to him to be a boy scout and the parade comes by and a dame in one of the cars starts giving with the shrieks and screams. So I got out of there and a cop puts the arm on me, of course, to make a fast score and maybe earn a nod from Genung. And that's all."

"Is what he said at the station, I am inform." Pokh nodded.

North scowled down at the lurid figure on the bed. The trouble with this outlandish character's story was that it just possibly could be true, or at least true enough to separate Aloysius Robinson from any plot against Hans Bracht. Hugh had no doubt that the Macanese had slipped up on Bracht with the idea of picking his pocket or possibly mugging the scientist, but even so, a bit of sidewalk banditry did not place this unpleasant young man in the main picture.

As for the key alibi—North turned abruptly and walked to the phone. "Who is in Room 539?" he asked the operator after the sleepy acknowledgment of the call.

There was a wait and then the sleep-laden voice said: "Misser Ah—aah—Misser A. Robinson of Macao, pliss."

Hugh hung up to meet Robinson's triumphant smirk. "You satisfied now, Strong Man?" the oily-haired hood asked.

North said, "No, but I'm letting you out of here this time. And I warn you, Robinson; from now on I'll have my eye open for you, and if you make any more of your honest mistakes I'm going to lean on you. Hard. Now get out."

Robinson got off the bed and walked uncertainly toward the door, straightening the appalling jacket. When Pokh handed him his key he asked: "How about m'knife? You got no right to keep m'knife, copper."

74

"I know." The G-2 colonel smiled. "Suppose you make a complaint to the police. In court maybe I could find out how a crumb like you can afford a room at the Imperial. I could find out who pays for your liquor—I could find out a lot of things."

Aloysius Robinson gave a short, nasty laugh. "I can tell you right now, Snoop. A dame is payin' my way. A fat old dame that likes her men young and often. Dig me?"

"Get out of here before I change my mind," the colonel said disgustedly. "And don't cross my way again."

Aloysius Robinson teetered out into the hall and headed toward the elevators. Hugh watched him until the lift finally arrived to take him in and then turned back into Room 437.

"What you think now?" Captain Pokh asked.

Hugh shrugged. "It could be coincidence but it could also be something else. I don't know who'd hire an article like that for any important job." He thought of Mary Hollberg and her open pitch to him, her inexpert picturization of the concert pianist.

"But," he added, "maybe They operate differently in Thailand than anywhere else."

"Who is They?" Captain Pokh wanted to know, and hastened to append: "But maybe is not permitted to tell, hey?"

Hugh North measured his man. He had known this little Thai police officer only a short time and yet the undersized captain had given certain signs of eventually deserving his trust, something that the colonel gave or withheld by instinct more times than by objective reasoning. It was too early to take Pokh into his confidence, but Hugh had no doubt that sooner or later he would need an assistant, a fellow worker who understood the situation, and despite some of Pokh's comic-opera qualities it might be good to have a man like Pilanung Pokh available, if and when the time came.

"Let's just say for now that They are the Opposition, Captain." Hugh smiled. "And how about another drop?"

6.

Colonel North waited five minutes after Captain Pokh had left, promising to report back in the morning ("General Genung tell me to do anything you say, he don't care what"), before the G-2 operative went into silent action.

His first move was to the attaché case that rested on the floor near the baggage rack that bore the cowhide portmanteau. He scanned this case thoroughly, saw that the hairline thread that would have signaled tampering was in place, and unlocked it. From the assortment of odd items in the case he selected a small, compact article similar to a stethoscope but with a narrow, flat, bladelike piece in place of the stethoscope's round ear. The blade he inserted under the connecting door to Room 439 and fitted the earpieces in place.

Now Hans Bracht's breathing sounded as though it were only an inch removed from Hugh North; the street sounds filtering through the fourth-floor windows of the room next door were greatly magnified. The G-2 colonel listened for what would have seemed a long time to anybody who might have been watching this tableau until, satisfied at length that Bracht was indeed asleep, the colonel took the listening device from his ears, fitted the instrument back in its case.

Next he took out an array of tiny tools, some hooked at the end, others curved, some resembling keys and others files, and all composed of a material as strong as steel yet with the precious quality of absorbing sound like a sponge absorbing water. No matter how sharply one of these tools was struck against metal there was no more than a tiny dull thud, inaudible a foot away. (Proving that not all of the Army's scientific research was directed at the development of missiles, high explosives, or submersible tanks.)

It required Hugh only a few seconds to throw the latch on Bracht's side of the connecting door. The colonel stepped out of his cordovans with a practiced scuff and padded back to the attaché case. From this he extracted a pair of tinted glasses and a flashlight that looked as though it might have come from the dime store. His next step was to don the

76

glasses, snap off the lights in his room, press the flashlight button.

A bar of light streaked across to the farther wall, but the G-2 colonel was the only one who could have seen it; it was "black light," the miracle of ultra ray used by the Navy in World War II and brought to perfection in some of the nation's most secret, most closely guarded laboratories.

North went to the connecting door, eased it open, gently, gently, and slipped inside. He stood by the door for a full twenty seconds, measuring Bracht's fitful breathing. This was a touchy job, with the doctor such a light sleeper, so likely to be awakened by his horrid dreams born of his worry. Certain that Bracht was truly asleep for the moment, at least, North shot the lamp's black beam at the telephone on the bedside stand. Using the strange implements such as those he had employed on the door-latch, Hugh unscrewed the base of Bracht's phone, did things with wires, including the addition of a separate strand of cobweb-thin wires which he molded to the regular cord, then led it down to the edge of the wall-to-wall carpeting.

Out of sight from the phone's user and invisible to anyone who would not be looking for it, Hugh separated the cobweb wires from the cord and used its adhesive covering to mold it to the baseboard. He led this wire to the connecting door and through, into his room.

The whole operation required a little over one minute, and after Hugh had made a connection to his own telephone he was in business; now when Bracht got that telephone call from the people who were holding Tao Muong, Army G-2 would be listening in, in the person of Colonel Hugh North.

He did not have too long to wait. It seemed that three seconds after he lay down on top of his bed, fully clothed and with the listening device under the (carefully relocked) connecting door and attached to his ears, North was rocketed out of his sleep by the shrill of Bracht's phone. Actually it was something just over four hours; the colonel's wrist

77

watch showed the time at quarter to eight when the deafeningly amplified bell clamored its summons.

Hugh raised his own phone, clicked a switch, and heard the missile scientist's gruff hello.

The voice that spoke to Hans Bracht brought a deep crease to Colonel North's forehead. Was it man or woman, was that faint accent real or faked?

"Hans Bracht?" North checked the fact that these people were sure of themselves; they did not bother with the pseudonym the space-travel genius had used on his way out here.

"Yes!" Bracht was wide awake now and eager, hopeful. "Yes, I have been waiting for your call." So Bracht had spoken to this same person before; he recognized that muffled, distorted voice. "You said you'd call last night. I waited and waited but you didn't call—why not; has something gone wrong?"

"We call when it suits us, Doctor." There was the suggestion of the Germanic *Doktor* in the pronunciation of the word. "All you have to do is wait for us to contact you." That was an Americanism, "contact" used as a verb. "You are alone?"

"Yes, oh yes. I've been alone ever since I got here."

"But not on the way here, eh? We have reports that you violated our instructions." The stilted speech of the kidnaper was very noticeable; taken at face value it was the speech of one who thought in some other language while he spoke in English, but that was a ruse easily employed and often used.

"I didn't, I didn't!" Bracht protested. "I don't know what you're talking about!"

"No?" Coldly. "We have been told that you spoke to at least two persons aboard the plane from Hong Kong, that you dared strike up an acquaintance with the American movie slut, Lita Naline. You were seen entering the hotel with her."

"That—that was an accident," Bracht said wildly. "On the plane some man—somebody thought he recognized me. I—I told him he was wrong. What could I do, just sit there and refuse to speak?"

78

"But there was another person involved, a man named Boyden. Who is he?"

Hugh North held his breath while Bracht hesitated. Just how far would he go in protecting North's identity, this un-co-operative genius, who thought he had reason to mistrust all government operatives assigned to protect him? He exhaled a sigh of relief as Bracht replied.

"He says his name is Boyden, Charles Boyden. He interfered when this other man might have ruined everything by telling my real name. That's all I know."

"And you shared a taxi with him from the airport to the hotel—or at least you started out with him. Why?"

"There was no special reason. We went through customs together—Barrows and Boyden—and he asked me if I wanted to ride with him. You gave me no instructions about the trip from the airport to the hotel; it would have made him curious if I'd said no."

Good boy, North breathed. *Spoken like a pro.*

There was a moment's pause at the other end of the line and then the unusual voice indicated reluctant acceptance of Bracht's story. "All right, tell us about the accident."

"I don't know much about it," Bracht replied. "All of a sudden this car smashed into our cab. I was thrown out and I guess I was dazed. I thought—I don't know what I thought; anyway, I knew you didn't have anything to do with it so I ran away. I wandered along the streets until some cars came past and Miss Naline hailed me. She'd been on the Hong Kong plane with me but we hadn't even spoken to each other; I swear it! She said somebody was trying to attack me from behind when she saw me. I don't know whether that's right or if she imagined it. Anyway, there was some commotion and the police escort took after somebody, some man."

"You saw this man?"

"No. But that's the reason I rode to the hotel with Miss Naline. The only reason—on my honor!"

Another pause. "Well, it has not been good, Doctor. All this attention centered on you is bad. It will require investigation to see if you are telling the truth. If you're not

79

—I suppose you can guess what will happen to your wife if you're trying to play tricks on us, Hans Bracht."

"I'm not!" The scientist's protest was a wail. "I tell you I'm ready to do anything you say. I have the money with me. Tell me how to pay the ransom and get Tao Muong back."

"It is not that simple," the voice said, suddenly more alive than it had been, as though the speaker were angered. "If you had not become involved with all these people it would be easy, but now we must have a delay."

"No," Hans Bracht croaked. "No, you promised that when I—"

"I tell you we are giving the orders here! There will be a delay of at least three days, maybe more, before the transaction can be completed. Stay inside the hotel, close to your room, for the next several days, Doctor." Again the hint of the word *Doktor*. "You will hear from us. Do not show yourself on the streets of Bangkok; it will be dangerous for both you and your wife."

"Several days!" Bracht cried. "But you said— Oh, all right. Tao Muong, is she well? You aren't—you aren't stalling because you haven't got Tao Muong with you? Nothing's happened to her, has it?" Desperation welled up in Bracht's last question.

"She is with us and well," the voice replied, turned cold again. "You will be permitted to speak to her on the same terms as in Hong Kong. You will ask no questions, you will not even open your mouth while she is talking to you. We will be listening. Try to give her a message or learn where she is and we will act. I think it will be one of her lovely eyes that will be gouged out first if you try to play tricks with us, Doctor. You understand?"

"Yes, I understand. Let me hear her speak."

There was a moment's wait and then a woman's voice came on the wire, a high-pitched, twittery voice of ineffable sweetnesss, a bird-song voice that thrilled North even in this situation.

"Ah, darling Hans," the girl said, "it will not be long. Do as they say and soon we will be in each other's arms again. Do what they tell you, Hans, and they will not hurt me, but if you do not obey them—ah, my darling, it will be terrible! Do what they tell you, Hans, and we will soon be together. Good-by, beloved."

North heard Bracht groan softly. *Poor devil,* Hugh was forced to tell himself, *he's really in the middle. His wife tells him to play ball with these rats or she'll be tortured, and still out of his loyalty to his country and his mission he walks a razor's edge, covering for me. My hat's off to you, Hans Bracht, no matter what I may have thought of you before—and may think of you again.*

The voice that had opened this conversation took over. "You heard what your wife said, Doctor," it warned Bracht. "See that you follow our orders. We are not pleased by this interference—"

"But I tell you it wasn't my fault!" Bracht insisted. "I tried to follow orders."

"All right, we believe you until we investigate, at least. But if you are up to something, your wife will suffer. Stay within the hotel, near your telephone, for the next several days, remember."

The receiver at the kidnaper's end of the line was lowered with a muted click. Then, after a second, Bracht's phone was hung up. Hugh flipped the switch on the "bug" and lay back on the bed, frowning at the ceiling.

So Tao Muong—if that had been Tao Muong—was in Bangkok. The kidnaper had mentioned something about the conditions of this conversation between Bracht and his wife being the same as in Hong Kong. There had been no chance to bug Bracht's phone in Victoria, on Hong Kong Island; passengers aboard the plane from Manila had been taken into the city from Kaitak Airport on Kowloon Peninsula and were lodged in a hotel, but just long enough to lunch and freshen up, catch a short rest, and yet the kidnapers had known what room Bracht had been assigned and had used that opportunity to talk to him, let him hear from the real or pseudo Tao Muong.

Hugh reached out to the night stand and got a cigarette from the rumpled pack that lay there. This latest development was getting interesting. If Tao Muong had been in Hong Kong the day before, how had she gotten to Bangkok? Had there been a later flight from Hong Kong to the Thai capital that had not been listed on the regular schedules?

It required only a brief phone call to Don Muang Airport to knock this possibility in the head. No, Flight 184 had been the last plane from Hong Kong to land at Bangkok on the previous day.

Well, then, either They had flown Tao Muong over in a private airplane or it simply had not been Tao Muong who had spoken to Hans Bracht. The Reds must have on their list of agents some woman who could mimic Tao Muong's voice to perfection, and the stern restrictions that had kept Bracht from speaking to his "wife," asking her any questions, indicated that a stooge was being used.

Hugh cautioned himself that if it seemed incredible that a man with Bracht's brains could be led across the world by a phony voice over the wire, it had to be remembered that here was an elderly man hopelessly infatuated with a beautiful young wife. In his fear for Tao Muong's safety the space-travel king must have been a soft touch for even the vaguest proofs that Tao Muong lay at the end of the trip to Bangkok.

"I've got to gain the old boy's confidence somehow," North murmured, half aloud. "Maybe I should have invited him in on that little party with Robinson—it might have impressed on him the fact that the cab crash, Robinson's mugging attempt, the greasy wart's trying to get into his room mean that somebody's out to get him."

He shook his head at his own conjecture. Bracht would have been sure Robinson was what the young punk claimed to be, a man accidentally involved through no fault of his own.

Which, Hugh thought wryly, the guy just might be.

The colonel abandoned his thoughts, crushed out his cigarette, and began stripping off his clothes. The kidnaper's remarks about several days' lull in activities notwithstanding, it seemed advisable for a hard-working G-2

agent to refresh himself with cold showers and such whenever possible; it looked like a busy stretch ahead. Hans
Bracht was under orders to stay in the hotel; thank heavens
for that, at least.

He was emerging from the bathroom, his close-clipped
pepper-and-salt hair glistening with water drops, when his
phone rang.

"Mr. Boyden?" asked Mary Hollberg sweetly. "I've been
waiting to hear from you."

North glanced at his watch on the night table; eight-
thirty and Mary was certainly wasting no time. She was
indeed a different-type Red agent, if that's what she was;
no woman operative Hugh had met in his long career had
ever tried the seduction gambit before noon unless it had
been a continuation of the previous night's activities.

"I was pretty tired after the trip and it was so late I
didn't think you'd want to be bothered," he explained into
the mouthpiece.

"And I sat up until all hours, waiting," Mary mourned.

"Well—"

"How about breakfast?" the self-styled concert pianist
suggested.

North considered. He wanted to—had to—find out where
this German girl fit into this setup, and it seemed unlikely
that there would be a better opportunity to put Mary Hollberg through the wringer than now. Bright morning was
hardly the time for whoever could be after Bracht to make
a move—if any time was more unlikely than another—and
the kidnaper had just spoken to the scientist; there was
almost no possibility that they would call back within the
time it would take him to eat breakfast with Mary Hollberg.

"Fine," he said heartily. "Give me a few minutes to bathe
and shave and get dressed. I'll meet you in the dining
room."

"I had an idea we could have breakfast in my room,"
the girl said, and North could almost see her pout.

"Well—well, I'm supposed to meet a fella in the lobby,"
Hugh explained. "I wish I could make it in your room—I
sure do—but—well, you see how it is, Miss Hollberg."

A tiny pause and then: "Well, all right. I'll meet you in the dining room."

North's wide mouth quirked as he hung up the phone. Just what in hell was the blonde up to? Had she planned knockout drops in the Rice Krispies or was she one of that small but select sorority who considered it more fun in daylight? Or had she just now gotten her instructions from higher up, orders that had told her to get busy on the double?

He took his time dressing, waiting for some sound to tell him that Hans Bracht was up and around, but by the time he was ready to go there had been not a murmur from next door. North rapped on the connecting door, rapped again as the scientist ignored the first summons. Finally Bracht's harsh voice sounded with a "What is it?"

"Doctor, are the shades of your window drawn?" Hugh knew they had not been during his nocturnal visit; the question was merely an icebreaker.

Bracht apparently studied this question from all sides, found nothing in it to which the all-seeing eye and all-hearing ear of the kidnapers could object. "No," he said gruffly.

"Then please draw them for a moment," North said mildly. "I want to talk to you for a second and I promised I wouldn't do anything that the people who hold your wife might object to."

"Damn it, North, why don't you keep out of this? Why don't you leave me alone?"

"Because I want to see you get Mrs. Bracht back as soon as possible," Hugh returned. "I want to get you back safely in the States. Just draw the shades; certainly nobody can object to you being normally modest while you dress."

A grunt and then the sounds of Hans Bracht crossing his room to pull down the blinds. Hugh took advantage of this time to remove and pack the listening device. He waited until Bracht unlocked the latch on his side, then turned his own latch and pulled open the door.

The space-missile genius was in his pajamas, his frizzy hair starting wildly about his bald dome, his face haggard

84

despite the hours of restless sleep he might have had. Without his glasses, Bracht looked even older, wearier, than with the spectacles; his skin was gray with the strain he was under, and wattles that North had not noticed before hung from his jaw about his stringy neck.

"I'll be brief," Hugh rapped out. "Did you get your phone call?"

"You must have heard the telephone ring," Bracht growled. "Why do you ask me, then?"

"All right; answer me this. At any time since your wife disappeared have you had proof—positive proof—that these people you're dealing with have her?"

"I don't have to answer that," the scientist said in a surly voice.

"No, but I ask because I've got reason to believe that Tao Muong is still in the States, that whoever these people are, they've led you out here on a wild-goose chase."

He deliberately used an irritating know-it-all tone and it worked. Hans Bracht's thin-lipped mouth almost sneered openly. "Which shows how much you know," the missile man said harshly. "What would you say if I told you I spoke to my wife on the telephone a few minutes ago and she was here, in Bangkok?"

The G-2 operative donned a smug, supercilious smile. "And what would *you* say if I told you that it's a ten-to-one bet that the woman you spoke to wasn't your wife?" he asked. "That's an old trick, imitating voices."

It worked again. "This was Tao Muong!" Bracht graveled. "I guess I ought to know my wife's voice! And anyway, when I spoke to her in Hong Kong and before that, in San Francisco, she told me things that only she could possibly know. Intimate things; things I did not like her to be saying in the hearing of those animals who stole her. It *is* Tao Muong, I tell you."

North rubbed his chin. "You're positive?" he asked.

"I've never been more positive of anything in my life," the scientist said, and the utter sincerity, the complete lack of doubt, rang through his words.

"All right." Hugh nodded. "There's one more thing. I won't

85

go into it now because I haven't time, but I'm pretty sure that somebody, not necessarily these people you're dealing with, is out to kill you." He ignored Bracht's scornful grunt. "I don't know who they are or what their pitch is, but that cab crash, the man who tried to collar you before the movie people picked you up—"

"All accidental," Bracht broke in. "I admit I was jumpy and when that car hit us I lost my head. As for the man they say tried to approach me when Miss Naline happened by, I still don't believe he meant any harm. You've seen Miss Naline; she's excitable and she imagines things."

"Just the same," Hugh argued, "it would be smart for you to be careful. If you go out today, watch for—"

"I'm not going out. Not today nor tomorrow or probably the next day, if that gives you any satisfaction," Bracht broke in.

"It does," Hugh returned quietly, "if you really mean it— if you're not just saying that to get me out of the way."

"Believe me, I'd like to get you out of the way," the missile scientist said flatly. "It so happens, though, that I really do intend to stay in the hotel for the next few days, for reasons of my own."

"Then keep your door double-locked and have all messages pushed under the door," the G-2 colonel advised. "I'd also be very careful of what I ate."

Bracht thrust his head forward at the end of the long, scrawny neck. "Are you making the ridiculous suggestion that somebody might try to poison me?" he asked.

North hunched his shoulders. "It has been done, you know," he replied.

The sneer was back on Bracht's lips. "I don't know how you arrive at these deductions, North," the older man said. "Do you really believe that the people who kidnaped Tao Muong would bring me out here to pay the ransom and then poison me before they got the money?"

"No," the colonel conceded, "but this might be somebody not interested in the kidnaping of Tao Muong."

"Who?"

Hugh North sighed; could the man be so naïve as to

believe he wasn't the greatest prize a Red agent or a whole troop of Red agents could grab? Bracht read Hugh's expression and answered the silent question. "You mean the Communists? But why would they poison me? Kidnap me, yes, they might try to do that, but they certainly wouldn't try to kill me."

It was a question that had been bothering North. Why had They staged the taxi crash? Why had Aloysius Robinson tried to get his hands on Dr. Hans Bracht? Was Robinson a Red agent; had that Chinese knife wielder been a Red agent? Pokh had snorted at the idea of Robinson being anything but a cheap hood, never a man the Commies would pick to kidnap Hans Bracht, and the Manchu knifeman certainly had been no better than a crude cutthroat. The two incidents, the crash and the attempted encounter on the street, did not show evidence of the fine Communist hand. As for Robinson's try at getting into Bracht's room, that had been a bungled job that bore the amateur's stamp, if, indeed, it had not merely been a drunk's mistake.

The voice on the telephone had wanted to know details of the cab crash. Did that mean that the people who held Tao Muong were as much in the dark about that incident as North himself, or had that question been thrown in as a red herring?

"Well?" Bracht was asking.

North drawled, "Just the same, I'd be careful. Do you know who owns this hotel?"

The frizzy head wagged in a negative headshake. "No, and I don't care—what's that got to do with it?"

"Only this," Hugh said. "The owner is Chu Hoong."

Again that jolted reaction, but this time minus the fear that had shown in Bracht's face when he had met Chu aboard the plane. Now the scientist was surprised, concerned, but he was not afraid. Hugh followed his reasoning; Bracht had recently spoken to the kidnapers, and they had told him the deal for Tao Muong was still on despite Marchet's appearance on the scene, Chu's presence on the plane. Now Hans Bracht did not have to be afraid that the ransom deal might be wrecked, but at the same time he was disturbed by North's announcement.

"Chu Hoong? The Chinese who was on our plane?"

"The man I asked you about," the G-2 colonel reminded Bracht. "You said you never heard of him."

"I've never known anybody named Chu Hoong in my life," the missile man said stubbornly.

"Maybe you knew him under another name," Hugh suggested.

The other hunched his shoulders. "I've met a lot of Chinese people," he said. "They all looked alike to me, and who can remember their names? I'm sure about the name Chu Hoong, though—never heard it before."

"And Marchet?" North went on. "Do you want to tell me a little about Marchet so I can see where he might fit in?"

Hans Bracht shook his head again, savagely this time. "You said you wanted to speak to me for a second," he rapped out. "Your second's up and five minutes besides. Good day, Colonel North."

With which he turned and stalked through the connecting door, back into Room 439. The door slammed and there was the snap of the lock being thrown.

When this is all over, Hugh North told himself, *I'm going to give you a medal, Doctor. Most un-co-operative man I ever met. I hope I don't have to hang it on your tombstone.*

7.

Mary Hollberg looked charming. Dressed in a smartly cut suit of light green linen and wearing a hat that was stylish but not too absurd, she sat over an untouched cup of coffee at a table in the hotel's main dining room, waiting, as Hugh North crossed toward her.

Her smile was as sunny as the Bangkok morning and her blue eyes looked very young, very open, as she gazed up at him. "You're late," she said with mock severity. "You told me to meet you here in a few minutes. It's been"—she con-

88

sulted a tiny jeweled wrist watch—"exactly twenty-three minutes. I don't call that a few."

"I was held up," North explained, slipping into the chair opposite. As the waiter drew up at his side, poured a cup of coffee, the colonel glanced across the gleaming white cloth. "Have you ordered?"

"Nein." She used the German word instinctively but followed it in English. "I thought I'd leave that to you. You seem to be so well acquainted with this strange part of the world that I thought you could probably get me what I wanted instead of some nasty native dish."

"And what do you want?"

"Oh"—she waved a spike-nailed hand, and the emerald ring glistened—"ham, eggs, toast. Do you suppose they have them in Bangkok?"

"No reason why not." North laughed. "They have pigs here, and hens. I wouldn't say their ham is likely to be Smithfield, but we can be pretty sure of the eggs." He used French to give a double order of ham and eggs, took a sip of the coffee, and made no effort to repress a wry face before he emphatically asked for tea. Miss Hollberg laughed delightfully.

"Is the coffee not terrible?" she asked gleefully. "I was waiting for you to try it. But surely I should have known enough to get tea, as you did." She sighed. "It is so much better to have traveled as you have and know these things."

Nice try, Mary, but I'll still bet you've been here before and know all about Bangkok coffee. Still, a subtle touch, duly appreciated.

Miss Hollberg was peering across the table at him. "You said your work brought you to the Orient many times, did you not, Herr Boyden?" she asked.

"Fairly often," Hugh said carelessly, and moved a conversational pawn to block a play aimed at opening up his defenses. "And you said this was your first trip out here. Has most of your concert tour work been in Europe, Fräulein?"

She sure uses her hands a lot when she should be sitting on them if she wants to be taken for a pianist. Or are all

89

these hand motions signals to somebody else in the room?

He dropped his napkin, recovered it smoothly, but in straightening from his bent-over position he swept the large dining room with a gaze that missed nothing. The Russian, Boris Salenkov, sat near the doorway; Lex Ross and John Wallen had a table next to the window across the room. There was no sign of any other headliners of the *Tiger, Tiger!* troupe nor of Marchet or Chu Hoong.

". . . and my teachers have just now said I am ready for concerts," Mary Hollberg was explaining, perhaps a shade too rapidly. "So I am new at this, *mein Herr.* That is why I hope so much that you will befriend a frightened little pianist. You have the look of—of a strong protector, Herr Boyden. That is why I have chosen you to be my friend."

Hugh gave a slight bow across the table. "I'm flattered and delighted," he said, "but I do have to tell you, you won't need a bodyguard in Thailand, Miss Hollberg. You spoke of elephants and tigers last night—you won't see any wild animals at all unless you go the Royal Zoo, a trip I'd advise, by the way."

The girl pouted. "Then my shameless overture is being answered by a no?"

"Not at all," Hugh said gallantly, "but I'm afraid old Charley Boyden won't turn out to be much of a protector if the need should arise, by any wild stretch of the imagination. You see, I'm scared to death of house cats, let alone tigers."

"I don't believe it! I see you as a—a—oh, as a man engaged in some very dangerous secret work, Herr Boyden," Mary bubbled. She cocked her head to one side. "What are you really, Herr Boyden? A policeman, as Herr Barrows called you on the plane? Perhaps a—a jewel smuggler? Or a spy?"

All these questions were asked in a laughing voice, but Hugh North, although his face bore a wide, almost inane, grin and although his eyes reflected nothing, caught the intensity that lay beneath the gaiety in those questions. Mary Hollberg was as anxious to find out who he really was as he was to learn what her game might be.

90

He was saved the necessity of answering these too-bantering questions by the arrival of the waiter with breakfast. The ham and eggs proved remarkably good, by Eastern standards, and the tea was superb. Hugh took the offensive again while Fräulein Hollberg was busy with her meal.

"Where did you study?" he wanted to know. "Were your teachers anyone I might know?"

The blue eyes came up and met his. "You are well acquainted in the music field, Herr Boyden?" she asked.

The wide shoulders lifted a fraction of an inch. "I'm not what you'd call any great student of music," he replied, "but—well, I'm not totally unversed, let's say. I told you I spent a great deal of time in your country and there were the festivals, the great schools and teachers—" It was his turn to move his hands expressively. "How could a person help but become interested in music? And the piano has always been my favorite."

The pretty girl opposite Hugh took a swallow of tea, touched her lips with a napkin. "That is very nice," she said. "And what took you to Germany, Herr Boyden? Forgive a woman's curiosity, but what kind of work is it that sends you all over the world?"

"I might ask you the same thing, Fräulein," Hugh said, very quietly.

The girl's eyes were round as she looked up from her plate to stare at him. "But I have told you," she said wonderingly. "I am—"

"You're not a concert pianist, Miss Hollberg," Hugh broke in, his voice icy.

The German girl started a protest, abandoned it as she saw the steel in North's stare. Astonishingly, Mary went on to the attack. "And you're no commercial traveler," she flared. "Oh, I was not fooled by that story you told me on the plane. I know who you are, Herr Boyden or whatever your name really is. I know, all right!"

There was an odd bitterness in her voice that North could not account for. *Unless,* he told himself, *she's a fanatic Commie who's been trained to regard all anti-Red agents as more evil than the devil himself.*

91

"Then if you know," he murmured, "you realize you're on a spot. You can't make a move we don't know about." (He hoped she would accept that *we* and take it back to her superiors.) "We can put a hand on you any time we like. Walk carefully, Mary Hollberg—very carefully, indeed."

The German girl's face was white, but her eyes met his with a sort of desperate courage. "You cannot prove anything!" she choked. "I will say you lied."

North spread his hands. "If you can find anybody to listen," he said. "There are places even here in Thailand where a person could yell—even scream—and not be heard. I hope we're not forced to use methods that were perfected by your own countrymen, the Gestapo, Fräulein."

Now the eyes flashed with—yes, by God, indignation! "I told you I was never a Nazi!" Mary cried. "At least I told you the truth there. And you would torture your prisoners, eh, Herr Boyden—*ach*, how gentlemanly are the *verdammte amerikanische Polizei!*"

"Hear, hear," applauded a quiet, cultured voice behind Hugh North. "What's the matter, Miss Hollberg; did you get a traffic ticket coming through Los Angeles?"

Hugh cursed the arrival of Lex Ross even as he rose, his face unreadable, and turned toward the motion-picture actor. Ross wore a white silk suit and an amused smile on his handsome face. His brown eyes under the heavy brows were curious as they looked past North at Mary Hollberg.

"What's all this about the damned American police?" he asked. "Why spoil such a beautiful morning with memories of traffic cops, Miss Hollberg?"

The German girl did not move her hot eyes from Hugh. She sat still for a moment, transfixed by her strange fury, and then she pushed back her chair, threw her napkin beside her unfinished breakfast, whirled, and half ran out of the dining room, a doubled hand to her mouth.

Lex Ross uttered a low exclamation, then turned to Hugh. "What's eating her?" he asked. "Something I said?"

"No," the G-2 colonel replied slowly. "It was something I said—but I'm damned if I quite understand her reaction."

8.

The G-2 colonel resumed his seat, erasing the puzzled frown from his face. He had cursed Ross's arrival, but now that the aging star was here he welcomed the opportunity to talk to the man. Lex Ross knew that Henry Barrows was Hans Bracht. So did Georges Marchet and so, possibly, did Chu Hoong, although this last was open to doubt. Ross, from what little information Hugh had on him, was a sideline patriot, bond and USO tours during World War II, a Korean troop entertainment junket; things like that. He might be convinced that he would be serving his country best by deciding that he had made a mistake in identifying a smooth-shaven Henry Barrows for the bearded missile genius, Dr. Hans Bracht. *If* the conviction could be put over without admitting that Barrows was Bracht. *If* anybody could take a publicity-conscious motion-picture figure into agreeing that silence and secrecy were worth a thousand times more than a headline in certain circumstances.

"Have you eaten?" he asked Ross, to break the silence that had followed Hollberg's stormy departure.

"I'll have a cup of tea with you," Lex said, his charming smile returning. "We'll celebrate your escape from the Bangkok police, shall we?"

Hugh signaled a waiter, chuckling. "Oh, that." To the Thai waiter he said, *"Encore du thé pour m'sieur et moi, s'il vous plaît."* To Ross he said, "Seems there was a slight case of mistaken identity there."

"What was it all about?" Ross asked. "I tried to find out who'd been murdered, but nobody knew anything. Or is it a state secret?"

"Somebody killed in an auto accident, I understand," Hugh shrugged. "All I know is that it only took a phone call to that cop's headquarters to clear me." He finished his last piece of ham. "For which I was very grateful," he added.

"I don't imagine you were very worried," Lex said idly.

"Well, no, not exactly. No shield like innocence, eh? But I was afraid it would be a bit awkward, not knowing Siamese.

93

Luckily, most officials speak French and a good many know enough English to get along."

"I wasn't referring to your innocence," Ross said calmly. "I knew a G-man wouldn't have any trouble getting out of a jam like that."

North's brows rose in twin crescents. "G-man!" he exploded.

"That's what you are, aren't you?" Ross smiled. "The G-man assigned to protect Dr. Bracht?"

Hugh North laid down his fork deliberately, leaned back in his chair, and brought out his cigarettes. He offered the pack across the table and, when Lex accepted one, leaned forward again to hold his lighter. That done, the G-2 colonel blew a stream of smoke toward the ceiling, leaning back in his chair again.

"Mr. Ross," he said pleasantly, "first of all, let me swear to you by all that's holy, I'm not a G-man. Boy Scout's word of honor. Second, even if it were true that Henry Barrows is this Dr. Bracht you speak of, wouldn't it be your duty to keep it to yourself rather than go around telling every Tom, Dick, and Harry—and Charley Boyden?"

"My duty? I don't get you."

Hugh tapped a fragment of ash into the tray in the middle of the table. "You say this Bracht has shaved off his beard, that he's incognito. Okay, if you're right about this bone-structure business—and for all of me you may be that good at spotting people—isn't there the question of why Bracht should be hiding his identity? As I understand it, he's in some pretty top-secret stuff. Aren't you taking a chance of the Iron Curtain boys overhearing you and getting curious?"

"Then you admit it is Bracht," Lex Ross said.

North stirred irritably. "I admit nothing. What difference does it make? If he is Bracht you'd be doing a damned bad thing for your country. If he isn't Bracht you might be getting a completely innocent stranger into a peck of trouble. Either way, to be blunt, I'd advise you to button your lip."

Lex Ross flushed beneath his tan, but his smile held. "I'm not known as a loose-mouth, Mr. Boyden," he said. "I haven't mentioned this to anybody else. I wouldn't have said anything to you if I hadn't known you were Bracht's guard."

"Did you get that from my bone structure?" Hugh asked acidly. He reached for the cardholder in his hip pocket, slipped a business card free, and rudely scaled it across the table at Ross. "I don't suppose you'll believe it," he said, "but there's my business card."

Ross read the card: *CHARLES P. BOYDEN, Boyden, Chase & Bryn, Importers, 30 Rockefeller Plaza, New York 20, N.Y. Phone: CIrcle 6-2750. Cable Address: Chabroy.* The actor ran a thumb over the engraving and nodded, smiling. "Very nice," he said approvingly. "Twenty bucks says it was printed in New York too. Very thorough, you fellows."

North began a cuss word, stopped, and broke out laughing. "Okay, Ross," he said. "Have it your way. I'm a G-man and Barrows is Bracht and you—well, you can be a Russian spy to make it complete, huh?"

The waiter arrived with a fresh pot of tea and a cup for Ross. He looked sadly at the remains of Mary Hollberg's breakfast and tried out his English on North. "Missee come back, pliss?"

"No," Hugh replied. "Missee gone."

When the waiter had left, Hugh found Lex Ross still undaunted.

"Listen, Boyden," the actor said, "what you told me about keeping my mouth shut makes sense. I don't intend to make your job any tougher. Matter of fact, my idea was that I could make it a little easier."

"Keep going," North said with an expansive wave. "Don't mind me."

"No, seriously. I thought maybe you could use somebody to—well, sort of look around, listen around, and see what was going on."

"Oh, come now," Hugh groaned.

"I have a unique talent, Mr. Boyden. I told you I was a master at disguise. I am. I can make myself into practically any other man. Don't laugh; I mean it. Ask anybody in Hollywood. You want to know what's going on in somebody's room, for instance? I can be a native bellhop, or whatever they call them here, in a couple of minutes and I

95

can get in that room and listen and report back. Do you want to know what X tells Y when they're alone? I can be X or Y and the other will never know he's not talking to the real thing."

"My aching back," Hugh North wailed.

There was a bite to Ross's voice. "Try me," he challenged.

"Okay." Hugh grinned. "Suppose you make up as that director Anton Carss, and report back to me on whether his girl friend, Lita Naline, wears falsies or not. Or perhaps you know?"

The flush came and went in Ross's slender face. His smile faltered but returned. "I expected something like this," he said. "I didn't think you'd take me at my word. But honestly, Boyden, I do want to—to *do* something. Give me a chance to prove I mean it."

"Afraid I can't play games with you, Ross," the G-2 colonel said. "Sorry." He looked around for his waiter.

"Suppose I've got some information you'd like to have," Lex Ross said softly. "Would you trade? You use my services if I tell you what I know?"

Hugh North's nerves tingled. This man had been edging around this for some time and now he was going to come out with it. To Ross, the colonel showed the derisive grin once more and turned back, hunting the waiter. *Ross has got to talk; he's constitutionally unable to keep from talking to get this "job" he wants.*

But Lex held his silence longer than Hugh thought possible. The waiter came, finally, and accepted North's money, thanked the colonel for his tip, and departed, and Hugh was about to follow when the master of disguise finally spoke in a low voice.

"Watch Jack Wallen, Boyden. Watch him like a hawk. He knows something about Hans Bracht's wife, a woman called Tao Muong."

96

CHAPTER 4

1.

HUGH NORTH had to walk away from that dynamite-packed statement. He had to shrug helplessly, shake his head, keep his back to Lex Ross, and walk away. He might have wanted to grab Ross by the lapels of that beautiful white silk suit and shake down the actor for every scrap of information he had about this new, shattering angle, but he had to walk away.

Colonel North had had to make many tough decisions in his career as a G-2 operative, but few had come harder than the choice between staying at the table, admitting to Lex Ross that he was a government agent commissioned to protect Hans Bracht, and leaving there with that jolting statement still quivering in the air, unexplained.

Later Hugh might explain the practicality of his move; he might point out that he had all he needed, the word that John Wallen was somehow involved in the case of Tao Muong—the rest he could try to take care of himself without tipping the whole hand. He might further explain that Lex Ross was going to be around; if worse came to worst he could always take off his mask as a last resort and pump Ross then for the information the disguise artist possessed— or thought he possessed. He might say that to listen to Ross's spill at that first opening would have been to invite a flood of jealous hearsay, exaggerations, even downright lies, from an old actor envious of the younger man who had taken his place as the top-billed star.

Yes, he might have been able to offer a convincing brief

97

to back up his immediate action in that dining room, but the truth was that Colonel Hugh North, U.S.A., G-2, acted more on instinct than on any other factor. His blessed sixth sense told him that this was not the time to pay the sizable cost of Ross's information and he followed this warning as he had in the past. It had crossed him up on occasions, this sixth sense, but not often; usually it had paid off handsomely for his trust in it.

He left the dining room and started across the lobby, and despite his inner turbulence he saw several things happen. He saw the Greek hotel manager at the desk look at him and immediately reach for a telephone. He saw the chief porter (the bell captain in an American hotel) raise his pillbox cap six inches from his shaven pate and replace it. He saw the elevator starter slam shut the door of one elevator and open the door of another, two cars down the line, not the next car. He felt, rather than saw, a half a dozen pairs of eyes focus themselves on him, watching him.

The warning gong rang in North's head. He started for the open-doored elevator, then at the last minute turned abruptly aside and made for the stairs.

"Elevator here, sir, pliss!" the starter barked.

"Up Up!" the elevator operator chimed in.

"Telephone call for you, Mr. Boyden!" the Greek manager suddenly remembered. "Right here, sir."

Hugh ignored them all. He began to run before he hit the stairs, and he took the steps three at a time. He scrambled up the stairway faster than the elevator could have made it even if its operator had not been under instructions (as Hugh was convinced he was) to have a breakdown somewhere en route.

At the landing of his floor, Hugh took out his .38 and skidded around a corner, stopped in his tracks. His gun was held waist-high and pointed at the round belly of Chu Hoong, creator of Dragon's Tooth Elixir, multimillionaire, and, it just so happened, owner of the Imperial Hotel in Bangkok, where his orders could move any and all members of the hotel staff.

The Chinese looked at North impassively, glanced down

at the snub-nosed revolver with the same bland unconcern. The almond eyes returned to Hugh's and there was a faint smile on the small mouth over the goatee.

"Am I to understand that this is a robbery, Mr. Boyden?" Chu asked gently.

"No," North replied levelly, "I always back up my invitations with something solid to show my sincerity. I'm inviting you now to visit Mr. Barrows' room with me."

Chu's smile widened. "That would be delightful," he said. "As as matter of fact, I've just come from there."

"I had an idea you had," North grunted. "I trust you left him in good health."

The Chinese turned, shrugging. "I presume he was in good health. At least he was in good voice. He seemed disturbed, but of course it was hard to tell, speaking to him through the door as I did."

"Through the door?"

"Ah, yes. He is somewhat strange, this Mr. Barrows, is he not?"

"He may have reason to be where you're concerned, Mr. Chu," the G-2 man said, his pistol muzzle never wavering. "Perhaps what you said to him through the door was upsetting."

Again the Chinese shrugged. "I don't see why it should have been," he said smoothly. "I merely called to inquire if everything was satisfactory, as I make it a practice to inquire of all the Imperial's guests when I am in Bangkok." He smiled over his shoulder at North. "The personal touch, you know— I got the idea from reading about your so successful American hotel operators."

"I can imagine." Hugh North smiled back.

They reached the door of Room 439 and the Colonel rapped.

"I said go away!" Bracht's voice was gruff, but now it was hoarse, strained. "Go away, Chu, or whatever you call yourself! By God, if you don't I'll—I'll get somebody who'll make you go away."

Sounds as if he's ready to co-operate with me, North told himself. *For which heaven be praised.*

"It's me, Boyden," he called aloud. "Are you all right?"

There was a moment's silence, and then Bracht's voice sounded again, relief dripping. "Yes—yes, I'm all right. I slammed the door on him when I saw who it was. That little devil, he'll stop at nothing. He—he'll kill me before I get to—"

"It's all right," Hugh cut in hastily. "I'll be with you in a minute. Sit tight."

Throughout this, Chu Hoong had stood there with a small, compassionate smile on his rosebud mouth. Now he whispered, "I understand. The poor man is ill, eh? Or he drinks unwisely and that is why you have to care for him, poor fellow?"

North backed to his door, used his key to open it. The .38 gestured and Chu Hoong placidly walked into Room 437. His eyes roamed the room and he clucked his tongue.

"You see why it is wise for me to personally check on the comfort of my guests, Mr. Boyden?" he chirruped. "Those curtains there—they're faded. They should have been replaced. One can't trust servants in these days no matter what one pays them."

He walked to the easy chair in the corner near the window and calmly seated himself, laced his fingers across his watermelon stomach, and regarded Hugh North half humorously.

"If you are that poor man's keeper you deserve an explanation," he said. "More than that, you deserve a million apologies from this miserable bungler. I did not know Mr. Barrows was ill. They should have told me down at the desk."

"Suppose," Hugh suggested, "we speak Cantonese. And please go slowly; I am not very good at it."

"A generous gesture," Chu singsonged in Cantonese. "The genuine knight meets another's embarrassing inability to speak his language correctly by changing to the unscholared one's dialect. Truly a splendid example of manners."

"I want to speak Cantonese so the one in the next room does not understand," Hugh explained bluntly. "Now, Chu Hoong, why do you fear Henry Barrows?"

A veil descended over Chu's eyes, a veil Colonel North

100

had seen come down over a thousand Chinese eyes and seldom had been able to pierce.

"It is unforgivable to contradict a guest, but I must," Chu said humbly. "I do not fear Mr. Barrows. If it did not sound like the boasting of a worm I would tell you that I do not fear any human."

"I saw fear in your eyes when you met Barrows on the airplane."

"You did, honorable guest? Then, if you thought you did you did, for what a man thinks he sees is true in his mind. Consider the man who loves an ugly woman; love makes him see a beautiful woman and so she is beautiful and who can say she is not? Not this insignificant one." He unclasped his hands long enough to point a sharp-nailed index finger at his chest. "You may think you see in this person an evil demon who will harm your patient, honorable guest, and so, to you, I am a menace. But try to see me only as an innkeeper who desires that his guests have comfort and, succeeding in that, you will find no demon—only an old and weary man who is ashamed that his oversolicitude disturbed an ill person."

He bowed his head, his face woebegone. "What can I do to repair this thoughtless error?" he asked.

"You can stay away from Henry Barrows," North said coldly. "You can make sure no harm comes to him while he is your guest. Because if ill befalls him I will feel duty-bound to go to General Genung with certain thoughts and views."

Chu's face, raised again, did not move a muscle, but there was something, a passing shadow in those agate eyes, an inner change behind that impassive mask, at the mention of the name Genung.

"The general of whom you speak has long been one of my most valued friends," the Chinese said. "I have the shameless conceit to think any man, even you, would find it difficult to alter General Genung's regard for me."

"I, too, am not unknown to General Genung," North countered gravely in meticulous Cantonese. "The general was gracious enough to be concerned about the taxicab accident

101

last night and he may be interested in the two attempts to enter Room 439 of the Imperial Hotel."

The ghost of a smile played on Chu's lips. "I infer that my hospitable visit is to be reported as an attempt to enter Room 439?" he asked.

"It may be," North said steadily.

"And the other?"

"Was attempted early this morning by a man who calls himself Aloysius Robinson of Macao."

Now, for the first time, Chu Hoong let his face mirror his emotions. Black anger surged through the multimillionaire's expression for a fractional moment before Chu brought his features back under control. "Aloysius Robinson," he said rigidly, "is a foolish, irresponsible young man, as anyone in Bangkok will tell you. His father once did me a great favor, and since the father's death I have taken it upon myself to try to help the boy find himself. I must confess I have had little success and a great deal of disappointment. To you, honored guest, I must admit I am at my wit's end about what to do with Aloysius Robinson."

"Perhaps if you ceased putting a cushion under him to ease his every fall the pain of a bruise might cause him to hesitate the next time he is tempted," North suggested. "I believe it has been you who have always rescued him from the hands of the police when they would chastise him?"

The little fat Chinese bowed. "It is wrong, I know," he admitted, "but I have allowed myself to think that Aloysius has been persecuted, as he claims. You may not know it, but the Chinese in Thailand hold no enviable position. Although we have been free with our money and talents to help the country progress and even though we control a great percentage of all Thai trade and industry, the native Siamese looks upon the average Chinese as an inferior person. The Chinese defendant in a Thai court seldom receives the same kind of justice as a Siamese."

He held up a hand to cut off North's remark. "You may be about to say that Aloysius Robinson is Macanese, not Chinese. The same discrimination exists against a Macanese as against a Chinese, Mr. Boyden. I will admit that Aloysius has

102

been seriously at fault in several incidents that have occurred in Thailand—I will even admit that the Thai police have little reason to be kind to him—but when he finds himself in trouble I always fear he will be unjustly treated and so I come to his aid."

The shadow of a smile came again and Chu added: "The strange thing is that my own sons consider me unjustly strict in dealing with their affairs. But what would be unforgivable error on their part can be condoned in Aloysius Robinson because he has not had the advantages the gods were good enough to enable me to provide my sons."

With which Chu Hoong arose from his chair and walked toward the door. "I knew nothing of Aloysius' attempt to enter Room 439," he said sincerely. "As for the earlier incident that resulted in his arrest, Aloysius assures me he meant only to assist the gentleman. I will speak to him about this more recent affair. I know he was drinking last night and possibly he became so befuddled that he mistook that room for his, one floor above. I shall have him moved so that same mistake cannot occur again, if that is the explanation. If there was some other motive I will try to find it out and Aloysius will be punished."

He smiled at Hugh North. "Does that answer all your questions?"

"Unless you'll tell me where and when you knew the man in the next room," the G-2 agent said seriously.

Chu flicked a glance at the connecting door. "You mean Mr. Barrows? I have never known a Henry Barrows before now. I swear it."

"And he has never known a Chu Hoong," North said grimly in English, then added: "But I'd bet my last dime you knew each other under different names at some time—and you weren't bosom pals, either."

Chu paused, his hand on the doorknob. "Conjecturing is a dangerous pastime, Mr. Boyden," he said pleasantly. "Curiosity is hardly less perilous. We have a saying: *He who reaches into the tomb of Time risks being bitten by the roused serpent.* It loses in the translation but I think you can see its wisdom. Good day, Mr. Boyden."

103

2.

When Chu had gone and Hugh North was sure he was out of earshot, the G-2 agent crossed to the connecting door to 439 and rapped. Bracht's response was immediate; the hostility with which the scientist had greeted every other approach was gone.

Instead of growling behind the panel when Hugh spoke his name, the missile scientist unhesitatingly unlocked the door and came barging into North's room the moment the colonel turned the knob on his side. The older man glared wildly about the room, then turned toward Hugh. "You're sure he's gone?" he demanded. "Is that door locked?" When North nodded the scientist walked to the window and pulled down the shade. Turning back, he showed a certain defensive belligerence. "I know this looks foolish, but that man—you don't know him, North. He's a killer. He tried to get to me so he could shoot me or stick a knife in my ribs. I know it!"

"Why?" Hugh asked softly. "Why would a millionaire like Chu Hoong want to kill you, Doctor?"

The mulish look came back to Bracht's face. "I don't intend to tell you," he said. "All I can say is that it has nothing to do with Tao Muong."

"You're sure of that?"

"Positive!" There was no doubting Bracht's sincerity there.

"Well, then, is Chu hooked up in any way with Georges Marchet?"

The scientist's first reaction was a headshake, but he qualified the negative after a moment's thought. "I don't know," he said slowly. "To be honest, I can't say. Possibly."

North walked to the edge of the bed and sat down. "Doctor," he told Bracht earnestly, "it's time you leveled with me, as I asked you to in the cab before the accident. Which was no accident, as you must realize by now."

Bracht took the chair Chu had just vacated and rubbed his forehead with long, bony fingers. "I thought it was," he said. "Now I'm not so sure. Perhaps you're right. Perhaps somebody's out to kill me." His hand came down and knotted itself in a fist that thudded on the chair arm. "Damn them, if they'd only leave me alone until I get Tao Muong back they could try anything they wanted. I'm worried for fear they'll interfere in the ransom negotiations, that's all."

"By they, you mean Chu Hoong and company?"

Bracht nodded. He was a far different man than he had been when North had seen him last. Chu's appearance at his door had shaken him badly and, North had no doubt, for the reason he had just given; it was not primarily that he feared what Chu Hoong would do to him in this mysterious vendetta but that Chu's moves might ruin the ransom nego- tiations to which he clung with such naïve faith.

"We'll see that they don't interfere if you'll work with me," the colonel said. "Otherwise you'll be playing a lone hand against what looks like a lot of power on its home field."

Bracht's haggard eyes dragged up to meet Hugh's. "I—I'd like to," the space-travel genius admitted grudgingly, "but if the ones who have Tao Muong found out about it they'd think I was playing tricks on them and they'd—" He broke off, shuddered visibly as he imagined the kidnapers' revenge on his wife.

"They won't know," North said urgently. "I can almost promise you that the kidnapers won't know I'm working with you, not if you give me full co-operation." He saw Bracht shake his head drearily and gave up that tack momentarily.

"All right," he said, "can you do this—can you tell me who Georges Marchet is?"

Bracht hesitated a long minute, his long hands twisting between his knees. Finally—and it was a decision that Hugh hailed as the first big break in Bracht's determined silence —the scientist nodded.

"Georges Marchet was a small sometime planter in Indo- china," the missile man explained. "When I escaped from Germany and made my way to the Orient—and I'll never tell *anybody* how I did it or who helped me; there still might be reprisals—I was directed to Marchet. The Japanese occupied that territory, of course, but Marchet seemed to get along well with them. Perhaps it was because he was a drug addict and would kowtow to anyone to get his dope."

He looked down at his long hands and shook his head. "I suppose I shouldn't speak of him so, seeing what he did for me, but I can't help it," he went on. "I hate drugs and drug addicts with all my heart, North, and Marchet helped me only because I had money—lots of it and in gold."

"How did he help you?"

"He guided me through Indochina to the Siamese border," Bracht explained. "Thailand was not as dangerous as Indochina from the standpoint of Jap patrols; the invaders' posts were pretty well confined to the rivers. Of course there were pro-Japanese irregulars and bandits and always the jungle, but I found I could cope with them. I holed up in a native village near Ciang Mai until the war was over. The people were friendly; they hid me whenever a Japanese patrol came through. When it was safe I started for Bangkok on foot. On the way I met Tao Muong in Chainat. We fell in love and—well, you know the rest."

Hugh North kept his eyes fixed on the doctor. "That's the whole truth?" he asked. "You didn't leave anything out?"

Bracht swung his hollowed eyes around to meet the colonel's. "It's the truth," he said simply.

"And Georges Marchet recognized you only as a man he guided through Indochina? Did you use your own name while you were hiding out? You must have been clean-shaven or he wouldn't have known you on the plane."

Bracht nodded. "I used another name but—well, on the way to Thailand one time, when we seemed almost certain of being taken by the Japs, I told him that if he got out alive he must let somebody know what had happened to Hans Bracht." He smiled mirthlessly. "It's strange how a man's ego will demand that somebody know of his death, when it can't possibly matter to him."

"And you were clean-shaven during all this?"

"While I was with Marchet, yes. In that native village I let my beard grow again."

Hugh frowned. That didn't fit. "Then how is it that Chu Hoong recognized you?" he asked. "Was he with Marchet? Did you meet Chu during the escape from Indochina?"

"No. No, Chu, or whatever he calls himself, was not with

Marchet, nor did I ever see him while I was out here, hiding from the Axis."

"And that's the truth too?"

Bracht's eyes were steady. "That's the truth too," he said, and North believed him.

"Well, then, where did you know Chu— Oh, don't give me that rigmarole about never knowing a Chu Hoong, please! Where did you know the man who now calls himself Chu Hoong, Dr. Bracht?"

The old rejection was back in the missile master's eyes, the wide mouth was set in that familiar tightened line again. "I said I wouldn't tell you," the genius told the G-2 colonel. "I meant it. All I can say is that this Chinese has nothing whatever to do with Tao Muong."

"And yet you say he wants to kill you," the colonel said grimly. "You want protection from him and you won't tell me why you think—"

"I've told you too much already," Bracht broke in desperately. "If the people who have Tao Muong knew I was sitting here telling you everything I know, they'd—they'd—" His head dropped to his big hands and he uttered a low groan.

North studied the missile scientist, wrenched between frustrated anger and sympathy for this great man who was going through torture. He abandoned Chu Hoong and tried a new slant.

"How well do you know John Wallen?" he asked abruptly.

Bracht's head came up with a jerk, his eyes wide. "Wallen? You mean the movie star? Why, I don't know him at all. He was on the plane with the rest of them; that's all I know about him."

"Did your wife ever know him?"

Bracht shook his head violently. "No, of course not! Tao Muong never met anybody unless I was with her, and I tell you I never saw Wallen outside the movies until he boarded that plane at Hong Kong."

Hugh reached for a cigarette, stuck one between his lips, and hunted for his lighter. As he spoke, the cigarette moved up and down. "You say your wife never met anybody except

107

when you were with her—she must have met somebody alone."

"It's impossible! Whom did she meet?"

"Her kidnaper," North said quietly.

The scientist's face was ashen as his eyes fell away. "Yes," he muttered. "Yes, you're right. I've wondered about that. She—she used to complain about not being able to leave the apartment when I was not there. She was under strict orders not to let any stranger in the house—even the tradespeople were not allowed inside. You see, I was afraid for her. She is so tiny; she is so trusting. I was afraid she—she'd be molested. I was very strict about her not letting anybody come close to her when I wasn't there and yet—and yet the kidnaper got to her; she must have let the kidnaper in the apartment."

"Tell me, Doctor," Hugh North said, "were there signs of a struggle when you came home that day and she was gone?"

"No, but that means nothing. She's such a little thing, and fragile—what kind of struggle could she put up?" He peered at North. "Why did you ask me about knowing Wallen?"

"I was told that Wallen knows something about Tao Muong," the colonel replied. As agitation rose in Bracht, North continued swiftly. "It came from a source I'm doubtful about and there may be nothing to it."

"B-but Wallen! It's ridiculous! Why would a man who makes the money he must be involved in a kidnaping?"

But this is more than a simple kidnaping, Hugh said silently, *and the Reds find their converts in strange places.* "I told you I haven't put much faith in it," he said aloud.

"Who told you that? Who knows about the kidnaping? You promised you wouldn't do anything that might—"

"And I haven't," North broke in. "This was a word dropped out of nowhere. I said I'd level with you and that's the only reason I told you about it; otherwise I'd have gone ahead and given Wallen a going-over to find out what he knows. As it is, I said I'd keep hands off and I will unless I'm forced to make a move."

The missile man's face was tortured. "Please, for God's

sake, don't do anything to wreck the situation. They're edgy enough now; if you tried to find out about Wallen They'd certainly take it out on my wife."

"I've said I'd leave it alone unless I absolutely had to go into it," North said. "Will you co-operate with me a little in return?"

Bracht's eyes were wary. "What do you want me to do?"

"I want you to sleep in here," the colonel said. "I want you to spend your time in here; you can leave the connecting door ajar; you won't miss your phone call. I don't like those windows—they're fine for cross ventilation but they're fine for a sniper, too."

Bracht scoffed: "But They wouldn't harm me—at least not until after they get their money."

"I think we're dealing with two sets of people," Hugh returned. "One gang is holding your wife and wants you kept alive; the other wants you dead, from the looks of things. It's the second bunch that makes me afraid of those windows. How about it; will you use my room? If you're worried about the kidnapers knowing the difference we'll keep the shades of both rooms drawn."

It took some time, but Hans Bracht finally nodded reluctantly. And Hugh North, considering his previous progress at earning Bracht's nods, scored it as a major victory.

The missile genius had no more than given his assent to North's plea when the telephone on Hugh's night table shrilled. Pokh? The G-2 colonel answered and listened to an arrogant voice on the other end of the line.

"Boyden? This is Jack Wallen."

North clamped down in his surprise, pressed the receiver tightly to his ear so Wallen's voice could not possibly carry to Bracht. "Yes?"

"I saw you talking to Lex Ross at breakfast, Boyden," the actor went on. "Did he say anything about me?"

"I don't think I understand," Hugh countered.

"Look, Boyden, don't play games with me. Either Ross said something about me or he didn't. I want to find out."

"Why not ask him?"

There was the harsh bark of a laugh at the other end.

"You think he'd tell me? He knows I'd kick the living hell out of him if he admitted it. I ought to anyway, just on general principles, the old jerk. That's it—he's so old he knows I can't slug him, but I can go to Carss and have him cut out of *Tiger, Tiger!* And I will if he keeps telling lies about me. What did he say about me this morning?"

Hugh's eyes switched to Hans Bracht. The missile scientist had walked to the connecting door and was entering his own room, obviously to avoid the appearance of eavesdropping. The G-2 colonel lowered his voice. "What makes you think he told me anything?" he asked.

"Oh, I can tell whenever the louse has dropped another one about me; he gets a smirk on his face like he'd just won an Oscar. And he kept looking over toward my table to make sure I wasn't coming up on him while he was spilling the hot poop."

"Mighty flimsy evidence you've got, don't you think?" North asked. "Or are you extraordinarily good at reading a man's face from fifty feet away?"

"Don't hand me any of that stuff, Boyden," Wallen said roughly. "If you knew Ross you'd know his word isn't worth a plugged nickel. Ask him who Walter Wells really was sometime when he gets sounding off about other people and then watch him curl. Yeah, I know a couple of things about *him* that I could shove down his throat if I wanted to."

"Look," North said, "I'm not sure what this is all about, but I don't want to get involved in any grudge between you two fellows."

"So you won't tell me what he said about me, huh?"

"Why should he say anything about you to me? I just met the man on the plane yesterday. Why should he—"

"I told you he's a screwball," Wallen interrupted. "A stinkin' snoop. He's— Ah, to hell with him. Listen, the main reason I called you is I'm having a little cocktail party this afternoon. How about dropping by?"

"Well—" North hesitated. He had promised Bracht he would not follow up the Wallen lead, but would accepting this surprising invitation break that promise?

"Come on, come on," Wallen was saying. "You'll have a

good time. Lita will get stoned and when she's plastered she usually does a strip tease. Of course Anton takes her away before she gets going real good, but once in a while she gets peeled before he knows what's going on. How about it?"

"Why—ah—I'll certainly do my best."

"Four o'clock," Wallen said. "Depending on you."

The receiver went down with a crash and North replaced his own phone, looking down perplexedly at the instrument. Why had Jack Wallen suspected that Lex Ross had cracked about Tao Muong? Had Lex dropped a word to Wallen? Was this room bugged and Wallen at the earphones, listening to him talk to Hans Bracht a few minutes before?

For the second time since he had checked into Room 437, Hugh North gave the place a going-over and this time he made it thorough. When he finished his work he was as sure as he ever permitted himself to be about anything that there were no listening devices in this room. When Bracht moved over to 437 he would give the scientist's room a complete shakedown, but North was reasonably certain that They— neither group of Them, if there were two—had put an ear in either room.

He went through the connecting door and found Bracht stretched out on his bed, his hands behind his head.

"That was John Wallen," the G-2 colonel said bluntly.

Bracht sat up with a lurch. "What did he want?"

Hugh said, "He wanted to invite me to a cocktail party he's giving in his rooms this afternoon. Or at least that's what he said. I don't know what he really—"

Bracht's phone sounded. The scientist's long arm flashed out and he answered eagerly, "Yes—yes?" His face fell as he heard the voice which Hugh knew, by its crackle across the room, was Wallen's. Disappointed because it was not the kidnapers, Bracht listened listlessly and said at the first pause: "I don't believe I can, thank you, Mr. Wallen. I—I haven't been well and I've got to rest. But thank you very much for your thoughtful invitation."

He hung up the phone and turned to North. "Imagine him inviting me to a silly cocktail party." And added reflectively, "But Tao Muong would have enjoyed it so, wouldn't she?

111

All those motion-picture people—she would have been in her seventh heaven."

North nodded, but absently; he was realigning some conclusions. His first thought when John Wallen, a movie star, had invited Charley Boyden, a nobody, to a cocktail party had been that Wallen either wanted Bracht left unguarded or wanted him, North, to come to his rooms at four o'clock for a talk about those suspicions of Ross's blabbing. The invitation to Bracht had changed the aspect—unless Wallen had anticipated something along that line of reasoning and had made the Bracht call to meet that possibility.

"Do you have any objections to my going to the party?" the colonel asked Bracht. "I mean, would you think I was interfering with your ransom negotiations?"

(Be it explained here that Hugh North usually did not show such tender regard for the feelings or opinions of others connected with missions to which he was assigned. Ordinarily, the colonel considered only the best way to deal with the problem at hand and seldom if ever the effects of his operations on other persons. But in the case of Hans Bracht his first need as he saw it was to establish a rapport between his ward and himself, build Bracht's faith in him. If the missile man, always the temperamental genius, insisted on playing his lone hand North's job would be that much tougher, that much more liable to meet disaster through Bracht's refusal to co-operate. Therefore, North held it a small concession to make to Bracht's fear and ego to ask permission to attend a cocktail party, in view of the closer relationship it might lead to.)

Bracht considered the G-2 agent's question and finally shook his head slowly. "I suppose not," he said with no great enthusiasm. "So long as you don't pry into—" He caught himself and looked up at North from under his shaggy eyebrows. "I didn't mean that," he said gruffly. "I take you for a man of your word."

"Thanks," Hugh said. "And if you'll move into my room while I'm gone I think you'll be reasonably safe from whoever might have ideas about harming you."

He did not add, because he could go only so far with this

frank and earnest business, after all, that he intended to take added precautions for Bracht's safety by asking Captain Pokh for plain-clothes protection (if the Bangkok Imperial Troop possessed such things as plain-clothes men) for Rooms 439 and 437 while he was sipping martinis (unpoisoned, he hoped) with John Wallen.

3.

The cocktail party was in full swing that afternoon when Colonel Hugh North pressed the ivory doorbell button of Suite Seven-D. Barely muffled by the door were the typical cocktail-party sounds, the rumble of intermeshed voices spiked occasionally by women's shrill laughter.

An American whom Hugh recognized dimly as a *Tiger, Tiger!* underling opened the door in response to North's ring and the colonel was greeted by a billowing wave of tobacco smoke, perfume, and the warmth of close-packed humanity. He wedged himself down a short entrance foyer crowded with Westerners he knew to be lesser lights of the location company and managed to get into the suite's living room, where the jam was only a little less rib-crushing. Most of the throng were Americans, but there was a sprinkling of Siamese men, apparently Bangkok and national Thai officials with whom the movie people wanted to maintain good relations.

He looked about for his host and failed to find him. He did see Lita Naline, more beautiful than ever and even at this distance noticeably drunk; Lex Ross, Anton Carss, Boris Salenkov (and who would have thought that Comrade Boris would have been included on the guest list or would have accepted?), and Mary Hollberg.

Mary apparently had gotten over her breakfast-table mad. When she met Hugh's eye she waved delightedly and detached herself from Lex Ross, bore down on North as fast as the crowd would permit.

"Ah, it is so nice you came," she enthused when she came

113

up to Hugh. "They told me you'd been asked, but Jack—Herr Wallen—wasn't sure you would come."

She was wearing a white dress with a square-cut neckline that did not have to plunge; it started low and stretched across one of the most perfectly rounded pairs of breasts it had ever been Hugh North's pleasure to try not to ogle. As though to assure the colonel that these proud promontories were not the product of Akron, U.S.A., Fräulein Hollberg almost immediately dropped her handkerchief and, before Hugh could move, bent to retrieve it. Hugh, always the gentleman, veered his eyes away—when he finally managed to tear them loose from the beauty so generously displayed.

"I am so clumsy, *nicht wahr?*" Mary asked as she straightened.

Or so adroit, Hugh told himself. Aloud he said, "Wallen seems to have gotten quite a crowd together on short notice."

"Oh, he told me he invited everybody who was on our plane," the German "pianist" explained. "Also, there are some people of the motion-picture crew who were here in Bangkok earlier, making ready for the picture."

"I see." North nodded. He looked around the room again. "And where's our host?"

Mary gestured with her blond head toward a closed door. "In there," she said. "He is a little *betrunken.* Oh, very charmingly drunk, but he said he thought it advisable to lie down for a moment. Meanwhile, the party goes on." She looked at Hugh's empty hands. "But you have no drink—come, we will fix that."

North saw there would be no danger of a Mickey Finn, because in the absence of a bartender (perhaps Wallen had started out in this capacity and had sampled his own concoctions too freely) everybody was mixing his own. North and Mary fought their way up to the soaked and spotted cloth-covered table and the G-2 colonel mixed a mild scotch for himself, gave the German girl the double martini she asked for.

"*Viel Glück,*" Mary said, and drank. She eyed Hugh over the rim of her glass. "Perhaps I should not do this," she said. "I am apt to become—what is the word?—reckless after so

114

many of these. And maybe I would shock the oh-so-proper Herr Boyden if I did, no?"

"No." Hugh grinned. A surge of the crowd behind him pressed him against Mary, and the German girl's body responded in a manner hardly recommended by the book of etiquette. Despite his years, his long experience with women on the make for diverse reasons, Hugh felt the back of his neck turning red. Just what the hell did Mary Hollberg intend, a torrid session in this crowded room?

"And you have forgiven me?" the girl was asking as she ostensibly maneuvered to make more room for herself and succeeded only in undulating closer to North.

"Forgive you? For what? Oh, the *verdammte amerikanische Polizei* bit? Consider it forgotten—and I'm *not* a damned cop, you know."

"I know." Mary looked down at her glass and sighed. "It was that I am so—so ill-tempered in the mornings, Charles." *Ah, so we're now Charles, are we?* "I should never, never see anyone before noon unless—" She did not finish the sentence; she did not have to; the implication was there that she could be quite charming before noon if not forced to leave her bed.

"We all have the same trouble," Hugh said heavily.

"And you did not mean it when you said I was no—"

"Well, for God's sake, look who's here!" caroled a soprano voice in North's ear. "Did you bring that cute little old man with you, the one I rescued last night?"

The G-2 colonel turned to greet Lita Naline, a Lita Naline who either had had a head start on everybody else here or who let alcohol take over with no checkrein at all. If Mary's dress was low cut, Lita's was lower, but this seemed to be the result of some disarrangement rather than the design of the afternoon gown. Lita appeared to have been mixed up in a rassling match sometime during the party, by the slewed bodice and the condition of her coiffure.

Still, she was beautiful, possibly the most beautiful woman North had ever seen from the standpoint of pulchritude and nothing more. Lita Naline or Lily Novotny, the fates had endowed this young woman with perfect, flawless symmetry of feature, a body that might be exaggerated in places but never bovine. It had been suggested by a columnist that Lita had been born a couple of hundred years late; in other days she doubtless would have been a king's mistress and would have shared history's limelight with Madame Pompadour.

As it was, even Hugh North—no movie fan by any definition—knew Lita was doing all right. In claiming the affections of Anton Carss she seemed assured of roles her histrionic abilities never would have earned for her, and her pay check was one of the biggest in Hollywood. She had had five husbands for varying stretches of married bliss and according to the thinly veiled remarks of the gossip columnists she had burned out all five before tossing them onto the discard pile. Only the fact that the word "nymphomaniac" was taboo had prevented the columnists from coming right out and telling their readers that Miss Naline was insatiable.

And also, at the present moment, quite drunk. Hugh saw that she was one of the fortunate women who did not become bulbous about the eyes, nose, and mouth when stoned. Her beauty did not suffer from her inebriety; indeed her dishevelment rather added a titillating note to her allure as to a girl flushed by excitement beyond bothering to care if her hair was precisely arranged.

"Where is he?" Lita demanded now, looking blindly around the room. "Where's cute little ole man I rescued?"

"You mean Mr. Barrows?" North asked. "Doesn't look like he could make it."

"What's his room number?" Lita asked. "Give 'm a call; invite 'm personally."

Anton Carss, short, bulgy, his dark face creased by a soft, tolerant smile, was suddenly at Lita's elbow. "He'll probably be here later, darling," he said quietly.

"Give 'm a call," Lita said, and lurched away. Carss threw North a tilted-eyebrow look, shrugged his dumpy shoulders in a silent plea for understanding, and trailed after the star of *Tiger, Tiger!* Hugh turned back to Mary Hollberg. The German "pianist" was looking after Naline and Carss and for the first time the colonel saw a hardness in those blue eyes, a cold calculation that vanished as the girl felt Hugh's glance upon her and looked up to meet it.

"Those jewels; did you notice them?" she asked North.

"I've often heard the term 'dripping jewels' "—Hugh nodded—"but this is the first time I've actually seen jewels drip from a woman. And speaking of jewels, I've admired your ring so much, Miss Hollberg."

The girl held up the emerald on her knuckle, wriggled her finger to make it give off green fire. "Is it not an excellent imitation?" she asked with a laugh. "Our German scientists are unexcelled at ersatz—they had to learn to be during the war, you know."

"Oh? I never would have guessed it wasn't real." *And it is, sister, it is!*

"Nein. I bought it in West Berlin for a few marks. It was too expensive for me to afford, perhaps, but it is worth far less than the smallest diamond in Miss Naline's cheapest bracelet." She heaved a sigh that swelled the square-cut bodice to the danger points. "Oh well, there is no use envying her her jewels, Mary *Liebchen.* No man will ever think you so—so delectable that he will give you diamonds and rubies."

"Perhaps a silver wedding ring is more precious," North suggested.

The German girl's eyes flashed up. "You think so? Hah, how old-fashioned that sounds, Herr Boyden. Perhaps you are right, but most of the women I know would prefer to have the jewels first and later the precious silver wedding ring. I"—she darted her eyes up at North and dropped them again—"would ask for neither if I found the man attractive, if he pleased me."

This was getting into deep water, but Hugh North sailed on. "That would be a very fortunate man indeed," he murmured. "I envy him."

Hollberg's lips curved in a smile. "You have no need to because I am trying to say—"

"Good afternoon. I am Boris Salenkov, textile commissar in the government of the U.S.S.R. How do you do?"

Hugh North's first thought was that Mary Hollberg came close to throwing her drink into Salenkov's face for inter-

117

rupting. His second thought was that Boris Salenkov was the most Russian-looking Russian he had ever met. If he was a Red agent, the MVD had outdone itself in putting on the Bracht case the best double-switch operative conceivable.

In his career Hugh had matched wits with many Soviet secret agents, dating back to the old OGPU days. He had met and dealt with a range of operatives that had included every type from brutish strong-arm torturers to cultured women in the highest circles of society, but this was the first time (if Salenkov actually was an agent) that he had faced a man who fitted so exactly the picture of what a Red undercover man should look like and never did.

"You are Mr. Boyden," the Russian said, his accent thick, "and you are the Fräulein Hollberg. Of the People's Republic of East Germany?"

Mary Hollberg shook her head. "I am of West Berlin," she said briefly, and deliberately turned her back on Salenkov. To Hugh she said, "Please excuse me. It has become unbearably close all of a sudden and I must have fresh air." Then she was gone.

North found Salenkov looking after the departing "pianist," his stare murky. "She is hiding something, that woman," the Russian said without looking at Hugh. "I know she is not what she says she is."

"Oh?"

"Always when I have tried to speak with her she has run away from me," Salenkov rumbled. "I think she fears me because she thinks I am from the police."

"And you're not?" Hugh asked calmly.

Comrade Salenkov transferred his stare to the G-2 colonel. "No," he said seriously. "As I explained, I am a textile commissar. I am on a world tour, seeing the factories of the United States of America and also those of Southeast Asia so I can make a report to my government. It is all set forth in my credentials."

"I see," North murmured.

"And this Fräulein Hollberg, why does she fear the police? Because she is a deserter from the People's Republic of East Germany, of that I am almost sure. She has betrayed her country for"—a contemptuous wave of a thick hand at the surrounding hurly-burly—"this depraved luxury and now she fears she will be taken back to justice."

"She says she's a concert pianist," North offered.

"Ho, who would believe anything a German says?" Salenkov scoffed. "They are an ungrateful people, the Germans; they accept all the generosity of the U.S.S.R. and give nothing in return. And then they desert their country and tell lies about us. They are undependable, the Germans."

He fixed Hugh with the small eyes behind their spectacles. "Why are you traveling in this country?" he asked bluntly.

"Have one of my cards," North countered, masking his amusement. He proffered one of the engraved cards that Lex Ross had seen. The self-styled Soviet textile commissar studied the slip gravely, nodded, and tucked it in his breast pocket.

"The U.S.S.R. has no need of importers," he informed Hugh. "The U.S.S.R. produces the finest goods in the world and so we do not need to bring in a single thing. Instead, we export and the day will come when every nation will depend upon the Soviet's good will to obtain the products they will need to survive. Good-by, Mr. Boyden."

With which Boris Salenkov of Moscow trudged off. Hugh watched him attach himself to one of the lesser lights of the *Tiger, Tiger!* company and introduce himself, as stolid, as stupid, as he had made himself appear to Hugh North.

It was about time he was getting out of here, the colonel told himself. His only interest in making this party had been the possibility that John Wallen might volunteer something about his possible connection with Tao Muong or somehow settle in his, North's, mind that Lex Ross had come up with a bum steer. If the latter had proven the case, Mr. Ross would have had some explaining to do—something that was on Hugh's list for Lex Ross in any case.

However, with the host passed out and with this affair developing into such a rat race there seemed no chance to do any work here. Hugh decided to have one more drink and then leave. He had contacted Captain Pokh and the little captain had assured him that Rooms 437 and 439 would be well covered by an invisible Thai plain-clothes man, but North's doubts about the efficiency of the Bangkok Imperial Troop made this absence from his ward a somewhat uneasy time. There also was the question of what claim Chu Hoong might have on the plain-clothes man. If Chu had been telling the truth when he had claimed close friendship with General Genung, would anybody in the Bangkok Imperial Troop prove trustworthy when the chips were down?

He went back to the bar, tipped a light scotch into his glass, and added ice and soda. He was turning away when Lex Ross sidled up to him.

"My rooms are next door," he murmured. "Can't we get out of this madhouse and talk?"

"I read somewhere that the best place to tell secrets was in a crowd like this," Hugh retorted. "Nobody listens to anybody else."

"Whoever said that never meant a Hollywood cocktail party," Ross grunted. "Some of us have developed the fine art of hearing everything said across a room while talking at the top of our voice. You'd be amazed. I sometimes think we're turning into a nation of lip readers or perhaps it's extrasensory perception. Those who can't hear do their damnedest to. For instance, I understand Wallen called you up and asked you what I said to you."

Hugh nodded.

"Did you tell him?"

"No," North said. "I didn't want to get mixed up in any personal feud between you two. Anyway, I'm not interested in scandal about somebody's wife."

Ross looked about him, lowered his voice another notch. "You're interested in Tao Muong, all right," he muttered grimly. "You're interested in everything about Dr. Bracht."

"Ah, yes." Hugh smiled. "That's right, you did say something about this—Kayo Mung, is it?—being the wife of this guy Bracht."

Ross's face darkened, "God damn it," he growled, "when are you going to admit that's Hans Bracht you're with? I tell you I want to help you."

North fired one round into the darkness. "Look, you ask

so many questions perhaps you'll answer one for me. Who was Walter Wells?"

Jack Wallen's suggestion that the colonel put this question to Ross produced results. Ross had been scowling; now he lost his scowl, dropped his attitude of near belligerency, let his eyes drift away from North's stare.

"So that's it," the actor said in barely a whisper. "I should have guessed." His eyes came back. "But that was a long time ago," he protested. "I—I thought I'd made up for that. I was told you fellows wouldn't hold that against me."

North waited. Ross looked about him again and then burst into a smothered, impassioned protest. "I made a mistake, sure, but do I have to have it hung around my neck all my life? I didn't know they were—well, yes, I guess I did toward the end, but as soon as I found out I quit, didn't I? I told you fellows everything I knew, didn't I? You've got to remember that this was when being a pinko was the fashionable thing to do. Hell, most of us went into the damned thing just to go along with the crowd. I never really believed any of that Marxist stuff."

"And Walter Wells was your Communist party name, huh?" Colonel North asked.

Lex stared at him. "Of course—you knew that, didn't you? That's why you won't give me the time of day, isn't it?"

Hugh shook his head, his smile in place. "To be honest, no. Somebody just told me to ask you that question, that's all."

The graying actor turned a black glare toward the closed bedroom door.

"That bastard Wallen, wasn't it?" he grated. "Someday I'm going to kill that guy, I swear."

"Whoa," Hugh counseled. "Don't talk like that."

"Well, I will! Who does he think he is, smearing anybody? Look up his record, Boyden. Oh, you'll find plenty there. Didn't he refuse to testify before that congressional committee and wasn't he almost blacklisted on every lot in Hollywood before he finally got scared and went to Washington and told a lot of lies? He's a bigger Red than I ever thought of being and he spreads stuff about me, does he? He's not going to get away with it this time!"

He wheeled and started for the bedroom door. North's hand shot out and caught the actor's elbow. "Easy, Ross," the colonel warned.

"Leave me alone," the other man snarled.

"No, I'm not going to let you get yourself messed up," Hugh said. "Take a swing at him here, with all these people around, and you're going to start a lot of talk, attract a lot of attention."

"Who cares?"

"Well, suppose I care," North said quietly. "Suppose a fight between you two got some people upset whom I don't want upset? You say Wallen knows something about Tao Muong, Bracht's wife—what if this personal battle between you and Wallen interfered in some way with Dr. Bracht's plans, the plans of the people Bracht works for?"

Ross stopped his struggle to get free and turned around to face North. "You mean you're finally admitting that it is Hans Bracht?" he asked. "Do you mean—"

"Never mind what I mean," North said in a clipped voice. "Just take it as I've put it. Any commotion involving a man who knows something about Hans Bracht's wife, as you say Wallen does, could be a damned dangerous thing at this time. Take my word for it."

Ross hesitated a moment and then nodded. "Okay," he said. "I'll be good. Someday you might find out that if you'll take me into your confidence I can— But never mind; I guess you will in your own good time."

"Now, what's this about Wallen knowing something about Tao Muong?" the colonel asked in a low voice.

"I don't know," Ross admitted. "He only said—well, we were having breakfast together this morning and the talk got around to missiles and rockets and moon shoots and things like that, the way they will, and—"

"Who brought it up?"

"I guess I did," Lex said after a pause. "I'm not positive but I think I was the one who started it. Anyway, I couldn't help asking Wallen if he'd ever seeen Hans Bracht and Wallen said no, he hadn't. Then he gave that nasty laugh of his and said he knew something about Bracht's wife, Tao Muong, that one of the scandal rags would pay plenty to get. I asked him what it was and he said what did I think he was, asking him to give away a million-dollar piece of information like that?"

"Million-dollar information? You mean the scandal magazines pay big?"

"No, he was talking about blackmail—oh, maybe not in cash but something he could use to put pressure on somebody when he needed it in his career. He's done that before, plenty of times. Oh, he's the filthiest, rottenest heel that ever struck Hollywood, that no-good bastard!"

The master of disguise remembered what had been said before his break for Wallen's door, and his voice deepened with intensity. "About that Walter Wells business, I swear to you that—"

"Wheeee! Look, everybody! If a Turk belly dancer can do it halfway in Rome, I guess I can do the complete job in Bangkok!"

North spun, as did everybody else in the room, toward the shrilled announcement.

It was Lita, and she quite obviously had somehow gotten away from Anton Carss's restraining care. Her black hair was loose and swirling about her shoulders, which were bare.

As was the rest, every lovely inch, of Lita Naline.

4.

There was a hush for a moment and then two male voices split the air simultaneously.

"Lita!" cried Anton Carss in outrage.

"Atta girl!" howled Jack Wallen from the door to his bedroom.

Carss fought his way through the transfixed crowd toward the naked Lita, who was beginning a shockingly lascivious writhing grind of jerking torso and heaving breasts. Wallen

123

clung to the doorframe, his face red and swollen from alcohol and laughter, and bawled his drunken hoots.

"Aw, leave her alone, Anton!" he yelled. "What the hell, everybody's seen it all, anyway."

Carss, the director, hesitated in his frantic efforts to reach his star-mistress long enough to cast Wallen a look that was as lethal as a kris. The drunken man in the bedroom doorway caught the glare and laughed louder.

"Ask anybody!" he bellowed. "You think you're the only one that ever had any of that? Be honest with yourself, Carss, like your head-shrinker is always telling you—admit you're getting the leftovers after everybody in Hollywood and Malibu got tired of banging it!"

He guffawed again, then ducked as an ash tray came sailing at him, thrown hard though wide by the party's impromptu nautch dancer. Lita hurled herself at Wallen, her full breasts bobbing, her fingers crooked into claws, her beauty gone as her face distorted in hate.

"God damn you!" she screamed. "God damn you, you god damn pervert. You fairy. You—" There followed a blast of epithets that made even Hugh North shudder.

Carss caught her a moment before she reached Wallen. The pudgy director seized her about the slim middle, heaved her over his shoulder, and bore her, kicking and yelling, toward the door. En route, one of the *Tiger, Tiger!* underlings recovered from his paralysis enough to strip off his madras sports coat and throw it over the part of Lita that was nearest to him. One of the motion-picture industry's highest paid stars, therefore, exited from John Wallen's cocktail party with her bottom covered in handsome red-, black-, and green-striped cloth.

The door banged behind Carss and his burden and the suite was quiet except for Wallen's gasping chuckles. The host recovered his breath enough to wave his hands at his guests. "Come on, come on," he said. "The show's over but the party's just beginning. Belly up, folks, and we're off and drunking again!"

He fumbled his way toward the array of bottles on the cloth-covered table, and Hugh noticed that at his side was

124

Fräulein Mary Hollberg, smiling invitingly up at Wallen as she steadied the drunken actor.

She must have her eye on a pair of emerald earrings to go with that rock on her finger, North said silently, and then laughed at himself; how much had jealousy to do with that thought? Hell, the girl probably was as awed by motion-picture stars as Bracht had said his Tao Muong was, and who could blame her for cozying up to the most glamorous man in the business?

And that reminded North; he had been too long away from Hans Bracht, Chu Hoong had not been among the party guests (Hugh could not imagine the Chinese accepting an invitation to such a brawl, even if he had been invited) and at the present moment Chu was the number-one menace to Bracht in North's mind.

He did not try to do the correct thing by bidding his host good-by and thanking him for his hospitality. Instead, he slipped out of the throng unnoticed, descended to the lobby's cable desk to send off a coded query to Washington. Then he went up to Room 437.

Pokh's man turned out to be surprisingly good at hiding, at least. Colonel North had to look closely to find a small individual in a niche shielded by a potted palm. The G-2 agent gave the signal agreed upon with Captain Pokh, a left-handed salute, and used his key to open the door of Room 437. Hans Bracht lay snoring on the bed, obviously worn out from the days and nights of tension that had been his lot since Tao Muong had disappeared.

Hugh checked the scientist's breathing, smelled his breath, and knew that this was a natural sleep not induced by any of Their subtle additions to the lunch he had shared with the scientist. Hugh walked next door and spent nearly ten minutes checking Room 439 for a possible bug, finding nothing other than the connection that he himself had stretched between the two phones early that morning.

He was stripping off his shirt preparatory to taking another shower (for the Bangkok day was very humid) when the phone in 437 jangled. He got to the instrument before it rang again and answered in a muted voice that could not disturb

125

the sleeping Bracht. His instinctive check of his wrist watch showed the hour as 5:57.

"Hey, Boyden, where'd you get to?" It was Jack Wallen.

"I had to leave," Hugh explained. "Sorry I missed you."

"But somebody told me you were there for the show Lita put on. Hot stuff, huh?"

"Very—uh—unusual."

"Unusual's the word, son. Hey, what I called you about, I've got to see you privately. I got something to tell you. Something that's maybe right down your alley if you're a cop, like Ross says."

North kept his curse silent. "Ross says what?"

"Oh, don't worry, I won't tell anybody. But I've got a piece of information you might like to have."

"Look, Wallen, I don't know—"

"Oh, cut out the horse crap, Boyden. Ross may be an old jerk but he wouldn't have any reason for saying you're a cop if you weren't, would he? Does the name Tao Muong interest you?" As North held his breath Wallen laughed hoarsely. "I thought that'd jar you. You come on back up here in—well, I've got a little business to finish up, but I ought to be free in fifteen minutes. Tell you what—I'll give you a call when you can come up."

Before Hugh could speak the phone went crashing into its cradle. North hung up slowly, glancing at Bracht on the bed as the missile scientist groaned and stirred in his sleep.

The G-2 colonel asked himself just how far he could go in adhering strictly to the assurances he had given Hans Bracht. His duty on this case was to protect the scientist from anybody who might try to harm him, help recover Bracht's wife, if possible, and get the space-travel genius back to Cape Canaveral. Would Wallen's information, whatever it was, help expedite any of these things?

Well, certainly it could not hinder, and unless he used the information Wallen might give him to grab Tao Muong's kidnapers before the snatchers made their move it could not be considered breaking his word not to interfere. North decided that when Wallen called back he would say yes, he'd be right up.

Meanwhile he had fifteen minutes in which to grab that shower. The G-2 agent stripped and submitted himself to a stinging needle spray that washed some of the weariness— and the griminess of that sordid scene in Suite Seven-D— from him. Then he dressed leisurely in a fresh shantung silk suit, mixed himself a highball with some decent scotch, and lay back on Bracht's bed to wait.

Fifteen minutes passed, twenty, twenty-five, then a half an hour. Hugh left the bed and walked the floor of his room, passing his hand over his close-cropped head. Had Wallen passed out again? Had he forgotten the call or was the "little business" he had had to finish up stretching out this long?

Or was Wallen in trouble, possessing that dangerous knowledge and as loose-lipped with drink as he had been?

The colonel went to the phone, had the operator ring Wallen's suite. There was a lengthy series of ring-clicks and then the sing-song voice of the Thai operator informed him that Suite Seven-D did not answer.

North told himself Wallen could be deep in another alcoholic slumber or in the shower or gone for a walk (in this heat?) or—or—

The colonel left the room, marked the plain-clothes man still in place, and mounted the stairs to the seventh floor again. Outside Seven-D he pressed the ivory button, bore down on it. No response. He tried the door and found it locked, so he went to his slender bunch of keys. The third key he tried fit the lock and the colonel pushed into the suite. His watch showed him it was 7:06.

Its crowd gone, Seven-D revealed itself as including a large, sunny living room gorgeously furnished with oriental pieces—although the place was littered with the remains of the party now—its picture window looking out over the Menam Chao Phya. A haze from the cigarettes smoked there that afternoon still hung low over the room despite the efforts of the air conditioner to draw it out. A cabinet radio near the picture window provided muted American dance music that had been drowned out by the clamor of the crowd earlier.

North walked through the room to the open bedroom door.

127

It required only a step over the threshold onto the thick carpeting of the bedroom to find John Wallen.

The handsome actor was not handsome now. Coatless but otherwise fully dressed, he sprawled on the bed, his sightless eyes staring at the ceiling, his arms outflung, fingers curled as though he had made a final grasp at life and had missed. His long body was as contorted as his face, and in his death throes his heels had dug into the coverlet, bunching the spread.

From his chest thrust the carved hilt of the dagger that had silenced John Wallen forever before he could tell Hugh North what he knew about Hans Bracht's wife, Tao Muong.

CHAPTER 5

1.

BEFORE HE PUT IN A CALL to Captain Pokh,
Hugh made a swift and searching examination of the body,
Wallen's effects, and the disordered suite.

Except for a tiny cut on the dead man's upper lip, the
body showed no other wounds than the fatal stabbing. Wallen's pockets yielded nothing at all. On the bureau were the
things he would normally carry in his trousers, wallet, keys,
handkerchief, lighter, cigarettes. His jacket, hung in the
closet—his trunks had not been unpacked—contained nothing beyond a fountain pen; the side pockets of the coat, in
fact, were still sewn shut as they had come from the tailor,
apparently to keep the star from breaking the jacket's perfect line by shoving his hands into his pockets absent-
mindedly.

Wallen's keys provided those needed to open his trunks
and it required only a few minutes for the G-2 colonel to
explore them and come up with nothing of value—unless
one counted as valuable a packet of pornographic pictures,
several of which showed "models" who bore at least a startling resemblance to well-known movie stars. Hugh's nose
wrinkled as he looked at them, but through his disgust came
the reminder that Lex Ross had said Wallen was not above
using blackmail to pressure his way ahead in his profession,
if not actually to wring cash out of his victims.

He stuck the pictures in a hip pocket (no use letting the
Thai police lay hands on them until he was a little more
sure of Siamese police ethics) and went on with his exami-

129

nation, moving into the living room. It proved a hopeless task to get any worthwhile clues from that mess if there were any there and the colonel returned to the bedroom.

This information Wallen was supposed to have about Tao Muong, was it written down, a picture, or had the actor carried it about in his head? And if Wallen did have anything tangible was it kept in some secret pocket, possibly a false heel compartment? It was a long shot, but the G-2 agent made a second swift search of the body, hunting for a hiding place on Wallen's person such as he, North, would use.

He found no secret pocket or false heel but he found something else. As he was removing the shoe from the dead man's right foot he smoothed over one of the folds of the rumpled coverlet. There, pressed deeply into a crease, was the emerald ring that Hugh North had last seen on the finger of the self-styled pianist, Fräulein Mary Hollberg.

North picked up the ring and stared at it, his brows lowered. So little Mary was mixed up in this thing, eh, and in what capacity? Was she the executioner They used to silence unsuspecting men They wanted removed, men who set themselves up for the death stroke when they lost themselves in anticipation of what she would bring to their bed?

Possible—hell, anything was possible with Them—but North's instinctive answer to his own question was no.

A Red killer would never be so careless as to leave an emerald ring on the murder scene, a finger pointing straight at her. Mary Hollberg might have proved a strangely inept bungler for a Red agent in her choice of roles, but this was too much to expect from even the most incapable operative on the MVD payroll.

This was a heavy knife and, popular belief to the contrary, it required considerable strength to drive a knife into a man's chest, as this blade had been driven. If the knife had gone in under the rib cage, slanting upward—but it hadn't. Mary Hollberg might have used both hands to do the job, but it would have been an awkward thing and one easily avoided by the man on the bed. If he had been awake; there was always the possibility that he had passed out again, after dalliance with the delectable Mary.

The G-2 colonel sighed, grimaced. Who was he, Fräulein Hollberg's defense attorney? He reached for the bedside phone to call Captain Pokh.

It was as though the instrument anticipated him; it rang with a shrillness doubly amplified by North's tension. The colonel hesitated only a moment and then lifted the phone from its cradle.

"Hullo," he muttered.

"Mr. Wallen?"

"Who's calling, please?" North hoped his voice somewhat approximated Wallen's but he doubted it.

"This is—are you Mr. Wallen?" The question was sharp.

"No," Hugh acknowledged. "Mr. Wallen can't come to the telephone right now. Who's calling?"

"Who is this, please?"

"A friend," North stalled. "Can I have Jack call you back?"

"Ah"—there was a moment of indecision—"no. No, never mind, thank you. Thank you very much."

The connection was broken by a click at the other end. North jiggled the cradle lever until the phone operator downstairs answered.

"Where did that call to Seven-D come from—outside or another room in the hotel?" the colonel demanded.

"The hotel, sir," replied the operator. "Penthouse. Mr. Chu Hoong, sir."

2.

Captain Pilanung Pokh was on the spot within three minutes of North's call. The captain was in his element; his brown eyes sparkled, his little body took on a bantam-rooster strut that North would have found entrancing under any other circumstances. The undersized officer headed a platoon of men, all of whom were almost identical to their commander, minus the strut.

"Always I want to solve high-class murder," Pokh told Hugh confidentially, and with relish. "Now you make present

131

of one. Excellent. I show you what I learned from books, Colonel. First we grill everybody who was in this room today, eh?"

North thought back to the crowd that had attended the cocktail party. When he had been there, there must have been at least thirty, possibly fifty, persons elbowing each other, fighting for talking space, guzzling drinks, munching canapés, and, at the end, eying Miss Lita Naline's opulent charms. If Pokh intended to question each one it was going to be one of the biggest mass "grillings" on record and doubtless the slowest.

"Maybe there's another way, Captain," he suggested. "I know Wallen was alive at five fifty-seven. He phoned me then and said he wanted to see me. He told me he'd call me back in about fifteen minutes, after he finished up some business. When he didn't call back I phoned him and then came up here."

"Finish up business? What business?"

"He didn't say. The party was over; I know that. There were no noises in the background, and even if he called from the bedroom with the door shut there'd have been some noise, with that mob."

But Mary Hollberg wouldn't have been noisy, getting ready for the tender scene—and murder. Or whoever came back to kill Wallen wouldn't have been loud about it.

"In such case," Pokh was saying, "we only got to find out who here at five fifty-seven and after that, till you find him at ten minutes past seven, eh? Is easy."

You think so? Hugh asked silently.

"Together we have murderer in double-speed time, you see," Pokh said confidently. "You help me with this investigation, Colonel North?"

Hugh rubbed his chin reflectively. "I'm sort of on a spot, Captain," he told Pokh. "You know I'm here on a big job, a job that's even bigger than murder. But this killing may be hooked to my mission. I want to find out everything I can about it, who killed Wallen and why, but at the same time I don't want to let anybody know who I am if I can help

132

it. And I want Henry Barrows, the man in the next room to mine, kept out of it altogether."

Pokh's face fell. "Had idea we could make team; you show me how big-shot American Intelligence colonel works."

"Well, I don't know about the big-shot angle but I'll do anything I can to help." North smiled. "Suppose we work it this way: I'll suggest a list of people to question and some of the things you'll want to ask them. I'll be just another suspect for the time being—be sure you treat me like one. Now if you could have the room where you do the questioning outfitted with a listening device I could sit in on your interrogation in another room and possibly come up with some ideas as you go along."

"Oh, sure." Pokh nodded. "Bangkok Imperial Troop has newest listening machines. You see. Who's on list of suspects, pliss?"

"We'll start off with Fräulein Hollberg," Hugh North said. He had not shown Pokh the emerald ring that nestled in his watch pocket; he had not yet brought himself to believe that the German girl could have been Wallen's killer and he was reasonably sure that to produce the ring found under the dead man's foot would mean the end of any investigation so far as Pokh was concerned. Which, if the ring had been planted, would be exactly what the real killer—possibly a Communist hatchet man—had intended.

Hugh North had always mistrusted too obvious clues, even in dealing with relatively minor cases. Now, with so much at stake on this mission, he was doubly reluctant to take the emerald ring's significance at face value. If this was a Commie killing linked with the Hans Bracht case, to snap up red herrings too quickly might result in a fatal bone in the throat. Mary Hollberg would not go far, even if she tried to run. Bangkok was not an easy city for a pretty German girl to move about unnoticed; Thailand was a difficult country to get out of except through the few easily covered transportation termini. Besides, unless this murder was entirely unconnected with Hans Bracht—a cornered burglar, a jealous rival, an outraged husband—the one who had used that

133

knife *couldn't* run. The main job was unfinished and any risk entailed in staying at the scene would be nothing compared with Moscow's displeasure at a task left uncompleted, no matter what the agent's predicament.

Pokh and his men set up a Siamese version of a "bug" (antiquated by American standards but still serviceable) in Wallen's living room with an earphone connection stretched to a room across the hall. Hugh realized that all these preparations would be known to Chu Hoong before they were completed, but that couldn't be helped. Besides, the Chinese multimillionaire had not been at the party; he had phoned after the killing, something he would hardly have done if he were involved, and he was clear of suspicion of murder in Hugh's private opinion. North was beginning to form his own idea of Chu's possible part in this whole involved drama, and nothing the G-2 man had come up with so far suggested that Chu Hoong, discoverer of Dragon's Tooth Elixir, would have any reason for wanting John Wallen dead.

Then, when they were ready to begin the questioning of the people Hugh listed for Captain Pokh, the strongest of the G-2 colonel's theories took a left hook smack in the eye.

Fräulein Mary Hollberg, it developed, had flown the coop. She was not in her room; she was not in the hotel. When last seen by the doorman at the main entrance of the Imperial Hotel she had been hurrying, nearly running, out of the building in what the doorman's translated description was "an extremely agitated condition, as though very frightened."

The time of Mary's departure? Six-ten, or just about the time that John Wallen had expected to finish up his "little business."

"Ho!" cried Captain Pilanung Pokh. "Now we have dragnet! Hot dog!"

The "dragnet" out, Pokh finally was restrained enough to get on with the questioning of the other people on the list. Lex Ross was the first man quizzed by Pokh.

Ross said he had left the party shortly after Lita Naline had been carried out and had not returned. He had stayed in his suite, adjoining Wallen's, passing up dinner because

134

of too many hors d'oeuvres and intending to eat a light supper later.

No, he had heard no screams, nothing at all, through the wall from Wallen's quarters. He didn't have a single idea of who might want to kill John Wallen.

"But you overheard to say you yourself kill Misser Wallen some day," Pokh pointed out. "You say that only hour before John Wallen found dead. How is this?"

Hugh North, sitting across the hall with the earphones in place, wished again that there had been a chance to install a one-way mirror somewhere so he could watch the faces of those questioned. Not, he consoled himself, that he would be likely to see much in Ross's face; the actor's long career in movies gave him complete command of his expressions when he needed to use it.

Ross: "I was joking."

Pokh: "You sure, Misser Ross? Informant says no joke the way it sounded."

"Who is your informant, may I ask?"

"You may ask but I don't tell. Why you want to kill Wallen, eh?"

A brief silence and then: "All right, I was burned up at Jack at the time. He spread some—some loose talk about me and I resented it. But I wouldn't kill him, for God's sake!"

"But your room's right next to Wallen's, eh, and connected by outside balcony? You in Seven-C, next door. You could come back in here when Wallen alone, after cocktail party, and use knife—"

"I tell you I didn't."

Pokh: "We see. You stay in hotel, Misser Ross, till we say okay for you to leave."

Anton Carss: "You'll have to forgive me, Captain, if I'm a trifle incoherent. This has hit me very hard, sir. I was not especially close to John Wallen as a person, I admit, but he had a great talent as an actor. A great talent. My picture will suffer from this shocking loss." There was the sound of a deep sigh. "And I had such great hopes for *Tiger, Tiger!*"

"You don't make movie now?" North heard Pokh ask.

135

"Oh yes, we'll go ahead with it. The studio will fly some-body out to take Wallen's part. We'll have to reshoot the footage we canned in Hollywood, but that's not too much, thank heaven. Yes, we'll go ahead, but it's Lita's reaction to this tragedy that I fear most of all. She was very fond of Jack in spite of their professional differences."

"Mebbe so fond you don't like it, eh?"

"What do you mean, sir?"

"I mean people at party say Misser Wallen said many things when lady takes her clothes off. You don't like these things. Mebbe you don't like them so much you come back and stab Wallen."

"Ridiculous," Carss snorted. "Wallen was drunk and Lita—Lita had invited insults by her reckless behavior. She should not drink, Captain, for when she does— But that has nothing to do with this terrible thing."

"Mebbe not. Misser Carss, Wallen tell somebody he has business with someone after party. You head of movie peo-ple here; was business with you?"

"No, not that I know of."

"Okay, does name Tao Muong mean anything to you?"

Hugh North tensed, trying to interpret the inflection of Carss's voice when he replied. "Tao Muong? I've heard that name somewhere. Let me think. I'm not sure but I think I heard Jack Wallen mention the name to somebody, not me. I overheard it, I think, and I believe it was Wallen who said the name but I may be wrong. And who is Tao Muong, Captain?"

"Don't know," Pilanung Pokh answered, truthfully, be-cause North had not told him. "Is all questions for this time, Misser Carss. Stay in hotel until we say all right to go, pliss."

"But we're scheduled to go on location, Captain! The camp's set up, everything's ready. If there's any delay it'll cost the studio a fortune."

"Ho, couple of days we catch murderer, all right. Don't you worry about that. You got to wait for new actor any-how, don't you?"

"Yes, but we can shoot around him on location until he's

136

ready to work. Please, Captain, it's imperative that we keep to our schedule."

"We see, Misser Carss. Good-by, pliss."

Lita Naline: "Omigod, my head. Can't I have just a little drink, Captain? I'm all shook up because I positively *loved* Jack Wallen even if he did have more enemies than *anybody;* there wasn't a shred of *decency* in the sonofabitch when he wanted to be mean.

"But there I go, that's just my hangover talking, and with all that liquor just *sitting* over there you could at least give me one little drink." A pause. "Thanks, but are you sure you can spare it? I said a *drink,* for crissake.

"And what do you want to ask me questions for? Didn't they tell you I was blacked out when it happened? If anybody's got an alibi it's me because Anton can tell you I was in bed all the time. Instead of asking dumb questions you'd better look and see if Jack took any pictures of me when I was—well, when I was undressed. He thought that was funny, getting a girl plastered and then taking pictures of her, the louse. But I don't mean that. How about another drink?

"Who'd want to kill Jack Wallen? Who wouldn't? When we busted up I came damn near doing it myself. But we made up, honest. We got along fine. Ask anybody.

"I don't know anything more about anything. I only hope the guy they send out to take Jack's place isn't some B-picture jerk that'll ruin *Tiger, Tiger!* How about letting me go, Captain; my head's splitting."

Boris Salenkov: "I know nothing about this. I protest against being questioned. It is an outrage. Have you never heard of diplomatic immunity?"

Captain Pokh: "It is understood you are not diplomat; you are industry commissar making inspection tour. Very sorry to disturb you but there are questions, pliss."

Salenkov: "I refuse to answer them. Unless you want to create an international incident you will not detain me any longer."

137

There was a lengthy pause and then Pokh asked, "In your country, if official Thai person making inspection journey happened to be on scene of murder would your police let him go without asking questions?"

Salenkov: "There are no murders in the U.S.S.R. They are forbidden."

And that was all that Pokh got out of the Russian, that and the promise that Moscow would protest to Thailand about this high-handed treatment of a Soviet textile commissar.

"Is nothing," Pokh said gloomily when North rejoined him. "Is all lying, look like. Except mebbe lady who was sleeping off too many cockstails. Mebbe-so Misser Carss, too. He so worried about movie picture he wouldn't stab leading man, you think?"

North shrugged without replying. That black glare he had seen Carss deal Wallen when the dead man had been hooting at Lita's nakedness had been murderous. However, a man's instinctive reaction to ribald comment concerning his mistress did not mean that man would wait nearly an hour before his flash-fire hate exploded into murder.

"Is Mary Hollberg, certainly." Pokh nodded wisely. "When we find her she confesses everything, I bet you."

"Could be." North nodded. "But let's face it, it could have been any one of that mob that was here this afternoon. Wallen had a pretty ugly background; how do we know one of the electricians or cameramen or assistant directors who knew Wallen in Hollywood didn't have a grudge against him? He seems to have been a grade-A heel, all around."

"Job is to question everybody at party, then," Captain Pokh said. "Misser Wallen invite everybody on plane, everybody in movie, to drink cockstails with him, so everybody now in Bangkok who knew him was here, hey?"

Hugh North pursed his lips. "Not quite everybody," he amended. "Besides Barrows there were two men aboard the plane from Hong Kong who weren't here while I was here, Chu Hoong and Georges Marchet."

"Oh, Chu Hoong never go to cockstail parties," Pokh said.

"Not even big SEATO affairs or Thai government receptions; he say no to all. Who is this Georges Marchet?"

"A planter from Cholon, Vietnam," Hugh explained. "A pretty shabby character. Wallen probably cut him off the invitation list; I don't think he'd have added much, even to this mob scene."

"You think mebbe this Marchet so mad he not invited he kill Wallen?"

"No." Hugh smiled. "It was just a thought. One of your men might check up on Monsieur Marchet, see if he's registered in the hotel, where he was when Wallen was killed. Nothing to it, probably, but we might as well cover the angle."

Pokh spoke a word in Thai to one of his lieutenants. The undersized officer exited, accompanied by a private. The telephone rang for Pokh and the captain seized it eagerly, listened, and replied in Thai, his face falling.

"Thought we got Mary Hollberg," he told North when he hung up. "Not so." He shook his head. "Don't know why dragnet has not found her. Most excellent dragnet in Southeast Asia and German lady who can be identified a mile away walks free. Very bad."

He squinted at North through his faintly slanted eyes. "Why you not sure like me that Mary Hollberg kill Misser Wallen?" he demanded. "Oh, I can see; you say yes when I say we catch her and solve murder but you don't mean it. Why is this?"

"I don't know, really," Hugh admitted. "First, of course, there's the question of how a little girl like Mary Hollberg could drive that dagger into Wallen's chest. If it were a belly wound or even a back wound I could see how she could have managed it, but a chest wound—and what was Wallen doing all this time? He was a pretty big man; even drunk he should have been able to protect himself against Mary Hollberg."

"Troop surgeon says there is cut on dead man's lip," Pokh offered. "Mebbe-so Mary Hollberg hit him in mouth, knock him out, before she use knife."

139

"You seldom knock people out with a punch in the mouth, even a roundhouse," North said.

"Mebbe-so Misser Wallen asleep."

"That's more like it," the G-2 colonel agreed. "But if he was, that wrecks the surprised prowler theory and another one you've doubtless considered, the girl fighting for her honor and picking up a knife that happened to be lying there and— What did you find out about the knife, by the way?"

Pokh sniffed. "Is common enough in Thailand," he said. "Cheap copy of old-time ceremonial knife, Phra Naret dynasty. Hundreds made here in Bangkok for export, valuable curio, but Siamese use it for everything, chop meat, carve wood, even women use it to cut cloth for dresses. Can buy in any shop, ten bahts, fifty cents, U.S."

"I saw a curio shop in the lobby downstairs," North said. "Are these knives sold there?"

"Oh yes." Pokh nodded. "Certainly be sold there; Chu Hoong own factory where ceremonial knifes are made and must surely sell them in his own hotel."

"He really owns the knife factory?"

"Oh yes. Chu Hoong own mostly *everything* in Bangkok, pretty near."

He turned as the lieutenant he had sent to inquire about Georges Marchet burst into the room, chattering in excited Thai. Captain Pokh listened and his round face glowed as the lieutenant rattled on. When the underling was finished at last the captain whirled toward North.

"Is important break in case!" he cried. "Hotel elevator man and porter both say Georges Marchet came up here to seventh floor and ask which way to Suite Seven-D, this place."

"So he was invited to the party, eh?"

"Not so! This was after party over. Georges Marchet did not ascend to seventh floor until after six o'clock. Was here when Wallen murdered!"

3.

Now, what the hell?

How could the seedy French planter, the drug addict who once had guided Hans Bracht through the jungle to the Siamese border when the missile scientist had been escaping the Nazis, be mixed up in the murder of John Wallen, the film star? Had Wallen's information about Tao Muong somehow implicated Georges Marchet and, if it had, how in the world had the Frenchman known Wallen was ready to spill?

Or was Wallen mixed up with dope? North had heard the dead man accused of a full list of crimes, but narcotics had never been mentioned. As for Wallen possibly blackmailing Marchet on the dope angle; that was pretty far-fetched. Ross had said Wallen used his blackmail information to pressure people into advancing his career, not to get money, and how could Marchet help Wallen, either professionally or with cash?

"Marchet is registered here?" North snapped.

"Oh yes." Pokh nodded. "Not high-class man like other guests, so they put him in little room near kitchen. Is back entrance nearby. Monsieur Marchet can come and go through back door without offending fine ladies and gents in lobby. Also can skip hotel bill easier that way. Very suitable."

"I should think Chu Hoong and his manager would want to put guests with doubtful credit somewhere where they could keep an eye on them," Hugh observed.

"Oh no! Monsieur Marchet is expected to skip bill. They put him in cheap room so they don't lose so much when he skips. Same time they make it easy for him to skip, save face all around."

"I see," Hugh murmured gravely, as though he did.

"Let us go arrest this Monsieur Marchet," Pokh said. He got up from his chair and shook his heavy pistol down into place. "This one we will give real grilling. My goodness, we got to grill *somebody*."

"Mind if I come along?" Hugh North asked.

"Pleasant honor. May need excellent American help in subduing suspect, eh?"

North remembered the wreck of a man he had confronted on the plane from Hong Kong, the instantaneous curling up of the French addict when the vague "International Department" was mentioned. "I doubt it," he said.

North followed the undersized captain to the elevator and accompanied Pokh to the ground floor, rear, and the door of Room 14. It was the shabby, behind-the-scenes part of the hotel, the hallway narrow and dark and dirty, the air full of stale kitchen smells mixed with a stench from the alley which ran behind the Imperial. North had been in these seldom-seen parts of luxury hotels before and he never ceased to marvel at their contrast with the glittering lobbies that were so few feet and yet so many worlds removed. Here, in this narrow, unkempt corridor under the same roof as sheltered John Wallen's luxurious suite, dwelt dingy disappointment and ignominy made more poignant by its contrast with the showcase that hid it from public view.

Pokh, the swaggering officer again, rapped sharply on the door of Room 14, waited a moment, and then drew his heavy revolver.

"Just a second, Captain," Hugh said mildly. "I've got a key here that will open it. No need to shoot off the lock."

"Oh, I have master key from hotel manager," Pokh said airily. "Was going to shoot off lock to show you Thai police know all modern methods."

Hugh smothered the impulse to give way to helpless laughter. "I'm convinced they do but you might as well—"

He stopped and clutched the little captain's arm to silence Pokh. Inside Room 14 there was the scrabble of feet, the crash of an overturned chair.

"*Arrêtez!*" shrilled Marchet, inside. And then: "*M'aidez! C'est le meurtrier de l'acteur! Mon Dieu, c'est—*"

There was the smash of a gun, deafening in the close confines of the room beyond. North's own pistol was out and speaking as it blasted the lock Hugh had just kept Pokh from shooting.

142

"The alley," the colonel yelped at the little captain, and yanked open the door, flung himself through.

He went in at a crouch, bent almost double, relying on an inexpert snap shooter's invariably high aim. He guessed right. There was another gun blast, a streak of orange flame cutting the darkness near the pallid square that marked the alley window, and Hugh heard the sizzle of a slug a foot above his head.

There was the crash of glass and a figure, indistinct in the dark room, crowded the window as the gunman flung himself at the opening he had clubbed free. Hugh's gun came down to sight on the fleeing figure—and that was when Captain Pokh of the Bangkok Imperial Troop went into action.

The little captain either had ignored or had not understood North's barked command to cover the alley. Instead, he was right behind the colonel and his heavy revolver blasted in Hugh's ear as he fired over North's doubled shoulder. The jarring concussion was enough to knock North's aim off the fraction of an inch needed to score a complete miss. Hugh had been trying for the gunman's shoulder— a dead man could not explain anything—and with that minute swerve of his aim his bullet went smacking into the window frame beside the disappearing gunman. As for Pokh's shot, it spanged into the ceiling above the window and lowered a curtain of plaster dust.

Cursing under his breath, Hugh went for the window, but Pokh was faster. The captain did not have to straighten from a crouch and so he beat North to the opening, hoisted himself to the sill and leaned out, his feet off the floor, to send four more thunderous shots echoing into the dark alley. The colonel knew as well as if he had followed every bullet that Pokh had scored four more misses.

North whirled and raced to the door of the squalid little room, ran down the hall to the rear door, and turned a corner into the alley. His man was gone—if it had been a man.

Instead, there was a burgeoning crowd of natives attracted by the fusillade flowing into the alley from all direc-

143

tions. If the one surprised in Marchet's room had been a target a moment ago, the mob had swallowed up that target now and Hugh turned back to the hotel entrance, bitter disappointment mounting within him. He had had a good chance to grab Wallen's killer, a man linked to the Bracht case by odds of ten to one, and he had muffed it. No use to blame Captain Pokh for his failure; if he had approached Marchet's room as he should have, on the alert and quietly instead of thumping along like a cop on the beat, chatting with Pokh, he might have grabbed his man and gone on from there to almost any success in guaranteeing Hans Bracht's security, his safe return to Cape Canaveral.

Hotel employees, cooks, waiters, and porters, were jabbering outside Marchet's door as he came back down the narrow hallway. The colonel rudely pushed his way through the throng and into the room, slamming the door shut on all those peering faces. He found Pokh standing beside the bed, looking down at all that remained of Georges Marchet of Cholon, Vietnam.

Even in the gloom that preceded Hugh's click of the wall switch, North knew that Marchet was dead. An ugly stain welled and spread from a wound under the Frenchman's left eye. No man could have survived a shot there.

The Siamese captain tore his fascinated stare loose and looked at North, grimacing. "We have two murders now," he announced. "No murderer. Too bad you missed when you so close."

Hugh bit back his rejoinder and kept his voice level. "Have your men check the whereabouts of everybody in the hotel who was on that Hong Kong plane," he ordered. "Also see if Chu Hoong is in his penthouse."

"Why you suspect Chu Hoong?" Pokh wanted to know. "He never murder anybody—he don't have to. He friend of everybody, got no enemies. His medicine is best in world. You tired, Colonel North? You cannot sleep because murderers all about? Take dose of Dragon's Tooth Elixir and you sleep good, you eat good, you run down to chichi quarter and you cry, *Hallo, hallo, ladies; tonight I take three-four—*"

144

"No thanks," Hugh said hastily. "I'm afraid I'm past the Dragon's Tooth Elixir stage. And we'd better move fast on checking up on those people—there are a lot of them."

"Oh, I go, I go." He paused and eyed North speculatively. "You say everybody on plane? You mean Misser Barrows too?"

The question jolted North. It had taken a little Thai who sometimes skirted the ridiculous to remind him that he had taken Hans Bracht's innocence in Wallen's murder, this killing, for granted. What right did he have to do this?

Then he remembered Pokh's plain-clothes man on duty on the fourth floor of the Imperial and he heaved an inward sigh of relief. That man ought to be able to account for Bracht's movements and give Hugh North at least one person who could positively *not* have killed Wallen or Marchet.

"Your man can give you that information," he told Pokh.

The little captain snapped his fingers at the reminder. "Ho, you can see now why I need expert American help, stupid me," he said, and with that he was off. North heard him orating at some length to the crowd in the hall outside and while North could not understand the Thai chatter it was fairly reasonable to assume that Pokh was explaining that another foreigner had been killed, murdered in cold blood, and that he, Pilanung Pokh, would see that the killer was brought to justice, never fear.

Hugh muttered his exasperation. By the time Pokh got around to checking the whereabouts of any suspects, the killer, if he was one of the Hong Kong plane crowd, could have a tub and a shave. Or maybe only a tub; the killer could have been a woman. North had gotten only a fleeting glimpse of Marchet's murderer, silhouetted as he or she took a header through the smashed window; it was impossible to say definitely whether the hand that had held the gun on Georges Marchet had been male or female.

There was only one reason this poor drug-soaked wretch had been killed; the dead man had answered that question with his last breath. *"C'est le meurtrier de l'acteur!"* he had cried: *It is the actor's murderer!* Marchet had somehow

145

found out who killed John Wallen; he had ordered his own liquidation by his discovery.

A good bet was that Marchet had seen the murderer, either leaving Wallen's room after the killing or even in the very act of driving home the knife. But why had Marchet been there at that time? Had he merely been late for the cocktail party or was he connected with the "little business" Wallen had said he had to finish up? Marchet had known Hans Bracht in Indochina. Bracht had met Tao Muong in China *after* he had parted with Marchet. That is, if Bracht had told the truth there.

It was, to take a line from a play about a long-gone Siamese king, a puzzlement.

The colonel went through the dead man's pockets, oblivious to the faces that crowded the broken window. In the dingy shirt's breast pocket he found a faded and creased newspaper photograph of Dr. Hans Bracht and his wife.

Hugh studied the clipping. Even though the print was smudged by long handling, despite the woman's stiff attitude, Tao Muong was indisputably a beautiful young woman. And, unless the news photographer was to blame for blanking out all signs of intelligence, only beautiful; Tao Muong's eyes, the cast of her mouth displayed plenty of sex appeal even in this foggy photo, but there was no indication of deeper, more substantial qualities.

This, then, was the girl who had made one of the world's greatest minds spend hours reading movie magazines to her —how far apart these two people must be, the world's greatest authority on space travel and a girl who must think movies the most wonderful thing in life.

It was in search of that beautiful, vain, shallow face that looked blankly back at Hugh from the worn and soiled clipping that Dr. Hans Bracht had dropped one of the most important projects the United States had ever planned, had deserted his laboratory to place his life in jeopardy. This empty, movie-struck girl had by her kidnaping endangered the future of the free world.

Movie-struck girl. In those words must lie the connection

146

between Tao Muong and John Wallen, the link that had cost Wallen his life. *Does the name Tao Muong interest you?*

Yet Bracht had said Tao Muong had never met John Wallen. Still, Tao Muong's voice had sounded over the telephone here in Bangkok; had Wallen somehow met the missing woman since he had come to this city?

Could Wallen have been one of the gang holding Tao Muong as bait to lure Hans Bracht into their clutches? Had the actor decided to defect, for some reason, and had he been killed before he could spill what he knew? Possible. Very possible. John Wallen might not be Hugh's idea of a Red agent (Commie operatives seldom made personal enemies any more than they made friends and Wallen was too completely the heel to fit the usual Red agent pattern), but the MVD stuck to no particular brand of undercover worker. Wallen's position in the movies could prove valuable to the Reds in many ways.

The movies—always the movies! Call the *Tiger, Tiger!* company's presence on the Hong Kong-Bangkok plane a coincidence, but one could not so easily dismiss Wallen's knowledge and the death it had brought him.

The movies were the field of Lex Ross, who admitted that he once had borne the Communist party name of Walter Wells. It was Ross who had recognized Bracht so quickly, Ross who had badgered North, trying to get the G-2 agent to admit he was Bracht's guard, who had plagued the colonel for some kind of post as "assistant." It was Ross, another movie star, who boasted that he could disguise himself as any other man alive and thus move about freely in any character that suited his needs in search of information—and murder?

There had been no signs of a struggle in Wallen's room. Did that mean that the actor had been asleep, that he had thought he was in the presence of a friend—or that the friend he had trusted was another man, in disguise?

147

4.

An examination of Marchet's effects showed the French-man had been nearing the end of his rope when the murderer's bullet had snuffed out his shabby existence. The battered suitcase gave up several letters from friends and relatives in France, all refusing to lend him more money. There was also a stiff letter from a Saigon bank, telling Marchet that unless he came up with a payment immediately it would foreclose on the drug addict's tea holdings.

There were other pitiful relics of a failure, a photograph of a much younger Georges Marchet, spick and span in pressed white drill and a clean toupee, standing on the veranda of a new plantation house; a Croix de Guerre he must have won in World War I, some tattered obituaries from French newspapers, an I O U for a thousand francs, dated March 16, 1927, and signed with an illegible scrawl.

There were an opium smoker's tools, the little alcohol lamp, the pipe with its tiny bowl stained by countless pellets of opium that had been kneaded on its side before the bowl was reversed over the lamp's flame to provide the drafts of smoke. There was a tin of the poppy-seed paste, the estate of the man who had given up his happiness for dreams.

There was also a hypodermic needle, a flame-blackened spoon, a pillbox containing several white tablets which were not aspirin. Georges Marchet had graduated from opium to heroin and perhaps the killer's bullet had been a merciful thing.

And last of all was a scrap of hotel stationery upon which was written in a shaky hand: "Suite 7-D." That was the number of John Wallen's rooms and Georges Marchet apparently had not trusted to his fuzzy memory to direct him to the scene of his own death.

Captain Pokh returned to Room 14 with the announcement that Carss, Lita Naline, Lex Ross, and Boris Salenkov had been checked and had not left their rooms since the police interrogation.

148

"Proves murder was done by other person," Pokh observed sagely. "Mary Hollberg."

"Perhaps," North sighed. He knew it would accomplish nothing to point out that the Imperial Hotel had half a dozen entrances that the killer could have used when he or she doubled back, several on halls that did not lead to the lobby. When Pokh had delayed outside this room to orate to the hotel employees the colonel had known that the checks were almost useless; there had been a faint possibility that the killer could have been caught off home base if the checks were made soon enough, but speed was not Pokh's forte.

"I've got to get back to my room," the colonel told the undersized Thai. "I've been away too long, as it is."

"You not going to stay here, take fingerprints?" Pokh asked. "Thought American police always took fingerprints, found murderer by strange automobile tire mark."

"Not this one," North said a trifle wearily. "Besides, I'm interested in these killings only so far as they affect my mission."

"Colonel North, you never tell me what your mission is," the Thai captain said wistfully. "Why you not tell me? Perhaps I work better with you if I know what you're doing."

Hugh considered briefly. The little man might not be G-2 headquarters' idea of the perfect confidant but he deserved something for his co-operation; not too much, but enough to keep him from feeling he was on the outside.

"Briefly, it's this," the colonel told Pokh. "The man in the next room to mine is a person my country wants to keep out of the hands of the Communists. His wife's been kidnaped and I'm pretty sure the Reds used her as a lure to get my man out here so they could grab him."

"So-o-o," Pokh breathed, nodding. "And you think murder of Misser Wallen and Monsieur Marchet mixed up in this somehow, mebbe-so?"

"I don't know," North said truthfully, "but just before Wallen was killed he phoned me and mentioned the name of my man's missing wife."

"Can give me name, pliss?" Pokh asked.

Hugh hesitated. Was this little captain sufficiently well in-

149

formed to connect Tao Muong with Dr. Hans Bracht, the space-travel authority? He crossed his fingers mentally and took a chance. "Her name's Tao Muong," he told Pokh. "She's a countrywoman of yours, I believe. Ever hear of her?"

The captain shook his head. North produced the creased newspaper photo he had taken from Marchet's body. He folded the slip of paper so that Bracht's half of the picture was kept from Pokh's view as well as the cutlines that told who the couple were. "Recognize her?" he asked the Thai.

Pilanung Pokh studied the clipping and heaved a deep sigh. "Is most beautiful Siamese lady, but I do not know her," he mourned. "Not that lucky. She is one who should be in motion movies, that one. Much more beautiful to me than Lady Lita Naline who makes a million bahts every time she displays overlarge bosom to audience."

He looked more closely at the photograph. "Can have excellent picture laboratory make copies of this," he offered. "Place pictures at all stations with lookout order, find her quick if she is in Thailand."

Like Mary Hollberg? North asked, but silently.

"No," he said aloud. "That would be the proper thing to do but we can't operate that way, this time. You see, above all we can't let the kidnapers know that we're tailing my man. He thinks his wife would be killed or disfigured if they get the idea they're being double-crossed."

"Is large possibility he is right," Pokh agreed.

"I don't think so. If my theory stands up, they don't want any ransom money; they want my man. But we can't take that chance. We've got to play it as a straight kidnaping until we're sure it's what I think it is—then we can say to hell with the rules and move in."

He put his next question after due deliberation. "Tell me, Captain, what's your department's stand on the Communists? I mean, I know Thailand is neutral; I know your country is small and has to walk carefully when it comes to being involved in any dispute between the Communist and non-Communist nations, but are your department's leanings to the right or left? Just between the two of us, of course."

150

"To the right," Pokh said firmly. "Oh, General Genung most fierce hater of Communists. They fool around with General Genung and—phttt!—they find themselves dead, most times. Whole Bangkok Troop same way. Also national army. We are not neutrals like India, sir; we tell Vietminh to stay out of Thailand or we shoot them quick."

"Fine," North said heartily. "One more thing; Chu Hoong told me he was a very close friend of General Genung." Pokh nodded. "Then how much pressure can Chu Hoong bring to bear through your army if he wants to play rough with me?"

The little captain puzzled over this question and finally hunched his shoulders. "I do not know," he admitted. "Never has happened, I can think of. But is true General Genung and Chu Hoong very close friends. Like I told you, Chu Hoong is friend of *everybody*."

"You know it's Chu Hoong who always gets Aloysius Robinson out of trouble, don't you?"

Pokh grinned uneasily. "Had big suspicion but never no proof," he said. "Chu Hoong never come right out and say this man must not be arrested; only pay fines, put up bail, things like that. Some say Aloysius Robinson is really Chu Hoong's son by Macanese woman but don't know for sure."

He peered at North. "You think because Robinson tried to rob your Misser Barrows that Chu Hoong mixed up in kidnaping, mebbe-so? You think Robinson not trying to rob Misser Barrows, hey? Trying to kidnap him too?"

"Or kill him," North said bluntly.

"Ohhh nooo," Pokh protested. "Even if whole world crazy and Chu Hoong is Communist man, he not send Aloysius Robinson to get Misser Barrows. That ponk not worth a tical at anything."

And that, North told himself, was rating Robinson about as low as a Siamese could rate anybody. A tical was the lowest coin in Thai currency, worth, as the saying among American travelers put it, "a 'tickel' for a nickel."

"There's one answer to that," North returned. "Robinson might have been trained all these years to build a reputation for worthlessness so that when he handled a big job for anybody the general reaction would be just as you've explained."

Pokh's disbelief showed plainly on his round face. "Mebbeso," he said politely, "but if true, Aloysius Robinson sure have good time getting trained. Would think rich man like Chu Hoong could hire *expert* and not spend so much time and money training Aloysius Robinson to be a—a bomb."

"Bomb?"

"You know, worthless fellow. Bum, mebbe?"

"I get you." North smiled. "Now I've got to check on Barrows. And not a word of what I've told you to anybody, you understand?"

"Mom's the word," Pilanung Pokh said fervently, and somehow Hugh North believed him.

Hans Bracht was awake and roving restlessly about Room 437 when North returned.

"What's going on here?" the missile genius cried immediately. "When it got to be the middle of the night" (it was then exactly 9:32) "and you didn't come back I got hungry and went downstairs to the dining room. On my way to the elevator I noticed this strange little man come out from behind one of those potted palms. He went down in the elevator with me and he sat across the room from me. I took particular notice and he didn't eat a thing. When I left, he left, and he came up on the elevator with me. I finally asked him who he was and what he wanted but he wouldn't answer me."

"Probably didn't understand you," Hugh offered.

"You forget I spent some time in Siam. I haven't forgotten the language entirely. He understood me, all right. Who was he? Did you set him on me? Is he a policeman? I warned you, North, that if—"

"Now take it easy," the colonel crackled. "I said I wouldn't interfere with your ransom payoff or do anything to wreck the deal. That promise still holds. If I have a plain-clothes man put outside the door to make sure somebody other than that kidnap crowd doesn't try to liquidate you it doesn't break my promise."

152

"Liquidate me—who would do such a thing?" Bracht scoffed.

"I don't know who, but it's being done right here in this hotel. Didn't you hear the news when you were down in the dining room?"

"I didn't speak to anybody but my waiter, giving my order, and that little snoop later. News about what? What are you talking about?"

"Two people were murdered in this hotel this evening," North said grimly. "Two people you knew, one pretty well. Georges Marchet and John Wallen."

Bracht's jaw sagged. "You mean—you mean they got in some sort of a fight?"

"No, they were killed at separate times, Marchet, I'm sure, because he saw who killed Wallen and had to be shut up."

The missile scientist looked stunned. "But—but why was Wallen killed? Have they found the murderer? When did it happen? You said you heard that Wallen knew something about Tao Muong. Did his murder have anything to do with that?"

"I suspect it did," Hugh said. "I'm not positive."

The G-2 colonel moved to his bottle of White Label and poured two sizable drinks, watered them and handed one to Bracht, took the other to the chair in the corner. "Doctor," he said matter-of-factly, "let's talk. We may not get another chance, the way things are beginning to move."

"Talk? Talk about what?"

"About everything. It's time to stop playing games with me, Doctor, and give me the whole story. Two men have been killed. They're getting restless, Bracht; they may jump any minute and when They do I want to be ready for them— I want to know what direction They're coming from."

"I've told you I can't talk, North. I've explained how They warned me—"

"Let's get this straight," the colonel grated. "They didn't kidnap your wife for ransom money, Dr. Bracht. They want you. They're Communists and the only deal they'll offer is to swap Tao Muong for you—and they won't live up to their word then. At best, They'll let her live with you in a Soviet prison laboratory while you work for them against the free world. Will you go for a deal like that?"

Bracht's face was gray, lined. Cling as he might to the hope that he could get Tao Muong back by paying x number of dollars, North knew that the master of space travel must have had the terrible suspicion nudge into his thoughts that this was more than a snatch, that this was a Red plan to make a slave scientist out of him. Still, the missile genius fought to preserve his illusion.

"They promised me! Tao Muong told me over the telephone that They would let her go when I paid the ransom. I've got to believe her, Colonel."

"But you have no way of knowing it was Tao Muong," North pointed out. "An accented voice is the easiest in the world to imitate."

"But I talked to Tao Muong, I tell you!" Bracht cried. "Even if I hadn't recognized her voice I'd have known that by what she said to me. Those were things only she could possibly have known. She mentioned some things that I'd almost forgotten—things like what she wore the night we met in Chainat, my first words to her, what we ate at our first meal together. *Nobody* would have known that except Tao Muong."

"This was in Hong Kong?" North asked.

"There and in San Francisco." Hans Bracht nodded. "Whatever else I may be wrong about, I'm right when I say I talked to Tao Muong, no imitator, Colonel."

"All right," Hugh said reluctantly. "Let's drop that for the moment. Did Georges Marchet ever know Tao Muong?"

"No, he never saw her. I'd separated from Marchet when I met Tao Muong."

North brought out the clipping photo and crossed the room to hand it over to Bracht. "When was that taken?" he asked.

The scientist looked down at the slip of paper he held in his faintly quivering hand. The tall, balding man's eyes moistened as he looked at the photograph and his voice was husky. "That was taken when we reached Seattle, the first time we came to the States," he explained. "It was published everywhere. At the time there was a great deal of commotion about my reappearance and my seeking American citizenship. I was what I believe is called hot news." His eyes rose to meet North's. "Where did you find this?"

"In Marchet's pocket."

Bracht pursed his lips. "I wonder why he kept it?" he mused. "Probably to remind himself that once—just once in his miserable life—he did a worthy thing." His stiff, unyielding expression altered a trifle as he looked back at the G-2 colonel. "That sounds egocentric, I know," he apologized, "but Marchet had very little to be proud of. Perhaps, if it had not been for the drugs . . ." He let the sentence trickle into silence.

Hugh paused a moment before he said, "You hate drugs and drug addicts with a particular venom, Dr. Bracht. Why?"

The old rigidity came back to the scientist's face. "Doesn't every decent man hate both?"

"The drug traffic, yes, and those who prey on addicts"— Hugh nodded—"but most more fortunate men feel a certain pity for the addict. I've noticed you lump everyone connected with the evil and hate them all. I'm curious to know why. Were you ever addicted to the use of drugs, Doctor?"

The other man's indignation was immediate and righteous. "Of course not," he rapped out. "I have more self-discipline than to let myself become the animal that drug addicts get to be. Oh, I know how low a person can sink. Believe me, I know!"

"It was somebody in your family, then?"

"My father," Bracht grunted. "My early life was hell because of him. He killed my mother as certainly as though he had driven a knife through her heart, he and his crazy need for drugs. I grew up hating him and everything about him—most of all the dope that made him a quivering wreck, the drugs that made poor people of us Brachts. Oh, it was kept a secret from the world and still is—we were a proud family —but I swore one day that I would get revenge for what drugs did to me and I have, in small measure—oh yes, I have!"

"And yet you depended on a drug addict to lead you

155

through the jungle, out of the reach of the Japs," North ruminated.

"Yes, it was a strange quirk of fate," Bracht said. "I gave my life over to the hands of one of that tribe I despised, an addict. I even softened to the point where I thought of him as a friend, told him who I was, tried to get him to throw off his habit. He—he had some good qualities, I admit. He may even have tried to free himself from his curse but it was no use. In the end, when we were out of reach of civilization and his supply of heroin, he smoked hemp, hashish, and became a wild man. He—we had a fight once when he was mad with the stuff and that was when I left him."

He looked down at the clipping he still held. "Perhaps I was not compassionate enough," he said slowly. "Perhaps I should have tried harder to help him. After all, he did save my life." He straightened. "But I did pay him," he said defensively. "I paid him a great deal of gold."

"Which must have run out some time back," Hugh said quietly. "The papers that were on him showed he was desperately in need of money."

"That was why he approached me on the plane, probably. He wanted me to give him more money for more dope."

It was then that the thought struck Hugh North; what was it the Greek manager of the Hotel Imperial had said when he had first met North? *A stupid clerk had put "Barrows" in Wallen's suite.*

Of course the change had been made almost immediately, when John Wallen had raised the roof about not getting a suite of equal splendor to that of the other stars of *Tiger, Tiger!* But couldn't Georges Marchet, kept at a distance by Hugh's vague threat of some "International Department," have trailed Bracht to Suite Seven-D, jotted down the number of the room because he did not trust his drug-fogged brain, and next day, after the party in the suite he thought was occupied by his onetime companion was over, gone there to attempt a "loan" for old time's sake?

Hugh could almost see Marchet, loitering somewhere near the door to Seven-D, waiting for the merrymaking to finish so he could approach the man he had guided through the jungles of Indochina. Then, when it was quiet inside the suite, when Marchet was sure that Bracht was alone, he must have started for the door. He had seen the "International Department" agent come and leave again; he felt reasonably sure that this time there would be nobody to interrupt him when he made his plea for money.

Perhaps he had met Wallen's murderer face to face at the door when the killer fled. Perhaps he had entered the suite to witness the actual killing. Maybe he had seen the murderer come and then depart and, after the knife wielder had gone, had entered Wallen's rooms and found the corpse, known that the last visitor had blood on his hands. Or her hands.

What then? Had Marchet attempted blackmail, a phone call to the killer with an offer to trade silence for money? Or had the murderer seen Marchet and known that the planter, too, must die to preserve the dark secret?

That was something that might never be known and North told himself it did not matter much. What did matter was that it was almost certain that Marchet had stumbled into the middle of this plot against Hans Bracht, that he had no connection with the main problem. Wallen had, and Wallen's death had been planned by the same people who had kidnaped Tao Muong; that was almost sure. Marchet's killing had been an added risk They had had to take. First Wallen's move to break silence had thrown Them off schedule; then Marchet's blundering into the picture had further upset their plans. Now, the G-2 agent told himself, They must be revising their whole setup and what would be their next step?

As if in answer, the telephone in Bracht's room, 439, rang demandingly.

5.

Hans Bracht stared at the connecting door, then swiveled his head toward North. "It is for me?" he half whispered.

Hugh nodded. "At this time of night it's got to be Them,"

157

he told Bracht. "Better jump to it. I'll stay here and you can close the door if you like."

The scientist nodded mutely and hurled his angular length through the connecting door, slamming it after him. North waited until he heard the mumble of Bracht's voice speaking over the telephone and then went to his own phone and switched on the wire tap.

The same muffled, indistinguishable voice he had heard before was talking to Bracht.

". . . and now you know what happens to those who meddle," it was telling the space-travel genius. "Death came quickly to those two. It will not be so easy for your wife if you have ideas of disobeying us."

"You killed Wallen and Marchet?" Bracht asked.

"It is not for you to ask questions," the voice said rigidly. "But I said they meddled, didn't I? We know all that goes on, Doctor; be sure of that. Do you need more proof?"

"No. No, I believe you."

"That man who has the next room to yours—do not trust him, Bracht," the disguised voice advised. "It might be fatal to your wife if you talked too much to him."

"Who is he?" the scientist asked, and Hugh North could have blessed him; Hans Bracht dared play the colonel's game, unasked, to find out how much the kidnapers knew.

"It is enough for us to tell you not to trust him," the voice grated. "We know everything that goes on—we have eyes and ears that nothing escapes. If you go to the police we will know it and Tao Muong will scream in pain but never will you hear her in her agonies."

Doesn't Bracht see it? North asked himself fiercely. *They don't know anything, not even about Pokh's plainclothes man outside. They're not sure about me. They're trading on Bracht's fear to keep him under their thumb without having to watch him.*

"My wife," the scientist said brokenly. "She is not to blame for any mistakes I might make. Don't harm her; take it out on me. Let me speak to her."

"Later, perhaps. This call is to warn you to be ready to pay the ransom. You have the money?"

"Yes. All in small bills as you said."

"Then listen. It may be we will give you your wife sooner than we first thought. We must make certain arrangements but it may be tomorrow, maybe not. Stay close to your telephone, Doctor."

"I will, I will," the missile genius promised. "Now let me speak to Tao Muong."

"To whom do you presume to give orders, Bracht?" the voice asked harshly.

"I—— meant, please can I speak to my wife? I want to be sure."

"Sure of what?" the voice crackled.

"Sure that it's my wife I talk to," Bracht replied bravely. "How do I know it's not somebody who can imitate her voice?"

There was a second's silence and then the voice said gratingly, "Perhaps you would like us to send you her finger with your wedding ring on it? Would that convince you?"

"No!" Bracht's cry was heart-rending. "No, please!"

"Who has suggested it is not Tao Muong?" the caller demanded. "Quick! Tell me!"

"No one," the missile scientist lied stoutly. "I was sitting here thinking and it came to me that perhaps—"

"Perhaps," the voice broke in mockingly. "Perhaps some other than Tao Muong could invent the intimate things she said to you to prove it was she, eh? You must be reassured again, must you? Then listen—and remember that the mouthpiece is held to her mouth but the receiver is not at her ear. Asking her questions will get you nowhere and only bring terrible pain, terrible torture, to Tao Muong."

"I know, I know," Bracht said.

There was a moment's hesitation and then Hugh North heard the same sweet, birdlike voice he had heard before, the voice of the woman whom the kidnapers claimed to be Tao Muong.

"Ah, beloved Hans," she said, "do as they tell you. I will be safe so long as you do not disobey them. I love you and want you in my arms, dear Hans. Soon we will be together again if you do as they tell you. Good-by, my dear husband."

Then, in another second, came the muffled voice. "There, you heard her. Are you convinced now, Hans Bracht?"

"Yes," Bracht said dully. "Yes, I know it was Tao Muong. It couldn't be anyone else."

"Then you must be ready—"

Hugh North abruptly shut off the tap and put his own telephone through to the hotel switchboard. "I'd like Suite Seven-C, Lex Ross, please. Hurry."

The connection was made and Ross answered with almost the first ring. North took the receiver from his ear and cocked his head toward the adjoining room. Bracht's rumble told him that the scientist was still on the phone.

"Hello, hello?" Ross was saying. "Did somebody ring this phone?"

"So sorry," the G-2 colonel intoned in a singsong voice. "Wrong numbah, pliss."

He hung up, frowning thoughtfully. His call to Ross's rooms had been a hunch that had proved wrong. The disguise artist obviously couldn't be the voice speaking to Bracht—Hugh had half expected a "No answer" to his call to Seven-C.

But there was something wrong with the whole thing; something that Hugh could not quite put his finger on although he knew it was not far from his grasp, just a hairbreadth away. The "kidnapers" (North mentally put quotes around the word because he had long since discarded the idea that they could actually be snatchers operating on a ransom proposition instead of Red agents who wanted to lay hands on Bracht) could be using several men—or women to make their calls to their victim; the voice had been very like that which Hugh had heard earlier, but with the distortion the G-2 colonel knew he could have been fooled. If this was a cell of agents who were working this deal it would be easy for the top man, the Brain, to delegate the phoning duties to an underling North had never seen, but the colonel was convinced in his own mind that his most dangerous adversary was somebody who had been on that Hong Kong-Bangkok plane, somebody in this hotel.

How else, he asked himself, could Wallen's killer have

160

known he was about to talk? Of course there was always the possibility that a phone operator could have tipped the Opposition and a killer could have been sent in from outside to silence Wallen, but North could not buy that too easily. It did not fit with that first phone call and the caller's knowledge of what had happened on the plane, Bracht's having been accosted by Marchet, plus the fact that Muffled Voice had known that Bracht and North had shared a cab from the airport.

Again, there was the possibility that one of the *Tiger, Tiger!* company, a member of the camera crew or a make-up man, an electrician, could be the man North wanted to spot. It could have been the stewardess on the plane; it could have been one of the Thai pilots—who could it not have been when it came right down to it?

Boris Salenkov—why had Hugh's admittedly fallible hunch steered him away from suspicion of the most obvious suspect so persistently? Salenkov was a bulky man; surely he could have driven that knife into Wallen's chest. Could he have scrambled out the window of Marchet's room so nimbly? Yes, it was possible; North had encountered big men of Salenkov's outward stolidity and heavy-footedness who had been proven to own a panther's speed and a mink's agility in a tight spot.

Mary Hollberg? The emerald ring still reposed in the colonel's watch pocket, and whenever Hugh felt its pressure he experienced a twinge of guilt. Maybe he was suppressing evidence but he excused himself with the thought that Pokh's knowledge of the ring would not make his "dragnet" operate any better and the circlet could always be produced if future events warranted. Meanwhile, if it was a plant the real murderer, the Red agent who was behind all this, might bank too heavily on the ring having branded the German girl as the certain killer.

How about Wallen's death being something entirely apart from the Bracht case? True, the voice on the telephone had claimed that Wallen and Marchet were slain because they meddled, but that voice could easily have seized on two unrelated murders to throw more fear into Hans Bracht. True,

161

too, that Wallen had known something about Tao Muong, but coincidence had been known to play distracting tricks before this and it was not impossible that Wallen had been killed for an entirely different motive than to shut him up about Tao Muong. The murder could have been done by somebody totally ignorant of the actor's mysterious part in the Hans Bracht drama.

If this thesis was the right one the floodgates were opened to a whole tide of suspects. Wallen had had almost no friends but an abundance of enemies. Ross hated him, Anton Carss must have despised him as a former lover of Lita Naline (Hugh recalled Ross's saying that Lita and Wallen had been lovers before Naline had seized on Anton Carss), and Lita herself must have had reason to hate Wallen, by her hung-over conversation with Pokh. Wallen was said to have indulged in blackmail to push ahead in his profession, and that sort of thing was as dangerous as extortion for cash.

If, in fact, Wallen was murdered for reasons not linked with the disappearance of Tao Muong, the luring of Hans Bracht to Bangkok, Hugh North wanted to waste no time on the case. That was a police job, not his assignment, and years before Hugh had been trained in the difficult task of dropping a case, no matter how intriguing, if it was not directly linked with the mission at hand.

He was still sitting on the bed beside the telephone when Bracht came back into the room. The scientist's brows were lowered over the bespectacled eyes as he walked to the chair North had left and sat down heavily.

"What courage my wife has," he muttered, as though to himself. "Threatened with torture and yet she does not let her fear possess her as it does me."

So there it was, right there for Hugh North to see and curse himself for not having seen before. Tao Muong was not in Bangkok. It was very probable that she was not anywhere, alive.

162

6.

Now that Hugh North was sure—or as nearly positive as he was about anything not proven by concrete fact—there was a new problem to wrestle with. Should he tell Hans Bracht what he would have bet his life on being true, that the supposed kidnapers did not have Tao Muong to exchange for a ransom, even if they would?

How would the missile genius react; was there the slightest chance that he would believe such a startling conjecture? The answer: no, not possibly. To tell Bracht that he was almost sure that Tao Muong was not in Bangkok, never had been brought to Bangkok, probably lay in a hidden grave where she had been dumped soon after she was taken from the Cape Canaveral apartment, would serve only to throw the lanky scientist into a confusion that could make the situation even more dangerous than it was now.

First Bracht would scrap all thought of co-operation with his G-2 guard; that much was positive in North's mind. The blow of Hugh's announcement—and the colonel admitted that it would seem to Bracht only a wild guess—would make a loner out of the man North had been commissioned to bring home safely. Playing the single hand, where would Bracht wind up except in the grip of the devils who had plotted this whole thing?

He could hear himself making his explanation to Bracht: *You see, Doctor, that was your wife's voice you heard, all right, but she was not at the other end of the line. It was a tape recording.*

And Bracht's protest: *Impossible! How can you say such a thing?*

You explained it yourself, North would answer. *You said she didn't panic even under threat of torture. Just before she talked to you the voice asked you if you wanted to be sent her finger with her wedding ring on it. Moments later he or she spoke of pain, terrible torture. The voice said Tao Muong would scream in her agony. Seconds later, too soon for her to have been brought to the phone from someplace where she couldn't have overheard those threats, Tao Muong spoke to*

163

*you and her voice was calm, placid, showing no fear at all.
There's no woman alive who could do that; her voice would
tremble if nothing more.*

*She wasn't there, Doctor. She made those tapes that They
used as telephone conversations when she was completely at
ease, not afraid of the person who told her what to say.*

And there would be the stark fact confronting Dr. Hans
Bracht: Tao Muong had played the Reds' game right from
the start.

North groaned inwardly. How far would he get with that?
Nowhere. Bracht's love for his child bride would never
permit such a thought. He would hate anybody who dared
suggest it.

And if he told Bracht what he believed it would mean that
he would have to admit that he had listened in on the telephone conversation, that he had tapped Bracht's wire. That
would be the end of that tap as it would be the end of any
form of co-operation from the missile man. There was a
chance that in his fury Bracht would spill everything to the
Reds when they next called, naming North for what he was,
throwing the fat in the fire and applying a bellows to the
blaze.

Hugh decided he would keep his mouth shut. He had his
phone tap. Pokh's plain-clothes man was in the hall outside.
The Reds had to come to Bracht to make their final move. A
snatch from the fourth floor of the Imperial Hotel would not
be easy; the Commies would have to lure the missile man
outside to put the grip on him and he, Hugh North, intended to be ready to ruin that when the attempt was made.

Later, when he got the Brain of this Red plot and ran
him through the meat grinder, it was possible that he could
make the Commie himself tell Bracht all that the tall, gaunt
space-travel genius had to be told. He hoped he could do
this; he dreaded the task of telling Hans Bracht that the
woman he loved had let Them use her voice to lure him
into Communist captivity.

Now he yawned hugely, rubbed his close-cropped head.
"I don't suppose you're going to tell me anything They said
to you," he remarked idly.

The chief of Project Galaxy shook his head. "I can't," he said miserably. "Maybe I've talked to you too much as it is."

"Can you tell me when payoff time is due?" Hugh asked. "They must be getting anxious back at Cape Canaveral."

"No," Bracht said in a low voice. "It—it may be soon."

"Good. And inasmuch as They just called I guess there's no reason why we can't get some sleep. I'm tired."

He went to his closet and took down his pajamas, gathered up a robe and slippers, and headed for Room 439. Bracht looked up, began a protest, and then remembered he had consented to sleep in Room 437. He was still sitting in the chair, staring numbly at his feet stretched out in front of him, when North came back with the doctor's night things.

"I've got a sleeping pill if you think you need one," he offered.

Bracht rubbed a hand over his lined face. "I—I guess I'd better," he said hesitantly. "I'll never get to sleep without something and tomorrow—tomorrow I'll need all my wits about me."

"Get a good night's sleep and it'll help." North nodded. He went to his portmanteau and came up with a vial of specially compounded capsules, shook two out into his palm. "They're very mild," he explained. "You may need two."

Bracht accepted the sedative and the glass of water North brought him, swallowed both pills unhesitatingly. Which, Hugh told himself with satisfaction, guaranteed a harmlessly knocked-out Dr. Hans Bracht for at least eight hours.

Back in Room 439, the G-2 colonel heard the missile scientist fumbling about, getting out of his clothes and into pajamas, lowering himself to the bed with a series of gasping yawns. It seemed only about ten seconds later that the physicist's first snore growled through the silence.

Hugh smiled. Perhaps it was a dirty trick to drug such a trusting lamb as Bracht, but it *had* been for his own good and it *was* very possible that the scientist would need his wits about him on the morrow. The dose he had given Bracht had no aftereffects; its absence from the regular prescription files lay in the fact that an overdose of the tasteless and odorless compound with which the capsules were filled could kill a man without leaving one trace for a post-mortem to disclose. Made in a government laboratory, the formula a secret as closely guarded as a new rocket fuel's ingredients, there were only a very few of these capsules in existence and they were in possession of only a few picked G-2 and Counter-Intelligence operatives.

North lay down on top of the covers, his head cradled in his hands, and looked up at the blackness of the lampless room. He pondered the advisability of calling in G-2 help from Formosa, the Philippines, South Korea, to reinforce him in the coming showdown with the Reds. He decided against it. First, there was the time element; it was doubtful that agents could reach Bangkok before the showdown. Second, Hans Bracht was still the eccentric genius—there still was no telling how he would react if he learned that more agents were assigned to his case. Even after the climax of this deal there was always the danger that Hans Bracht would respond violently to disclosures that his government had kept only to the letter of its promise to him not to put security men on his trail. Regardless of the outcome, it was imperative that Bracht be returned to Cape Canaveral in a mood to continue work on Project Galaxy.

So although it admittedly was a risk and a big one, Hugh withheld his call for assistance. The egotistic idea that he didn't really need help in dealing with the Reds never entered the colonel's head; he thought of the future beyond the windup of this case and told himself he *had* to prove equal to the task ahead for the best handling of the whole problem.

He was close to drifting off to sleep when he came bolt upright in the bed, his head cocked toward the door.

Don't tell me he's making another try to get in, he said silently. *He's pushing his luck with me a little too far.*

For somebody was at the door of 439, somebody who was making a fumbling effort to unlock Hans Bracht's room.

Hugh slipped the .38 from its holster, swung his feet to the floor, and tiptoed noiselessly across the heavily carpeted floor. He reached for the knob, touched it, and started to turn it. The knob resisted; somebody was holding it on the other

166

side. At North's first pressure the grip of the person outside fell away—and Colonel North flung himself away from the door panel in one whirling spring.

He had nearly fallen for an old trick, bringing a person to the door by feigning an amateurish lock-picking job, then shooting through the panel when the one inside came to investigate.

Hardly had North cleared the doorway when there was the smash of a heavy gun in the hallway outside. Another. A third. Three clusters of splinters sprang out from the door, exactly where the G-2 agent's body would have been if he had held onto that knob one second longer.

7.

Something broke with a shattering smash across the room; one of the slugs intended for Hugh had shivered the window opposite the door.

North, his body kept under the protection of the wall beside the doorframe, blindly snapped one shot through the door, then raced through the communicating door to 437, past the drugged Hans Bracht on the bed, and burst into the hallway. He emerged in time to see a figure dodge around the corner of the corridor beyond the elevators and there was the slam of a door that boomed too loudly to belong to one of the rooms on the floor. Hugh, skidding around the corner, saw a red light glowing over the entrance to a service stairway. He hauled open the heavy first door and found himself in a concrete and steel stair well. Above him clattered the running footsteps of the man who had tried to murder Hans Bracht. Whoever it was, he was making time.

Hugh gave chase, two steps at a time, and was gaining on his man when another door slammed shut, a floor above him, the top floor of this seven-story hotel; the floor on which were the suites of Lex Ross, Anton Carss, Lita Naline; the floor where John Wallen had met his death.

All was silent when Hugh made the landing and came out into the corridor, panting from the exertion of the race up the steep service stairway. The colonel did not hesitate; he headed down the carpeted hallway back toward the elevators and turned up the stairs that led to the penthouse; Chu Hoong's penthouse.

For almost as surely as Hugh North knew his own name, the G-2 colonel was sure that the penthouse was the place to which Aloysius Robinson had fled. The gunman had been too familiar with the hotel's layout to have been Ross or Carss, guests of only a few hours, and those footsteps on the steel stairs had been a man's, never Lita's or Mary Hollberg's. As for Boris Salenkov, Hugh's "neglected suspect," the colonel could give him credit for possibly owning speed and agility but not enough to run up three flights of steps at that pace. Besides, Salenkov was registered as having a room on the second floor—his instinct would have been to take the easier way down than to go up.

That went for an outsider, too. With the Imperial's unusual design that offered a man half a dozen exits through a maze of hallways, no gunman in his right mind would head for the upper floors and the trap they threatened unless he thought he could find sanctuary there.

Aloysius Robinson had banked on the lateness of the hour, the silence inside both 437 and 439, to give him a chance to gun down Hans Bracht and get away before the man in 437 who had interrupted his previous attempt to assassinate the scientist could get into action. When his three shots had been answered by one from inside Room 439 he had panicked and had run for the nearest cover that had come to his jarred mind. He had raced to his benefactor, Chu Hoong, the man who had taken care of him in every foul-up he had made for himself.

North's thumb was heavy on the ivory buzzer button. Almost immediately the door was opened by a white-jacketed servant who began something in Chinese and was left spouting protests as Hugh North pushed past him, the .38 ready. The G-2 colonel found himself in a beautifully decorated foyer faced by three closed doors. He was reaching for the nearest knob when the door at the far end of the foyer opened to frame Chu Hoong.

168

The goateed patent-medicine king wore a gorgeously embroidered mandarin robe. On his feet were museum-piece slippers, and a gold-threaded skullcap topped his head. Standing there, his hands in the sleeves folded across his middle, he looked like something out of the Ming dynasty. His face was as placid as ever and the bow he gave Hugh North was calm, courteous, lacking all surprise.

"It is a great pleasure to welcome the honorable Mr. Charles Boyden," he intoned in Cantonese. "Even though he again greets me with a weapon in his hand he is a most honored guest in my humble abode."

"We can drop that right now," Hugh rapped out. "Where's Aloysius Robinson?"

"Aloysius? Why would he be here, Mr. Boyden? His room is on the fifth—"

"He didn't stop at the fifth floor," Hugh broke in. "He kept on running, headed for you. Do you want to call him out or do you want me to go in after him? And take your hands out of your sleeves, Chu. I don't think you'd do anything so crass as taking care of your own murders, but you never can tell, and a loose sleeve is a mighty handy place to stash a gun. Bring 'em out and bring 'em out empty."

Chu, smiling quizzically, brought out both hands and let them fall to his side.

"Now tell this butler of yours that if he interferes he's going to get hurt," the colonel ordered stonily. "I mean it."

Chu Hoong shrugged and directed a stream of Cantonese at the chattering servant who still stood beside the open door. Then the multimillionaire stood aside and gestured toward the room he had emerged from. "At least we can be comfortable while we discuss this, Mr. Boyden."

Hugh moved close to the Chinese, dug the muzzle of his pistol into the small of Chu's back. "Unless your Aloysius is a better shot than I think he is," he told the patent-medicine mogul, "he's going to hit you if he tries for me. And leave that front door open; I don't want him making a break from one of those other rooms."

Chu Hoong slippered his way across the room to a chair,

169

looked up over his shoulder at the G-2 agent. "Is it permitted to sit down?" he asked.

"Not till we've made a tour of this place," North growled.

Chu Hoong hunched his shoulders. "My dear Mr. Boyden, or whatever your name is, I haven't the slightest conception of what's going on but I will tell you this. Aloysius came dashing in a few minutes ago, panting something about having been in a fight, and ran right through to the rear entrance to this apartment. He did not tarry to explain what had happened."

"Just the same we'll go through this place," Hugh said grimly.

Chu shrugged again and led the way through the lavish rooms of his penthouse, North beside him, the gun never more than two inches from the Chinese millionaire's right kidney. Bedrooms, dining room, kitchen, and baths revealed nothing except three more servants, all wearing native footgear that made it impossible for them to have been the one Hugh had chased up the stairs.

Returning to the living room at North's direction, Chu Hoong took a chair without asking North's permission. He folded his hands in his sleeves again and looked up at the colonel, his round face imperturbable.

"If it is not too much to ask, will you kindly tell me what Aloysius has done now?" he inquired.

"I want to use your telephone," North said, and strode to the instrument across the room. He had the operator put him through to Bangkok Imperial Troop headquarters and Captain Pokh.

"Pick up Aloysius Robinson," he barked. "This time I'll guarantee you he won't be bailed out in a hurry. And check on the plain-clothes man you posted outside our rooms—he may be dead. Get a new man there on the double."

A spluttering stream of Thai came from the other end of the line. Hugh cut it short. "I'm in Chu Hoong's penthouse. When you get things moving come up and join the party."

The colonel slammed up the telephone to choke off the little captain's hysterical questions and turned back to Chu

Hoong. "This time," he announced, "your boy's fixed himself up right."

The Chinese permitted himself the shadow of a grimace. "What has he done now?" he sighed.

"What if I told you it was murder?" North rapped out.

If Chu started at the crackled question it was an imperceptible reaction. For a second the multimillionaire stared at the G-2 colonel and then the almond eyes fell away. "Ah well," Chu said softly, "I suppose I more or less expected something like this would happen someday. The way Aloysius was going it was only a question of time before he would become involved in some terrible thing."

He shook his head slowly. "And who was it?" he asked. "And why are you involved, Mr. Boyden? Ah, was it—was it the gentleman next door to you, whose name escapes me?"

"Barrows," Hugh supplied. "You knew him by another name."

The smaller man's eyes widened infinitesimally and Chu's placidity was ruffled just the slightest, a tiny cloud crossing the sun, a short-lived breeze rippling a pond. "I knew him?" Chu repeated. "Oh yes, I remember; you had the idea that I had known Mr. Barrows other than as a guest of the Imperial. But I assure you, Mr. Boyden—"

"And I assure *you*, Mr. Chu," North broke in coldly, "that my man knew you under some other name, somewhere, sometime."

He paused a moment and added bluntly: "And you wanted him dead."

Chu Hoong sat perfectly still, a tranquil Buddha. There was a silence that seemed to stretch for hours before the multimillionaire spoke. "To protest against such a statement would be to give it the serious intent which I know you did not mean it to have," he said.

"Oh, but I do mean it," North returned. "When Captain Pokh arrives I expect to lodge a charge of conspiracy to commit murder against you, Mr. Chu."

The Chinese scanned the G-2 agent carefully. His rosebud lips barely parted as he said, "I believe you *are* serious."

North nodded. "And the ironic part of it is that you didn't

171

have to go after Barrows with a gun, Chu. He wasn't out here to interfere with your business in any way, take my word for it."

Now the slanted eyes were wary. "Business, Mr. Boyden? How could this so-called Mr. Barrows interfere with my business? I have received information that—er—the gentleman is a nuclear physicist and although my interests are diversified enough I am not in the rocket or missile business."

Hugh held the .38 trained squarely on the rotund little man in the luxurious mandarin robe.

"But you are in the dope business, Chu," he said quietly. "Up to your fat, scaly neck in it."

8.

Chu's face was frozen as the colonel went on. "Don't stop me if I'm wrong," Hugh said, "because I know I'm not and I hate to be interrupted when I'm fitting the pieces to a puzzle.

"First, my man hates narcotics and everything and everybody connected with them. His father, as if you didn't know, was an addict, and when he was on the stuff he made life miserable for my man and his mother. This Mr. Barrows as I'll call him is a fanatic on the subject. Even though Georges Marchet led him through a jungle to safety, Barrows was never truly grateful because Marchet was an addict. Barrows' hatred for drug peddlers is still violent— imagine what it must have been when he was a young man, the memory of his father's cruelties still fresh in his mind, the days before he grew a beard."

Chu's lips moved. "Gibberish," he said.

"No," Hugh explained. "I mention the beard because you recognized Barrows on the plane even though he wore no beard and up to a few days ago he had worn a beard all his adult life, barring one spell when he was with Marchet. Barrows said he didn't know you out here in the Orient, so he must have known you in Alsace when he was quite young."

172

Chu Hoong stirred in his chair and North's revolver brought its muzzle down to those sleeved hands. The Chinese sighed patiently and disengaged his handclasp, brought his pudgy fingers out into view.

"You feared Barrows when you saw him on the plane," the colonel said. "I've asked myself why a thousand times since. You're a multimillionaire, you have a business empire out here, you said yourself you did not fear any mortal man. But I knew you feared Barrows, and why could you possibly be afraid of anybody?"

"Why, indeed?" Chu Hoong murmured acidly. "What lie did your lurid imagination give you?"

"The only man you could possibly fear would be someone who could threaten your business empire and, more than that, threaten your name," North said in a measured voice. "Your millions are precious, Chu, but not half so precious as your face."

Chu Hoong nodded involuntarily as Hugh went on. "With another man than Barrows I'd suspect that he knew of some dishonest thing you might have done years ago, a cheated partner, a swindled friend. But Barrows is hipped on the subject of dope. I'd say that aside from his work and his wife there's nothing that he's so intense about. So, I asked myself, why not dope as the connecting link between you and Barrows, the link that made you fear him?"

The Chinese multimillionaire made an effort to smile, but it was a failure. His voice held the suggestion of a hoarse note when he said: "This is better than a novel, Mr. Boyden."

North grimaced. "I hope you think so when I'm through because I'm going to make you the villain of this particular story. You see, when I finally got the narcotics angle I thought of Dragon's Tooth Elixir."

"Now there," Chu interjected smoothly, "is where you become utterly ridiculous. If you're accusing me of peddling dope in my Elixir you'll find that the authorities in Hong Kong, where the medicine is manufactured, have given me a clean bill of health. Dragon's Tooth Elixir may give its user

173

a powerful stimulant, but its ingredients have all been proven to be quite within the law."

"They are *now*," North agreed, "but were they when you began making Dragon's Tooth Elixir, Mister Chu? Didn't the original ingredients include some pretty potent drugs until Hong Kong authorities made you clean it up? And by that time weren't you already hip-deep in the dope racket? Or, I should say, *back* in the dope racket?

"The way I see it, you took a fall when you were a young man and Barrows was responsible for that fall. Probably you were in Alsace then and you were Bracht's father's supplier. The boy turned you in and you served time—oh, under another name, of course. Then you came back to the Orient, you started Dragon's Tooth Elixir, still pushing dope in a cure-all medicine, and when the authorities made you clean up the Elixir you already had set up your own dope ring with the Elixir as a front. By that time dope was the foundation stone of your empire; it still must be the biggest money-maker of all your interests or you'd have pulled out of it after you got respectable—unless, of course, you couldn't pull out. That racket doesn't let many people off the hook, users or pushers.

"Then you saw Barrows, as we call him, and you thought he'd come out here to ruin you, show you up as the scum he'd known under another name on the other side of the world. Chu Hoong, the most respected financier; Chu Hoong, the rat who pushed dope. You couldn't bear the thought of having the world know who you once were, not to speak of having the big dope money shot from under you.

"So you decided to have him killed. First, by phone from Don Muang, you dispatched that clumsy Manchu and Robinson to do the job in an auto crash or with the knife. When Barrows escaped, Aloysius followed him and tried for him on the street—Lita Naline ruined that. I interfered when Robinson tried to get his switchblade knife into Barrows' room the first time. You burned up about that when I told you what your man had done. Probably he was acting on his own that time, drunked up as he was. But tonight, I'm sure, he went to Room 439 on your orders."

174

Chu Hoong leaned back in his chair, his fingers tented under his goatee, his placid smile in place.

"Suppose there was the faintest possibility that some of what you have just told me is true," he said softly. "How could any of it be proved if you were brash enough to go to the authorities? Didn't you just tell me that Mr. Barrows—oh, let us call him by his right name, Hans Bracht—has been most unfortunately murdered by the misguided Aloysius Robinson?"

North started to speak, held his tongue just in time.

"Because, you see," Chu was saying, "all this you've told me is pure conjecture. And I told you once, Mr. Boyden, that conjecture is a dangerous thing. You could go to any police official in the world, even one who is not my good friend as is General Genung, and you would be asked for proof. And you, alas, have nothing but your own deductions to offer."

His smile widened. "So, you see, I have no reason to fear you now any more than I have to fear the dead man, Hans Bracht. He can't talk and nobody will listen to you."

"There's Aloysius Robinson," Hugh suggested. "He'd be easy to sweat out."

Chu made a motion with one hand, as though he were brushing away a gnat. "I have gone to considerable pains to establish poor Aloysius as a totally unreliable person," he said. "I doubt that anyone would take seriously anything he might say against me. You see, he is on record as having perjured himself a thousand times. Besides that, although you possibly don't know it, he is one of that unusual breed who can mix narcotics and alcohol. The combination seems to make its devotees especially despicable, unworthy of the slightest belief on any witness stand, I assure you."

The Chinese carefully smoothed the front of the embroidered mandarin robe. "No, my dear Boyden." He chuckled. "I'm afraid you'll have to be satisfied with my sacrificial goat, Aloysius. Do with him what you will; he has served his purpose well and now I am through with him. I trained him in his role, suspecting that someday I might need a brainless ruffian who would do everything I told him. Perhaps in my inner mind I thought that Bracht might reappear in my life someday to make a bad dream come all too true. He ruined what was a promising start in Europe in just the manner you guessed, by the way."

"I tell you Dr. Bracht's trip to Bangkok didn't have anything to do with you," North said. "You plotted a needless murder, Chu."

The Chinese shrugged philosophically. "Then I made a mistake." He smiled. "But what would you think? I saw Marchet, who I knew to be an addict, approach this man on the plane and be rebuked by you, who mentioned something about an International Department that obviously was concerned with drugs. You seemed to be traveling with Bracht— oh, of course I did not know it was Bracht until I made it a point to talk with you, try to find out who you were and what you were up to. It was then Bracht showed his face, older but unmistakably the man who had ruined me in Alsace when I had another name.

"This is Bangkok, my honored friend, and here meets the Southeast Asia Treaty Organization, which has begun to take an unhealthy interest in my drug empire. How could I help but link Bracht's presence here with a threat to that empire? It was to me a simple matter of putting two and two together and I decided that Bracht must be removed. The automobile smashup was bungled; Aloysius failed in his attempt to follow Bracht and knife him in the crowd; the stupid fool did disobey my orders and try to break into Bracht's room without my knowing it—some silly attempt to get back in my good graces after that first failure, I suppose."

"And then you tried your own hand at disposing of my man?"

"Ah yes. It was against my principles but I did. I could have carried it out, too, if you hadn't interfered. I had a passkey, of course, and in another minute I would have been in Room 439, but the call came to my lookout in another room that you were on your way up, having eluded certain delaying preparations. You didn't—what is the term?—frisk me that day, Boyden. You must be careful of that in the future. But not with me. I assure you that with Bracht gone

I am no longer your enemy. In fact, if you want to spare me the nuisance of laughing your charges out of existence I'll agree to help you send Aloysius to the hangman—and give you ten thousand dollars as a token of my appreciation."

"You'd abandon your hatchet man that callously?" North asked.

That bothersome insect gesture again. "Of course," said Chu Hoong. "Don't waste your sympathy on Aloysius Robinson. He is nothing but an animal. I will just be disposing of him before he gets the idea in his twisted brain that he could profit by killing me." Chu Hoong sighed. "Yes, it will be a relief to help send Aloysius to his timely and justified end on the scaffold. It will be a relief not to have to see those horrible clothes again, if nothing else. You can't imagine what a—"

The Chinese multimillionaire stopped, his eyes fixed on a spot behind Hugh North. The G-2 agent did not turn (it was a trick so old it was almost new) but he cocked an eye as far in the direction of Chu's stare as possible. He saw the dim outline of a figure and tensed to throw himself to one side.

"Aloysius," he heard Chu gurgle. "You came back. How dare you when I told you—"

Hugh North crouched and leaped to the cover of a heavy, carved teakwood chair at his left. He could have saved himself the effort; Aloysius Robinson was not aiming at him.

There was the heavy slam of the Macanese's gun, the meaty smack of the slug that plowed into Chu Hoong's forehead, an inch above a wide, staring almond eye. The embroidered cap snapped up into the air and fell behind Chu Hoong's chair. The discoverer of Dragon's Tooth Elixir slumped forward, curled, and slid gently to the floor.

CHAPTER 6

1.

"Hold it, Robinson!" North barked. "I'm right on you, man! Drop that gun."

The greasy-haired Macanese turned his head slowly until the dark eyes with their hot glare focused on the G-2 colonel.

"You heard him, didn't you?" Robinson panted. "You heard the sonofabitch tellin' what he was gonna do to me, didn't you? I had an idea he was puttin' in the cross. I coulda bugged outa here and been halfway to Bombay by now, but somethin' told me the sonofabitch would—"

"Drop that gun!"

Aloysius looked stupidly at the ponderous .45 he held in his hand. "Nobody's gonna frame me," he muttered. "Not even Chu Hoong. Big daddy—huh!" With which Aloysius Robinson abruptly dropped the gun and wobbled toward a chair, sat down heavily. His head dropped to his hands, his fingers combing the glistening black hair.

"Now who's gonna fix me when I need a pop?" he mourned. "Where am I gonna get the dough to keep my habit cool? Why did he have to leave me like this?"

Hugh was moving to retrieve the gun when the front door of the penthouse crashed open and Captain Pokh trotted in, followed by half a dozen Imperial Troopers, all with unholstered pistols. The little captain looked at Robinson, stared at Chu Hoong's body, and then gazed up at the colonel.

"Robinson shoot Chu Hoong?" he demanded. "Or was you, mebbe-so?"

178

"Was Robinson," Hugh said wearily. "What about my man downstairs? Is there somebody on him?"

"Oh yes." Pokh nodded, his eyes still busy roaming the strange scene. "Man on duty there fast asleep. Very strange. Teacup beside him indicate he get the—" He hesitated, sought the right words, came up with "Mikey Flynn."

"Chu probably had it sent to him, compliments of the house," North said.

"Chu Hoong? But why he—what is this, pliss? Everybody say they hear lots of shooting, on your floor, up here. Arrive to find honorable Dragon's Tooth Elixir inventor dead, Aloysius weeping. What is about, pliss?"

Hugh jerked his head toward the slumped Macanese. "I have an idea he'll tell you all about it once he's been kept from his fix awhile," he said. "In a few words, Chu sent Robinson to kill the man I'm with. I chased Robinson up here, but he left by another door. I was putting the heat on Chu when Robinson came back and shot him. I'll fill you in later. Right now I've got to get back to my man— he's been too long alone with a knocked-out plainclothes man guarding him."

"But pliss—" Pokh bleated, but North was already on his way.

"Get Robinson talking," the colonel advised over his shoulder. "Anything he doesn't tell you, I'll fill you in on. Check with me when you wring out this junkie."

Back on the fourth floor, Hugh found a new plain-clothes man on duty behind the potted palm. The mickeyed man had been removed.

The colonel frowned when he found the door to Room 437 still unlocked, but Hugh unburdened himself of his anxiety when the snores from the bed told him that Hans Bracht had slept through the whole thing. If it was Hans Bracht. The colonel went to the bed and carefully examined the sleeping man's features until he was satisfied that it actually was the missile master lying there. Lex Ross had boasted that nobody could penetrate his disguise, even in a close-up inspection, but Lex Ross had never had a G-2 agent inspect his handiwork. There were such things as neck

179

creases, a mouth emptied of two sets of dentures, that could never be faked.

North consulted his wrist watch. Two fifty-three and with the bang-bang uproar that had taken place in this vicinity so recently They certainly must have postponed a move on Bracht even if They had planned one at this hour.

Unless They were thinking a jump ahead of him; that was the danger. This Intelligence and Counter-Intelligence "game" was a never-ending struggle to anticipate the other side's thought processes and take advantage of their probable move. To be on the safe side, then, Hugh North would do well to sleep lightly, if at all, until the Reds made their play.

He locked the door of 437 and went through the connecting door into 439. Three thin pencils of light filtered through the holes Robinson's slugs had made in the hall door and one of these beams focused on the bed. North looked. North did a perfect double-take.

"And just what in the hell do you think you're doing there, Fräulein Hollberg?" he asked.

Mary Hollberg, self-styled concert pianist, presently a fugitive from Pilanung Pokh's "dragnet," owner of the emerald ring found under the foot of John Wallen's murdered corpse, lay with the sheet drawn up to her chin, smiling uncertainly through the gloom at Hugh North. On a chair beside the bed lay a neatly folded pile of clothes. It required Hugh only one glance to know that Mary wore very little under that sheet, if anything.

"*Guten Morgen*, Herr Boyden," the German girl whispered.

"And *guten Morgen* to *you*," North replied. "And I repeat, what do you think you're doing there?"

"Waiting for you," Mary explained, still with that faltering smile. "I have been trying to get to you ever since—ever since—" Her voice failed her.

"Ever since you killed Jack Wallen?" the G-2 agent asked brutally.

The head on the pillow went from side to side with desperate intensity. "I did not kill him, Herr Boyden. I swear

180

it. I struck him, yes. He was drunk and he threatened to tell about me if I—if I did not make love with him."

"And lost your ring when you hit him, I suppose?"

"No. No, I gave him my ring. First he said he would keep quiet if I gave him my ring, but when I did he demanded more." A bare arm came out from under the sheet and Mary Hollberg patted the bed beside her. "Sit down here, *mein Herr,* and I will tell you everything. Please."

Hugh walked to the side of the bed and sat down. The sheet was a thin one and if Hollberg had a gun or a knife with her it must be under her; her body was too frankly outlined for her to have it handy. Mary's fingers clutched one of his hands with trembling urgency, the giveaway nails biting into his flesh.

"You must believe me, Herr Boyden," she said. "I know you are of the American police and perhaps what I tell you will mean I must go to prison, but not for murder. Do you think I could kill anyone? Tell me, do you think it possible that I could murder a man, no matter how much he might deserve it?"

In her agitation the girl propped her free elbow under her and started up to a sitting position. The sheet slid down below the girl's full breasts and Hugh North marveled at the beauty exposed in the weak light filtering through the bullet holes before he gently pressed Mary Hollberg back, drew the sheet up again.

"Let's hear your story first," he suggested quietly. "You might start out by telling me who you really are. Not the pianist business, please. You know I saw through that right away, don't you?"

"Yes." The blonde nodded. "It was stupid of me—I should have called myself an ordinary tourist."

"And what exactly are you?"

The girl's eyes dropped. "I—I take precious stones through customs without—without paying the duty," she faltered. "You call me a jewel smuggler. I was on my way to Karachi where I was to join my sweetheart and I came to Bangkok because—because—" Her newfound honesty deserted her for a moment.

"Because you had a drop or a pickup to make here, *nicht wahr?*"

Mary nodded. "A pickup. Some very fine stones taken from the Wat Phra Keo, the Chapel of the Emerald Buddha, and imitations substituted, during the replacement of all jewels in the place that the Siamese make three times a year."

"So you're also in the jewel-stealing racket?"

"No, we merely transport the gems; we do not ask where they come from. In this case I was told more than usual because I objected to stopping off in Bangkok. I was anxious to rejoin my sweetheart, you see."

"Go on."

"When I boarded the plane in Hong Kong," Mary Hollberg continued, "I was given word by one of the people in our organization that I must look out for you. You were seen with the Hong Kong police, examining the plane's baggage."

So there was a smuggling-ring tipster present when we looked for a bomb, eh?

"Then bad luck put you in the next seat to mine. I—I tried to interest you in me so you might talk. Did I succeed in creating an interest, Herr Boyden?"

There was the suggestion of a quirked mouth, a coquetry that survived even the girl's fear. The hand that held Hugh's softened its grip, became an intimate clasp.

"Spectacularly." North grinned. "But go ahead with your story."

"Then you were involved in that incident with the Frenchman and later I heard Herr Barrows speak the word 'policeman.' I knew then that you were after me, or so I thought. You'll remember I went to the—the *Badezimmer* soon after that; I had two stones that were not very well hidden and I changed them to another place.

"Then that evening I heard of you being in an accident and it appeared you were not what I had thought you but some kind of *Vormund*, guard, over Herr Barrows. So I arranged the breakfast with you the next morning and you spoke as though you knew what I was. I lost my temper and —well, you know about that."

182

"Get to the cocktail party," Hugh said.

"Ah yes, the cocktail party. I got there before anyone else because Wallen told me the hour was three o'clock, not four. And when I arrived he told me that he recognized me. *Ach,* my bad luck! Once I was arrested in San Francisco and forced to stand in what you Americans call a line-up. At that very time John Wallen was making a motion picture in which he was a police officer of some kind ánd he attended that line-up to get—ah—what do you say?—the atmosphere of his role."

"And he recognized you?"

"*Ja.* He—I should not speak so of a dead man, Herr Boyden, but he was a beast. He said he would inform the authorities unless I—I gave him my favors. I pleaded with him —rather would I be dead than give myself to a man I hated so. Finally he said he would keep quiet if I gave him money, much money."

"So Wallen did go in for cash blackmail after all, eh?" Hugh murmured.

"I told him I had no such money as he demanded," the German girl went on. "Then other guests arrived and he told me to see him later and he would make a proposition. I kept close to him from then on except when he went in to lie down, he was so *betrunken,* and after the rest had gone I offered him my ring as payment. He took it and when he had it he laughed at me. He pulled me into the bedroom and— and made advances.

"I struck him in the mouth and ran out and went to my room. Then I knew he would not keep silent anyway, so I got up my courage and went back to get my ring. I told myself I would accuse him of stealing it if he did not give it to me. But when I got there I found—I found . . ."

Her voice trickled off into silence as she relived the grisly scene of her discovery, the dead man on the bed, the knife jutting from his chest.

"Then I fled again," she went on with an effort. "I did not know what to do. I had been seen to stay behind when the others left and—"

183

"Who were the last to leave Wallen's place?" North broke in.

The girl thought, shook her head. "I do not remember," she admitted. "Lita Naline, I think, and—"

"But Lita passed out," North said. "I was there when Carss carried her off."

"Oh, but they both came back," the German girl said. "She had on a dressing gown and she was drunk but she said she had mislaid a bracelet and she must look for it. They searched awhile, but Lita was too drunk to see anything and Herr Carss was only humoring her. They did not stay long but, yes, they must have been the last ones to leave."

So there goes Lita's passed-out alibi. "Go on."

"So I ran out of the hotel. I was half crazy with fear. Then I knew I had no hiding place in Bangkok; I would be noticed anywhere I went, a European blonde. I doubled back to the Imperial and now I wanted to find you instead of avoid you. I thought you would—protect me, Herr Boyden."

Hugh felt the pressure of the emerald ring in his watch pocket and smiled.

"You laugh?" Mary asked, hurt. "But I had the idea that I—that I was not unattractive to you, no matter what you said at breakfast." She waited a moment for some word from North, then went on when none was forthcoming. *"Jedenfalls,* I came here to the fourth floor by the back stairs and I saw a man watching your room—I had found out where you were staying, you understand. I hid myself in a little closet where they keep linens and wash buckets and so on. There I stayed, expecting someone to come at any time, until—until I was awakened by shots and the sounds of men running past the door. I looked out and the man watching was either asleep or dead. The door to your room was open. I ran into Room 437 and found Herr Barrows asleep in your bed and the connecting door to this room open. So I came in here to wait for you."

She stopped and there was a silence. Hugh North reached into his pocket and pulled out a pack of cigarettes, stuck one between Mary Hollberg's lips, and took another for himself. After his lighter had set both going he asked: "Did Wallen

184

make a phone call while you were with him, after the others had gone?"

"He made two calls. One was to you, but I do not know who the first was to. He talked in a very low voice in the bedroom when he called the first time, but louder when he spoke to you."

"You heard nothing of that first call?"

"Only once when he got angry and shouted something about if somebody would not—ah—play ball with him he was going to—what did he say?—lower the boom about the Chinese girl. Right after that he hung up the telephone and I could hear him muttering curses. Then he called you."

"Did he mention this Chinese girl's name?"

"No, he said only what I have told you."

So Wallen had thought that Tao Muong was Chinese because of her oriental features. If Tao Muong was not in Bangkok, that must mean that Wallen had seen Tao Muong in the States. *And who had he called?*

He scowled over the question, sitting on the edge of the bed, holding the warm hand of a fugitive jewel smuggler sought for murder, and the room was silent for a spell.

"The ashes," Mary Hollberg said apologetically.

North rose to get an ash tray, brought it back to the bed. As the girl raised herself to tap the ashes from her cigarette the sheet slipped down again, nor did Mary make any effort to replace it. Instead, she looked up at Hugh and smiled.

"I am not an ungrateful person," she said directly. "If you would—intercede for me with the police I would do anything you asked of me."

The G-2 colonel's mouth went up at one corner. "But how do you know I'm not like Wallen?" he asked. "Suppose I took you at your word and then turned you in anyway?"

"You would not," Mary said firmly. "I know you are a man of honor, Herr Boyden, otherwise—I am not one to make such an offer unless I am sure the man is—is *gut und liebend.*"

North dragged on his cigarette. "And how about the boy friend in Karachi?" he asked.

"He—we are of the modern age, Herr Boyden, Karl. We

are much separated and there are times when he dispels his loneliness and fear—for in our work there is always fear—with another woman just as I ease myself in the arms of another man. We have an understanding, we two."

In a sudden gesture she reached up and grasped the edge of the sheet, threw it back from her. "Do you not find me pleasant to look upon, Karl?" she asked, low and breathlessly. "Is that why you hesitate to claim what I have offered, because you think I have so little to give?"

Colonel Hugh North, U. S. Army, G-2, looked down on a perfect white body, presented unashamedly, and felt his pulses hammer. He was no anchorite, nor was he an aesthete whose senses demanded no more than enjoyment of the beautiful picture Mary Hollberg made lying there. North was tired, but in that nerve-edged way in which the animal appetites surged past the weary, slackening self-discipline the colonel always enforced; if there was ever a time when Hugh could shrug off all the responsibilities he bore to relax, revel, in the urgencies so recklessly aroused, it was now.

He took a step nearer the bed. *What the hell—why not?*

And Captain Pilanung Pokh of the Bangkok Imperial Troop rapped sharply on the door of room 437.

2.

Hugh's first impulse was to swear; his second was to thank his lucky stars. This was not the time to become so intimately involved with a girl, no matter how beautiful and eager, who still was not cleared by proof from the case of Hans Bracht and Tao Muong.

"Who is that?" Mary Hollberg gasped.

"Keep quiet," North said in a hushed voice. "Stay here—get some sleep if you can."

He moved into the next room, snapped on a light, and answered the door. Captain Pokh, bone-weary, fairly staggering from lack of sleep, entered and promptly collapsed in the nearest chair. The Thai officer cast one glance at the snoring Bracht and looked back at Hugh inquiringly.

186

"I thought it would be best to keep him in here," the G-2 agent said briefly.

"I see." Pokh nodded. He peered more closely at North. "Why you all hot in the face?" he demanded. "You been running some more, chasing somebody?"

"Perhaps I just had a narrow escape," Hugh muttered, half under his breath, and spoke loudly to cut off Pokh's next question. "Did Robinson crack?"

"He break in little pieces," the captain replied. "If we keep dope out of his reach long enough he will tell us everything we want to know." His face fell into gloomy lines and he shook his head. "Imagine man who makes Dragon's Tooth Elixir being hashish villain," he sighed. "Now he's dead, no more Dragon's Tooth Elixir."

"Cheer up, Chu said he had sons," North offered. "They'll probably take over the business without losing a single bottle of your business."

"You think so?" Pokh brightened. "Is case any better now Chu is revealed as bad man?"

North said, "Chu didn't kill Wallen, remember."

"Ah yes." Pokh shook his head again. "Mary Hollberg most elusive person. I catch hell from General Genung if she not found quick. And when General Genung give you hell you know you been given hell, all right."

"What would you say if I told you I'm pretty sure Mary Hollberg didn't murder Wallen?" Hugh asked quietly.

Pokh looked at the G-2 agent in aggrieved disappointment. "Don't you have pity on poor, overworked Thai cop?" he asked. "We have number-one suspect who flees and hides right after murder. Catch her and I go to General Genung and say case closed, girl murder him because she love him, he don't love her. Okay, everybody happy. I go home and sleep for a week."

"I'm afraid it's not going to be that easy," North said sympathetically. "First, if Mary killed Wallen and ran, why come back to kill Marchet? No, the murderer had to kill the Frenchman to keep Georges from exposing him—he or she is still sitting pretty, knowing the only witness is dead. Maybe if it weren't for Marchet's death I'd go along with you about

187

Mary; she might have killed Wallen to protect her honor, say. But I can't fit her in the picture as a cold-blooded killer who would run the risk of getting rid of Marchet, can you?"

Pokh studied the carpet at his feet and slowly, grudgingly, shook his head.

"No, goddamn," he admitted. He dragged himself to his feet, replaced the toupee he had pulled from his shaven head when he had entered. "So no rest for this humble servant of the King. What I do now?"

"As soon as it's light," North suggested, "I'd have your men go through the rooms of everybody who was on that plane from Hong Kong. Look for a tape recorder. It's a long chance but we may hit pay dirt. Tell them to say they're looking for a gun in the Chu Hoong case but to keep their eyes open for a tape recorder—they're easy to spot. Don't take it, if they find one; just let me know who owns it."

"Is simpler than that," Pokh said. "Customs rules say all such things of foreign manufacturer, radio, talking machine, tape recorder, must be registered, pay four-baht tax."

His momentary upsurge of spirits deserted him abruptly. "Is another thing, though," he added. "Movie company brought in great amount of all kinds of such things under one tax. Separate pieces not set down in books."

"I don't think the one I'm after was in that big shipment," North said consolingly. "I think this was part of one man or woman's personal luggage."

"Well—the Russian, Salenkov, had his baggage passed through customs without opening," Pokh went on. "Is courtesy to representative of foreign government even if Salenkov only textile industry snooper. But I call customs now, find out."

He put in a phone call and gave North the information he got from Don Muang customs. Arrivals on the Hong Kong plane declaring tape recorders were John Wallen—and Lex Ross.

Pokh said, "So we know those two had machines, anyway. But mebbe-so half a dozen more sneaked in past lazy, blind customs people. I have my men hunt for gun."

He went to the door, paused with his hand on the knob,

and cast his faintly slanted eyes in Bracht's direction. "He all right, he sleeps so sound?" he asked.

"He was tired," North explained. "He took a pill to make him sleep."

"Is very good pill," Pokh said decisively. "Lets man sleep through shootings and everything. Maybe I take one dozen such pills instead of going to General Genung and telling him my dragnet don't find Mary Hollberg."

Hugh North finally took pity on the diminutive captain. "Don't worry about Mary," he advised Pokh. "Call off your dragnet—she's given herself up."

Pokh's face was dazed with wonderment. "What are you saying to me?"

"I should have told you sooner, but Miss Hollberg turned herself in to me," the colonel said. "From what she told me I'm fairly convinced she didn't kill Wallen. I'll be responsible for her. Tell General Genung that I suggest she be placed under guard in her room but not arrested; not for the time being. Let's keep quiet about her—I want the killer to think she's still being hunted."

"Mary Hollberg is in this hotel?" Pokh asked slowly. His eyes flitted to the connecting door and back to Hugh. The G-2 colonel nodded.

"Yes, she's in there," North said. "She's been hiding in a broom closet all this time and during the commotion after Robinson's visit she slipped in here. She says she hit Wallen when he tried to force her but she didn't kill him. I believe her."

"In hotel all this time," the little captain mourned. "Wait until General Genung hear about that."

"There's no reason he has to," North said. "Just tell your headquarters she's been found and then give your general my suggestion about keeping her under guard in her room. Do you have policewomen here in Thailand, Captain?"

"Oh yes, have most excellent lady policeman. My number-three wife, Colonel. You hear joke about great American comic-paper detective, Dick Tracy and the lady policeman?"

"Yes," North said hastily.

189

"Is much funnier in Thai language," Pokh offered tentatively.

"But I don't understand Thai. Get a detail of policewomen to stay with Mary, for her own protection as much as to keep her from trying another escape. Can you do that now?"

"Use phone again, pliss?"

While Pòkh was calling his headquarters, Hugh North went back into 439. The advisability of knocking never entered his mind and so he walked in on Miss Hollberg while she was sitting on the side of the bed attaching a stocking to a garter at the top of a long and shapely leg. The only light in the room still was supplied by the bullet holes, but there was enough to see that Mary, in girdle and stocking, was as appealing if not more so than when she had been clad in nothing at all.

"I—uh—" the colonel stammered.

"Oh, *herein*," Mary said, busy. with the garter catch. "I have been listening and I thank you for believing me." She began slipping the other stocking up her leg while North tried to avert his eyes. "Someday, Herr Boyden, I will know who you are and why you are here in Bangkok, but now I ask no more questions. I only tell you I will never forget you. Never. And if that knock had not come at the door I would have real memories of you that would be most precious. I will think of you often, Herr Boyden—if that is your real name."

She finished with the stocking, stood up from the bed, and reached for her brassière. "Now I go with the Siamese officer and face what I must face, *nicht wahr?*" she asked. She snapped the gauzy band about her breasts and then took three steps toward Hugh until she was close to him, her scent heady.

"Before we say good-by I ask one thing," she whispered. "A kiss to take with me where I am going."

She reached up and pulled Hugh's face down to hers. It was not the kiss that would have been exchanged if Pokh had not knocked; this was a gentle, sorrowful caress which Colonel North would always remember as bearing only a faint, suppressed hint of what might have been.

190

Mary Hollberg broke the brief embrace and turned toward the dress on the chair. "Now I will soon be ready," she said briskly. "Tell the Kapitan Pokh I will be out in one little moment."

North started to leave, paused, and turned back. "Look here," he said, "you're not thinking of doing anything—"

"Crazy, you mean, like swallowing poison?" Mary broke in. "No, *mein Herr,* never fear. I love life too much for that, and what can they do to me in Thailand? They have no proof that I have smuggled jewels, and about Wallen they have your word that I did not do it."

She smiled up at him. "No, I want a moment in the *Badezimmer* to make myself pretty for my arrest, that's all."

And when she emerged from Room 439 into 437 a few minutes later North saw that she had indeed made herself beautiful for her appointment with Pokh. As the Thai captain led her out of the room on his way to her own room, Mary Hollberg managed a smile and a wave of one slim hand, capped by the long, long nails that first had told the colonel that she was not what she claimed to be.

At almost the instant the door closed behind Captain Pokh and Mary Hollberg the phone on the night table beside the snoring Dr. Bracht shrilled. Hugh jumped for the instrument before it could sound a second time. A reply to his cable to Washington?

Instead, it was Anton Carss.

"Mr. Boyden? Forgive me for calling you at this hour but I believe it is important. Tell me, are you acting in some capacity such as companion or possibly bodyguard to Mr. Henry Barrows?"

"Huh?" North asked in a sleep-sodden voice.

"I may be wrong," the director went on, "but I gained that impression. You don't have to answer me if you'd rather not. I called you to ask you this: do you know of any reason why my actor, Lex Ross, should disguise himself as Mr. Barrows, now, in the middle of the night, and wander through the hotel? Or has Mr. Ross suddenly gone insane?"

3.

North bit back the ejaculation that leaped to his lips. He tried to keep his voice level as he asked: "Where's Ross now?"

"I don't know. He went to the lobby several minutes ago, disguised as Barrows, and he hasn't returned to this floor. What's it all about, Mr. Boyden—have you any idea?"

"I'll call you back," Hugh said tersely, and hung up.

Hans Bracht was still snoring and looked likely to be for at least another three hours. The new plain-clothes man was in position outside. Hugh deemed it safe to leave the scientist alone, even though They might be getting ready to make their move with the dawn.

He let himself out of 437, locked the door behind him, tested it, and turned toward the rubber plant, pointed at the door and tried by facial grimacing and silent-mouthed English words to convey to the hidden plain-clothes man that this door must be watched unblinkingly. The Thai behind the palm nodded; he got the idea.

Colonel North then used the stairs to go down to the lobby, checking every floor briefly on his way. In the lobby he went to the desk and roused the sleepy night clerk.

Had the clerk seen Mr. Barrows? Oh, yes, honored guest just now walked through lobby and outside. When politely reminded it was five o'clock in the morning, honored guest explained he wanted to go see the opening of the Thieves Market, take pictures.

Hugh figuratively scratched his head. Just what in hell was Ross up to, posing as Hans Bracht, wandering around the hotel and then the streets outside at this ungodly hour?

As to that, why was Anton Carss up and about at this hour so that he could see Ross? It appeared to North more to the point to talk to the director than to go chasing after the disguised Ross through the dark streets of Bangkok, so Hugh took the elevator to the seventh floor and pressed the buzzer of Suite Seven-B.

Carss answered immediately. The pudgy director was clad in a blue watered-silk dressing gown and his feet were thrust into soft kid slippers. His face showed a heavy bristle of beard and the shadows beneath his eyes indicated a lack of sleep.

"Did you find him?" was his first question. "What's he up to now, that damned fool? With my leading man murdered does Ross think he can complete the ruin of *Tiger, Tiger!* by getting involved in some crackpot foolishness and landing in jail?"

He stood aside to let North into a suite that was an exact replica of John Wallen's. The confusion of the room, too, was almost as bad as the clutter of Wallen's suite after the cocktail party; there was a litter of crumpled newspapers, scenario manuscripts, empty or half-empty highball glasses, scattered pieces of hand luggage, a wardrobe trunk up against the wall, yawning open, the remains of a supper on a table in a corner.

Carss caught North's sweeping survey of the room and shrugged apologetically. "You'll have to excuse the looks of this place," he said. "I'm cursed with insomnia and I do most of my work after midnight. With Wallen having to be replaced, I've been trying to line up the sequences we could shoot without him when the police let us move on to location."

He remembered his main question. "What about Ross?"

"They said at the desk that he left the hotel, disguised as Barrows, and went to the Thieves Market to see it open."

"The Thieves Market!"

"Oh, it's not as bad as it sounds," North explained. "In the old days pirates used to bring their loot here to Bangkok to be sold in a market place that got the name of the Thieves Market. Today it's sort of a catchall proposition—produce, fish, curios, things like that."

"But why would Ross do such a thing?"

"I don't know," North admitted. "Maybe he's got insomnia, too, and wanted to exercise. Perhaps he was afraid of autograph hounds and disguised himself as Barrows to keep from being pestered."

Carss shook his heavy-featured head. "Not Lex," he said.

193

"He's past the age when autograph hounds are a nuisance. When an actor gets old he goes out of his way to find them." He pursed his fleshy lips, pulled at his chin. "There's something strange going on here," he said softly.

North gave a brief, humorless laugh. "You're putting it a little mildly, aren't you?" he asked. "Wallen was killed, Marchet was killed, I suppose you've heard about Chu Hoong." Carss nodded. "And the police tell me they've uncovered a big dope ring. There's something going on, all right."

"I mean with Ross," Carss said. "He—" The director stopped and eyed North speculatively. "Am I right in thinking you have some connection with the FBI, Mr. Boyden?"

"You're the second one who's made that mistake." North smiled. "Lex Ross was sure I was a G-man. I'm not."

"No?" Carss seemed crestfallen for a moment but then recovered. "But you're here in Bangkok in some official capacity, right?"

"That covers a wide field, Mr. Carss," North stalled. "But what did you want to ask me, in case I was something more than a traveling salesman, say?"

"It's about Ross," the pudgy director explained. "If—if it were discovered that a certain person had a link with the subversive Communists in the States, no matter how recent or how far in the past, could he be—is extradited the word? —to face charges?"

"I'm not too well up in my international law," North admitted, "but I'd say it would depend on the charges and Washington's relations with the country that was asked to extradite. Do you mean Ross?"

The director shoved his hands into the pockets of his dressing gown and began stalking back and forth in front of North, his brow deeply creased. "Let's say I've been wrestling with my conscience," he offered. "America has been good to me and I owe her a great deal and yet I dread to smear an innocent man's reputation. But I have discovered something. Lex Ross is a Communist. He operates under the name of Walter Wells or something like that— I suppose he has half a dozen names. I heard rumors of

194

this but I dismissed them as jealous slander—Hollywood is full of that, you know. But—well, I won't go into details but I've learned enough to know Lex is up to his neck in Communist filth."

"But didn't Ross make his confession to being a Communist some time back?" North asked. "As I understand it, he admitted his error and was cleared."

"So he claimed when I faced him with my suspicions," Carss nodded. "But recently, just before we left California, certain things were brought to my attention—"

"By John Wallen?"

"Yes, Wallen was one who came to me with stories about Ross but he wasn't the only one. If it had been Wallen alone I wouldn't have paid any attention to it. I know how bitterly the two men hated each other."

"That was more than just professional jealousy?"

"Oh yes. Ross's second wife—but it's a sordid story. Anyway, Ross never forgave Wallen and more than once he swore he'd kill Jack."

The pudgy director caught himself and darted his brown eyes at the G-2 colonel. "That sounds as though I'm accusing Ross of killing Wallen," he said. "I didn't mean it to come out quite that way."

"I'm sure you didn't," North said noncommittally. "By the way, how did it happen that you saw Ross when he started out on this tour of his disguised as Barrows?"

Carss waved a hand at the litter of papers on the divan against the wall to his left. "I told you; I have insomnia; I was working. Ross's suite is just up the hall, Seven-C. I heard his door close. There was a scene he was in that I was considering and I thought it would be a good time to go over it with him, clear up some details, if he was finding it impossible to sleep. But then I warned myself that Ross might have been entertaining a lady and I didn't want to embarrass her so I just opened my door a crack and peeked into the hall. There was Henry Barrows."

He spread his hands at shoulder height. "You can imagine how surprised I was. But then Lex apparently remembered something he had left behind. He used his key to let himself

195

back into his suite and came out again a few seconds later. I knew then that it was my actor up to his old tricks."

"Old tricks?"

"Yes, Lex delights in disguising himself and playing tricks on his friends—and enemies. They say there are some Hollywood wives who have been sure they were with their husbands until it was too late to do anything about it, but this might be gossip, nothing more. But I do know he has represented himself as other men in practical jokes and has caused them considerable embarrassment. I have not escaped; he once posed as Anton Carss and worked a company I was directing half the night on an emergency call, doing useless, idiotic bits. My studio thought I had gone quite mad."

"And after a trick like that you'd still have him in your picture, *Tiger, Tiger?*"

"Of course. The man's a genius even if his humor is a bit warped. And I am an artist, Mr. Boyden. Even if I hated Ross, which I don't, and he was the man for this role, which he is, I would insist on him. Personalities are forgotten when a director makes a picture."

"I see," North murmured. *Like hell.*

"And now you must be anxious to find Lex, so I won't keep you any longer," Carss said. "This may be unimportant to you but I thought—"

"Well, look who's here," caroled Lita Naline from the balcony doorway.

4.

She stood—clung to the doorframe—in disheveled beauty, this movie star whose publicity writers named the daughter of a maharajah. Over a black net nightgown was a filmy peignoir, and neither hid much of the sensuous body beneath. So, within a little over an hour, Colonel Hugh North gazed upon a second beautiful woman who had thrown modesty after the clothes she had taken off.

196

This, he told himself, *is getting to be a habit. Nice one, too.*

Quite apparently, Lita had cured the hangover she had had when North had listened in on her conversation with Captain Pokh; as obviously, she had eased her pangs by the old tried and untrue method of resorting to the hair of the dog that bit her and she had overdone it. Now she was plastered again, and if experience meant anything, North knew, she would be facing a new and more horrendous hangover on some never-to-be-evaded morrow.

North had always considered Lita beautiful; he did not alter his opinion now, no matter how stoned the star was. She was the one woman in a million who could fracture herself with alcohol and still not turn bulbous-nosed and slack-mouthed. Now at an hour when lack of sleep alone should have made a hag of her, even without the liquor, she was luminous of eye and creamy of skin, her hair was a perfect shining cap about her beautiful face. She might not be able to walk straight as she came into the room toward North, but she made a lovely staggerer.

Anton Carss moved quickly to support Lita by an elbow, led her to the paper-littered divan, and cleared a place for her to sit down. The star lolled back on the cushions with a total disregard of exposures and eyed the G-2 uncertainly.

"What're you two doin'?" she demanded. "Havin' a party all by yourselves without invitin' Lita? Don't you know that's bad manners? I wanna drink."

"Lita darling," Anton Carss said, "don't you think you've had enough?"

She pinned the director with an eye suddenly gone steady. "Anton," she said with enormous patience, "I said I wanted a drink, not a damn A.A. lecture."

Carss hesitated a moment, then shrugged and crossed the room to a cellarette, hauled out a bottle. While he busied himself with ice and soda, Lita turned to Hugh. "What're you havin', G-man?" she asked. "Gin or scotch or what, G-man?"

"Lita, dear," Carss said mildly. "Mr. Boyden assures me he isn't a G-man."

Lita giggled. "Too bad. Thought I could have you 'rrested f'r Mann Act, Anton. Transportin' females f'r lewd and lashvicious purposes. Mann Act. Woman Act. Man-and-Woman Act. Funny, hey?"

"Lita, please," Anton begged softly.

"Oh hell, Anton," the star laughed, "why do you keep thinkin' we're such a big secret? Everybody knows we're more than pen pals, buster."

She accepted the drink Carss gave her and applied her full lips to the glass. The director turned to North inquiringly. "Too early for you?" he asked.

"A little"—North nodded—"but go ahead—from what you say, this is the middle of your working day."

"Don't mind if I do." Anton smiled and mixed himself another, darker drink.

"Lissen," Lita Naline demanded, "what I wanna know is why you two fellas are buddy-buddying it up at this time of night. That's all I wanna know, see?"

"I had a question I wanted to ask Mr. Boyden," Carss explained smoothly. "He knows Thailand and there was a technical problem I had to straighten out."

"At five o'clock in the mornin', f'r gawd's sake?"

"Well—I'll explain it all later, dear."

"Like hell you will. Damn little explainin' you do to me." Her voice gave an almost perfect imitation of Carss's. "You just do what Poopsy tells you and everything will be all right. You just listen to Poopsy, never mind anything else." She reverted to her own voice as she appealed to North. "You'd think a guy that gets as much outa me as I give him would confide in me once inna while, wouldn't you? Naw, all he thinks of me is I'm good in bed, that's all." She gulped her highball as thirstily as though she needed it.

Carss gave Lita a pained glance, then turned to North with another hunch-shouldered grimace that asked the G-2 colonel to be tolerant, Lita wasn't usually like this.

"And another thing," Lita was reciting. "If you think you're gonna fly me up to Sara What's-her-name in that plane of yours you're crazy. Last time I flew with you I got scared spitless and there were plenty of landin' fields around

198

then. Catch me flyin' over a jungle with you at the controls—no, sir!"

She waggled her head and took solace in her drink. Carss was frowning when North looked at him. "I'll have you understand, Lita," the chubby director said with a hint of anger, "that I can fly as well as any pilot we have with us."

"Ho," jeered Lita. "Also, hah!"

North put in a question. "You're flying to this location camp?"

Carss nodded, still scowling. "If the police ever get this murder cleared up and let us leave Bangkok. You perhaps know that we're all set up and ready to go on location, but the police have told us we can't leave."

"Did Miss Naline mean Sara Kaeo?" the colonel pursued.

Carss gave another of his characteristic shrugs. "Something like that," he said. "They've bulldozed a landing strip farther up-country, but Sara-something is the railhead where the supplies are shipped."

"You have your own plane out here?"

"We chartered some planes for easy travel," the director explained. "I like to fly, so we got a light plane for my personal use."

"Personal use is right," Lita put in. "Nobody'll fly with Anton twice. He's the personalest pilot there is."

Anton Carss started a heated rejoinder, then paused and grinned sheepishly. "I guess she's right," he told North. "I'm just learning and I'm not very smooth at it yet."

"You can say that again," Lita Naline muttered, and drained her glass, held it out for a refill.

"Don't you think—" Carss began mildly.

"No, I don't think," Lita mimicked. "You just look out f'r Anton Carss and Lita will look out f'r Lita. Okay? Okay!"

Carss hesitated and then walked back to the cellarette. Lita gave Hugh North a grin and an elaborate wink. *See how I've got him trained?*

While Carss's back was to him, North threw his question. "You don't happen to have a tape recorder, do you, Mr. Carss? My office has sent me some tapes and my own machine got lost in the shuffle in Hong Kong."

"I don't," Carss said without turning, "but I can get you one easily enough—if it hasn't been shipped up to location."

"It's not important," Hugh said idly. "My own recorder will probably catch up with me today."

"How about yours, Lita?" Carss asked, rattling the ice in her drink as she stirred. "Couldn't you lend yours to Mr. Boyden?"

Lita straightened on the divan, squinted at her lover. "Whaddaya mean, mine?" she demanded. "You know damn well I don't own a tape recorder. What'd I do with a tape recorder, for gawd's sake?"

"Now, now," Carss chided, "don't be selfish, Lita; it's not like you. Lend Mr. Boyden your machine—you won't need it long, will you, Boyden?"

Lita was off the divan, her gauzy dressing gown flying out behind her in her lurch, and advancing on Carss. "What's the big idea?" she cried. "What're you tryin' to do to me, Anton? What's this tape-recorder jazz?"

"It's not important," North said hastily.

Lita whirled back toward him, her melon breasts heaving. "Lissen," she cried, "I don't know what this is all about, but this sonofabitch ain't up to no good. Sayin' I got a tape recorder when I never had one of the things in my life. What's the idea, Anton? What're you tryin' to put over on me, huh?"

Carss turned, the highball in his hand, his olive-skinned features showing perplexity and apology. "I must be wrong," he told North. "Yes, I'm sure I'm wrong. It was—it was somebody else who had a tape recorder. I remember now."

"Lex Ross has got one," Lita said, still belligerent. "Jack Wallen had one. But damn if I ever had one, and don't you say I did, neither."

"All right, all right," Carss said soothingly. "I'm sorry. Here's your drink."

Lita took it ungraciously and flung herself back down on the divan, revealing more of Lita Naline than even the most liberal censor would have allowed on the screen. "Don't say *I've* got a tape recorder," she grumbled.

"I'm sorry I asked," North lied. "I didn't know—"

"Oh, I'm sorry I blew my stack," the girl cut in, "but this is the second time— Well, never mind." She gulped her drink.

North got to his feet. "I've got to be going," he told Carss. "I'll keep in touch with you about—the man we were talking about."

"What's Lex done now?" Lita Naline wanted to know. As both men swung toward her she made a gesture with her glass, sending the liquor slopping. "Oh, I know it's about him. He's a maniac, isn't he? Didn't he kill Jack because he was goin' to squeal about Lex bein' a Commie? Didn't he knock off that other guy, that Frenchman, because—"

"*Lita!*" Carss's voice whipcracked across the room. The one word struck the drunken movie star with an impact so jarring that it seemed to sober her. The beautiful brunette raised a hand to her cheek as though she had been slapped.

"I—uh—I didn't mean it," she whimpered. "I forgot you told me to shut up about it or you'd—" She stopped.

The G-2 colonel turned to Carss. The director stood there with his hands balled at his sides, his face suffused by an ugly dull flush, his black eyes glittering in his anger.

"What is it, Carss?" North asked.

"Nothing!" the director said abruptly. "Don't believe her. She's been drinking, and when she drinks she talks nonsense."

"She said you'd told her to keep quiet about this," the Intelligence officer reminded Carss. "Exactly what was she supposed to keep quiet about, and why?"

Carss gave the girl on the divan a black scowl before he answered. "What will happen to my *Tiger, Tiger!* now?" he asked. "First Wallen and then Ross." He heaved a deep sigh and walked to a chair, dropped into it.

"All right," he told North. "Find Lex Ross, Boyden, and ask him where he was when Wallen was killed and when the Frenchman, Marchet, was killed too. Ask him to show you the knife he bought in the lobby curio shop right after we checked in. Ask him to explain the cut on his chin—a cut that could have been made by glass from Marchet's broken window. Ask him— But I don't have to tell you what to ask him. You're the detective, aren't you?"

201

"Yeah, ask him," Lita Naline shrilled. "He's in his rooms now, just beyond Wallen's suite. I know, 'cause when I came out on the balcony to come over here I saw his lights go on."

"I intend to ask him," Hugh North said grimly. "I intend to ask a lot of questions of a lot of people before I'm through. But first let me use your phone."

With Lita Naline staring at him, never heeding the cherry-nippled breast that was exposed, and with Carss scowling at him from across the room near the cellarette, Colonel North called the desk in the lobby. Yes, a cable had come for Mr. Boyden; they were holding it until a more convenient delivery hour. Yes, the clerk would be pleased to read the message.

Hugh North listened, disciplining his face to show his two watchers nothing of his reaction. Mentally decoded, the word from Washington was:

INRE WALTER WELLS; COMMUNIST PARTY NAME OF DANGEROUS RED OPERATIVE ACTIVE WEST COAST REAL NAME UNKNOWN BELIEVED HIGH IN PROFESSIONAL BRANCH MOVIE INDUSTRY. URGENTLY CABLE ANY INFORMATION RE HIM.

5.

North carefully replaced the phone, then raised it again to ask for Room 439. There were half a dozen long rings before the fuzzy voice of Hans Bracht answered.

"Hullo, hullo. I'm sorry, but I was asleep and I didn't hear—"

"It's Boyden," North cut in.

"Oh." Abysmal disappointment.

"I'm held up for a few minutes," the G-2 colonel explained. "I just wanted to check and make sure you were all right."

There was an indistinct grumbling at the other end before the scientist said: "Yes, yes, I'm all right. Don't keep this

202

telephone busy—They might call, and if there was a busy line They might be angry."

"Okay. I'll be back in a little while. You know the precautions to take."

"Yes, but what's happened? There are holes in the door that look like bullet holes and—"

"I'll explain everything when I see you. Good-by."

He hung up and with a nod to Carss, a final appreciative glance at the voluptuous Lita Naline, he left Suite Seven-B and headed for Seven-C, Lex Ross's quarters.

He did not press the ivory button this time. Instead, he used one of his slender bunch of keys to throw the lock of the door and eased himself inside noiselessly, his pistol out again and ready. There were sounds from the bedroom, and North crossed the dark living room to the bedroom door, stood there to watch Lex Ross busy himself with the removal of his disguise.

Although the actor had had considerable time, Ross apparently had been leisurely about changing character from Hans Bracht back to Lex Ross. The cap that elongated his forehead gave him a balding, friz-fringed pate, was still in place, as were the heavy eyebrows, the putty nose that made his profile an exact replica of the missile expert's.

Ross sat on the side of his bed, stripped to his T-shirt and shorts, the clothes he had worn in his masquerade on the floor beside him. Now he was removing a pair of shoes with built-up heels and soles that had given him the required height. Beside him on the night table were steel-rimmed spectacles such as Hans Bracht wore and a set of tooth caps that must have transformed the shape of Ross's mouth to Bracht's thin-lipped own.

Hugh permitted himself a moment of marveling at the actor's genius of disguise before he stepped into the room, the .38 held at waist level.

"Okay, Ross," the G-2 colonel said quietly. "Don't make any sudden moves."

The actor started, swiveled his head toward the door. When he saw the ugly snout of the revolver he gaped, then raised his hands to shoulder level. "I—I didn't hear you come in," he said inanely.

"Maybe I should have sent in my card—Mr. Walter Wells," Hugh rapped out.

His face still Bracht's, the actor widened his eyes. "Walter Wells? But I told you about that. What's the idea?"

"You told me you used that name a long time ago when you made a mistake and got mixed up with a fashionable pinko crowd," North said. "You forgot to tell me you're still using the name."

"But I'm not! My God, that was twenty years ago, Boyden!"

The Intelligence man shook his head slowly. "Washington's not that slow, Ross. I've just got word that Walter Wells is still a dangerous Red agent on the West Coast—and in the movie industry, at that."

Ross flung out his hands in a gesture of desperation. "They're wrong!" he cried. "I don't know who told you that but they're wrong, I swear it!"

"Maybe I'm wrong then when I say you've been parading around Bangkok disguised as Barrows, who you say is Hans Bracht," Hugh said tonelessly. "If you want to sell me that story you'd better wipe that disguise off your face first."

"I—I— Will you let me get this stuff off my face, Boyden?" Ross asked. "I admit I was posing as Dr. Bracht, all right—that's obvious enough—but some of this make-up application has to be taken off within a certain length of time or it wrecks the skin."

"Which would be too bad," North gritted. "You don't know how much I'd like to wreck that handsome face of yours—permanently—for what you've done to Tao Muong."

Ross's surprise showed even through the heavy make-up. "Tao Muong? Bracht's wife? What happened to her?"

"Suppose you tell me."

"But I don't know anything about Tao Muong that I haven't told you, about Wallen saying he had some dope on her that was worth a lot of money. I told you all that."

Hugh North had had plenty of experience in talking to men who had been falsely accused, men who had been guilty

204

but who were past masters at innocent protest, men who could lie more smoothly than they could tell the truth, and men who invariably telegraphed a lie with a shifting of the eyes, a tightening of the muscles at the corners of the mouth, some involuntary gesture that shouted their falsehood. Lex Ross, despite the disguise that prevented Hugh from noting every smallest nuance of expression, had at least a semblance of the ring of truth in his voice.

North hesitated, then jerked his head toward the bathroom. "Get that gook off your face and then we'll talk," he ordered. "Don't make a wrong move with your hands or anything you pick up or you'll be dead. I mean it, Ross."

Lex Róss got to his feet gingerly and walked to the bathroom, North close behind him. There the actor used cleansing unguents to wipe off the mask of Hans Bracht in a matter of minutes. And North watched a long, angry scratch on Ross's chin emerge from beneath the dissolved make-up but held his silence.

The actor returned to the bedroom and shrugged into a dressing gown. North patted the pockets of the robe, found nothing in either, and gestured to Lex to sit back down on the bed while he took a chair close by, the pistol still trained on the aging actor.

"Now start talking," he said coldly. "Tell me why you were disguised as Bracht. And you'd better make it good."

"Can I have a cigarette?"

"No. Just talk."

"Well—well, you know I wanted to work with you and you said no. Jack was killed, that Frenchman was killed, and still you didn't make a move toward taking me on as a helper. So I was lying in bed earlier tonight, thinking things over, and I came up with an idea. You never would admit it, but I knew that was Hans Bracht you were with and I decided there must be something or somebody dangerous to Hans Bracht behind all this. That could mean only the Reds."

The disguise artist unthinkingly reached for the pack of cigarettes on the table beside him and Hugh let him. After a long drag at the smoke, Lex continued.

"I've got a lot to make up to the United States for the

way I goofed off years ago. I suppose you know my christened name wasn't Lex Ross. My folks were immigrants from central Europe and we didn't have anything when I was growing up. This country gave me everything—money, a certain fame, a mighty fine life—and I'd thanked my country for this by dealing with a bunch of skunks who were trying to tear down all the fine system that had been so good to me. Oh, I didn't have much to be proud of, would you say?"

"Go on," North said noncommittally.

"So I was lying here, as I said, and the thought came to me that perhaps I could make some amends for what I'd done even if you wouldn't play ball with me. If the Reds were after Bracht I'd give them Bracht—only it would be Lex Ross in disguise."

"Wait a minute," North interjected. "You mean you got this idea and got out of bed and disguised yourself as Hans Bracht, at four in the morning, and then went out and walked the streets waiting for a Red agent to come down on you?"

Ross looked at his cigarette. "Sounds ridiculous, the way you say it," he conceded, "but that was the general idea. I thought the Commies would be sure to have this hotel staked out and when I showed myself as Bracht they'd just grab me and ask themselves no questions about why Hans Bracht would be up and around at that hour." The actor took another deep pull at his cigarette, blew smoke at the floor, as North tried to find his voice. "I'm that way," Lex went on. "I get an idea, I've got to try it right away. Besides, I sort of wanted to test-run the disguise. Hans Bracht was a tough one for me to copy, being so much taller and leaner and with that seamed skin. I thought I'd try it on the desk clerk and other people in the hotel before I worked it in broad daylight."

"And nobody saw through your disguise?"

"No. Of course the clerk was pretty sleepy and the elevator operator and the night bellhops were so busy yakking about Chu Hoong they didn't give me a real going-over but I was satisfied. I walked around the streets for about half an hour, down to the Thieves Market and back, waiting for the Reds to jump me. But of course they didn't."

206

Despite his first inclinations, North believed this weird story. Unless he was a clever Red agent with an almost perfect act, Lex Ross was one of the most naïve persons North had ever met. True, the actor had proved his ability to fool people with his disguises but to believe that he could act as a decoy for Hans Bracht, on whom was pinned the eye of what must be one of Moscow's top operatives, was—

Well, what is it—ludicrous? Can you say that the people watching Bracht wouldn't fall for it? They must be getting jittery with the Chu Hoong thing coming on top of Wallen and Marchet. Why wouldn't they get rattled at seeing Hans Bracht walk out of the hotel, against their every order, and just grab him?

"Tell me," he asked Ross, "what did you think was going to happen to you when they found out you weren't Bracht? Did you expect them to laugh heartily at the joke and let you go?"

"No," the actor said in a low voice. "I—I didn't give that a great deal of thought. I knew they'd be rough on me but— well, I told you I had a lot to make up for. I'm no spring chicken, Boyden. I've about had it. I was too old for the last war and before that—I guess you could call me a draft dodger in World War I. I went on Liberty Bond tours with Doug and Wally and the old crowd. We said we'd be more valuable selling bonds than shouldering a rifle, but we were only trying to kid ourselves; we knew the studios had ways and means of getting their stars deferred in that war.

"So what if the Reds did get peeved over grabbing the wrong man? I've had a good life and a full one, and if I went out doing something that was for the good of my country, what better way could there be for an old ham like me?"

There was a silence as North pondered the actor's strange story. Lex Ross finally broke the quiet. "Do you believe me?"

Instead of answering directly, North asked a question in turn. "Do you own a tape recorder?"

"Why, sure. I had the idea of taping some native music when we got in the jungle. I'm a deck bug, among other things. Why do you ask?"

"Does Lita Naline own one?" North asked.

Lex shook his head. "If she does I never saw it that I know of. Of course she travels with a mountain of baggage if she's only going to Palm Springs, but I never noticed a tape recorder among her things and they're pretty easy to pick out."

"Wallen had one?"

"Uh-huh. He had a collection of girls' voices taped while they were— But Wallen's dead, so why bring up his nastiness again? What's all this about a tape recorder?"

"How about Carss; does he own one?"

"I've never been in Carss's home, so I don't know. He didn't bring one on this trip, if that's what you mean. Or, again, I've never seen him with one since we left the States."

North pulled at his lower lip, frowning. "Tell me about the name Walter Wells," he suggested. "Where did you get it and how long did you use it?"

"Not long," Ross explained. "My cell leader just gave it to me one day. He said from now on I was to use the name Walter Wells in any work I did for the Party. I was starting to see I was in pretty deep by then and I wanted out. I did a few courier jobs after that and then I just quit. They weren't as tough on me as they were later on to people who defected; they didn't begin getting tough until Beria took over the whole setup. Oh, I got a few threatening phone calls but I told them to kiss my foot and I didn't hear from them again."

"Did you tell the FBI all this?"

Ross clamped his lips in a stubborn line. "I'm not going to tell even you what I said to the FBI," he told North. "They told me to keep my lip buttoned and I intend to—maybe I've told you too much already if you're no G-man, as you say you're not."

Hugh North hesitated a moment and then nodded. "I meant it," he told the actor. "I'm not FBI. Have you ever heard of Army Intelligence?"

"You mean spy stuff? Of course. But I thought that was OSS or something."

"There are a lot of branches."

"And you're from Army Intelligence? But why would an

Army man be in charge of Hans Bracht? I should think it would be Air Force, if anything."

"Never mind about why I'm with Bracht; I am. I'm telling you this because I think you're okay. I may be wrong, but if I am be assured I'll find out before you can do any damage with your information. And by doing damage I include telling anybody—*anybody*—who I am."

"I'm dumb," Ross said fervently. "Does this mean you're taking me on as a helper?"

"Not so fast. First, did you buy a knife in that curio shop downstairs when you arrived?"

"Yes." The word was dull, freighted with Ross's knowledge of what the admission probably would mean to his newfound ally. "Yes, and I suppose it was the same knife that killed Jack Wallen. It—I know how this sounds, but it's true—it was stolen from me sometime that morning, yesterday morning."

"Taken from your room?"

Ross nodded. "I left it on a table out in the living room. I distinctly remember putting it down and telling myself it was probably made in Hackensack. I didn't think anything more about it until I heard that Jack had been murdered with a knife. Then I realized it wasn't on the table when I came back from Wallen's cocktail party."

His eyes came up to meet North's. "I suppose my fingerprints were all over the thing."

"I don't know," North admitted, "but if it'll make you feel any better, I wouldn't worry too much about that. It was a carved hilt, and latent prints would be hard to pick up even for an up-to-date police laboratory. Here in Bangkok, heaven knows what kind of equipment or men they have in their fingerprint department. As for it being stolen, with these damn balconies running the length of this side of the hotel, almost anybody could have taken it."

"Who told you I bought the knife?" Lex caught himself immediately. "No, don't tell me. A dozen people saw me buy the damned thing and everybody knows how I felt about Wallen." The eyes held North's squarely. "You know I hated the sonofabitch, don't you?"

209

North shrugged. Wallen's death meant nothing to him except as it was connected with the plot to capture Hans Bracht, the dead actor's knowledge of something concerning Tao Muong. He was convinced by now that personal hate had had nothing to do with Wallen's murder; the star had been knifed to shut him up.

"You told John Wallen I was a G-man guarding Bracht, didn't you?" Hugh asked.

"I—well, I guess I did," Lex admitted in a low voice. "He was talking about having this information about Bracht's wife and I—well, I knew personally how he'd preyed on other women, so I told him he'd better watch his step because that was a federal agent sitting over there across the dining room who was in Bangkok on something I thought was connected with Hans Bracht."

There was a brief silence and then North sighed exaggeratedly. "So that's all you said, eh?" he asked heavily.

"Honestly, that's all. And I could see it hit Wallen hard, no matter if he did make some wisecrack about it. Then he saw me come over and talk to you and he braced me about it later. I knew then I'd blabbed too much and I said I was wrong, you were a traveling salesman, but he wasn't fooled."

"So he called me and invited me to his cocktail party to pump me or offer his information for a price, perhaps," North theorized.

"He invited everybody who was on the plane except Marchet," Lex said. "I happen to know that because he told me he wasn't going to ask the French or Chu Hoong. Not his class, he said. Then I told him Chu was a millionaire and he changed his mind fast enough about inviting him."

North remembered the telephone call from Chu Hoong that had come while he had been examining Wallen's body. So Chu actually had been invited and was no doubt phoning his regrets, that was all, and so had further snarled the tangled skeins.

"One more question before we move," Hugh North said. "How did you get that scratch on your chin?"

Ross involuntarily put a hand to his face. "That damn Lita, that's how. When I heard about Jack I was—well, I was knocked out, a little. You try hating a man and wishing him dead, even threatening to kill him, for a long time and then find out that somebody else has murdered him and you'll find out it's a hell of a shock.

"I was lying down, right on this bed, and Lita Naline came tottering in from the balcony, looking for a drink. I guess Carss had hidden her liquor—it wasn't long after she did that belly dance and she was in his doghouse, I figured. Anyway, to shut her up and get her out I gave her a bottle of bourbon and she—well, she was plastered and she wanted to pay me for it in Lita's own way. I wasn't having any and I tried to push her out the way she'd come and she got sore. Nobody was giving her the brush-off, by God, so she came at me with her nails. I got this before I really booted her tail out of here."

Hugh North stood there studying the scratch, pulling at his chin. And within his head there was the click-click of pieces fitting into place to make what had been a complicated puzzle a relatively simple picture.

He knew what he had to know now to put the finger on the Red agent who was at least directing the plot to seize Dr. Hans Bracht. With his complete confidence in his theory that Tao Muong was already dead, he was not bound by any promise to Bracht to keep hands off.

Now he could move. Now he *would* move.

"Okay, so you wanted to be of help in this case," he told Lex Ross. "Here's your first assignment. Phone Captain Pokh at the Bangkok Imperial Troop headquarters. Tell him to bring a squad of men here on the double."

He headed for the door and flung over his shoulder: "Tell him I know my man now and I'm going to make my move. *I'm going after Anton Carss!*"

6.

Hugh North burst into Suite Seven-B, his gun ready. The living room, the bedroom were empty; there was nobody in the bathroom. The G-2 agent made for the balcony, stepped out onto the railed ledge into the yellow-gray predawn of a Bangkok morning, and whirled around a corner into the living room of Lita Naline's suite.

The star was lying on a divan, half clad in the diaphanous costume she had worn when North had last seen her, with one long arm drooping to the floor, a knee doubled to thrust up out of the swirl of filmy stuff that was her nightgown, bunched up about her thigh.

The girl turned her head as Hugh entered and North saw that her drunkenness had finally caught up with her—that or something else had happened to make her an unlovely creature now. The luminous eyes were dull and teary, the full-lipped mouth slobbered, and even the full breasts that had swelled so entrancingly seemed to sag now in dismal weariness.

"Get out," the woman choked. "Get out before I have you thrown out, ya cop bassard. Get out."

"Where's Carss?" North snapped.

"Where's Carss?" Lita mimicked. "How'n hell do I know where the lil rat is? He's not here. He won't ever be here again. Never, never, never." She sat up and wiped the back of her hand across her smeared mouth. "Wanna see the goin'-away present he gave me?"

She labored to her feet, hauled peignoir and nightgown aside to reveal a purpling bruise just below her full breast.

She swayed as she looked down at herself. "Gave me that f'r a goin'-away present, the bassard," she mumbled. "He'd-a killed me if he could—if I didn't run."

Tears spilled over suddenly, and sobs wrenched the body that had been so glorious before this sudden degeneration. "He never loved me," Lita Naline sobbed. "He only made out he did so's I'd do what he told me to. Oh, the bassard. The rat. The . . ." She launched into a stream of slurred epithets that would have sounded better coming from a drunken dock-walloper than from the idol of the silver screen.

"How long ago did he leave? Where did he go?"

Lita was teetering her way toward the bottles that stood on a table near her bedroom door. "Right after you went

212

to see Ross he made a phone call. To that guy—you know, Barrows. I heard'm. I— He thought I went back to my room to go to the john, but I didn't. I stayed on the balcony out there and I heard him through the bedroom window. Called Barrows, he did. Then I looked through the window and one of those suitcases of his turned out to be a tape recorder. Had a false bottom, the suitcase, and there was a reg'lar little tape recorder. Said *I* had a tape recorder and he had one alla time."

She sloshed liquor into a glass, drank it neat, her throat working thirstily.

"How long ago?"

"Right after you left, I told you. He's been gone a long time. I tried to stop him—sonofabitch sayin' I had a tape recorder when it was his alla time. Special built—you couldn't tell it was in the suitcase. He said he was Austrian—sonofabitch is *Russian*, that's what, or a Communist, anyway. Imagine me givin' a goddamn Communist spy bassard what I gave him. Imagine me lettin' that lil rat—"

Hugh North waited to hear no more. If Carss had used the tape recorder he must have given Hans Bracht his final message from Tao Muong, the one that told Bracht to trust Anton Carss, that Carss would lead him to her.

That plain-clothes man Pokh had stationed in the hall—had he stopped Carss in time?

The colonel ran down three flights of stairs with total disregard of the risk of a fall, a sprained ankle. It was the time to take risks—pray God the time had not been put off too long.

He made the fourth-floor landing, hurtled around a corner, and headed for 439. On his way he passed the rubber plant behind which the plain-clothes man had been stationed. Pokh's man was still there, but now he was slumped in a huddle, blood welling from a blackjack wound over his ear. Carss's helpers, then, had spotted the hidden man and had waited only for a word from their leader to dispose of him when the time came.

He reached 437 and stopped, raised a hand to the frame

213

to steady himself against the shock that was only slightly dulled by having been expected. The door was open and so was that of 439. Dr. Hans Bracht was gone, kidnaped, or, more probably, departed on his own, full of foolish, suicidal hope of being reunited with Tao Muong, believing the promises of the man who had led him away, Anton Carss, Moscow's new "Walter Wells."

CHAPTER 7

"HAVE ALL GETTING OUT PLACES COVERED,
Colonel North," Captain Pilanung Pokh reported. "General
Genung says lookout for Carss put on all airports, railroads,
vessels, highways—especially places where he can fly plane
out of."

"Good." Hugh nodded. "He hasn't got much of a start.
We got too close to his heels too soon and he had to jump
his own gun. We ought to get him and—uh—Barrows before
he can get out of Bangkok."

"Except one," Captain Pokh said.

"Huh?"

"I say General Genung got all places covered like you
say except one. Is little place, though. Not important."

"What is is?"

Pokh shrugged apologetically. "Movie company chartered
little private field outside city for planes they hired. Been
flying from here to Sara Kaeo alla time."

"Oh my God, that's the one he'll head for. He's got his
own plane there. *Why can't Genung alert somebody there?"*

"Is no one to alert. Can get men there but not right away.
Bangkok Imperial Troop, police, army, always have men at
all regular airports but not that little field and no telephone
there. Take a little time to get men to private airfield."

"We haven't got a little time," Hugh barked. He ran his
hand over his stubbled hair and then asked, "Can General
Genung get me a military plane?"

"Can get you anything!"

"Get hold of him and tell him I want a fast pursuit ship

215

with a pilot who knows the eastern frontier country. Somebody who can speak English or French."

"You think Carss heading east, hey?"

"Yes, he'll go for North Indochina, Vietminh country. Those people are the nearest out-and-out Commies and he needs friends in a hurry." He started for the door. "Is your car out front, Captain?"

"Official auto parked in No Parking place in front, key in switch." Pokh nodded. "But not bulletproof like I can get for you if you wait one little minute. Have big Cadillac limousine for important people like you, Colonel North, all bulletproof and air-condition and—"

"Keep an eye on Lita Naline," North barked. "Is the closest Thai Air Force base at Don Muang?" Pokh nodded. "Tell General Genung to give me a plane from that field, then. I'll meet him there if he wants to hear the details."

"But—"

North was out of the room and racing down the stairs to the first floor. He half ran through the lobby to the front door and there he was met by the Greek manager. That portly individual wore an injured expression as he put out a hand to slow Hugh's rush.

"Ah, sir," he said in his too meticulous English, "I understand you are a high official in your country. Can you not do something about the terrible events in this fine hotel? Our owner has been killed, there are murders and stabbings all over the place, and the guests are greatly upset."

"Out of the way," North snapped. "I'm in a hurry."

"But Mr. Salenkov says he will make a complaint to his government and the missionary in Room . . ."

North was outside by then and jumping into the tiny Fiat that sat at the curb, its side emblazoned with the seal of the Bangkok Imperial Troop. As he pup-pupped away from the curb he found himself wishing for the speed, not the air-conditioning or bulletproofing that Pokh had said the important persons' Cadillac possessed. This midget seemed to crawl.

There was a siren almost as big as the hood, and North did something he humanly loved and almost never got a chance to do; he pressed the siren button on the dashboard and went through Bangkok with the accelerator jammed to the floorboard. Elephants went lumbering out of his way, squealing, and cars and trucks panicked into the curb as the Fiat rocketed through the streets at the little car's dizziest pace, a hammering sixty. He made Don Muang airport in record time and crawled out of the car to find himself confronted by what looked like the Joint Chiefs of Staff of the Thai Army, Navy, and Air Force. General Genung of the Bangkok Imperial Troop stepped from the front rank of this imposing array, saluted, and identified himself, wherewith his interpreter took over.

"Carss took off from the private airfield with Dr. Bracht nearly an hour ago. Dr. Bracht appeared doped, according to mechanics at the field. Radar stations and antiaircraft bases throughout the country are alerted and it will require only a word from you to have the plane shot down. Carss has been tracked and appears to be making for the Laos frontier, north of Cambodia. Our friends in Laos and Cambodia have been advised and are ready to shoot him down, too, if you so advise, Colonel."

Hugh shook his head. "Anything but that—at least not until we've tried everything else. I presume Carss's plane carries radio?"

Genung's interpreter addressed a question to one of the generals. The man nodded as he replied in Thai. "Yes, but we haven't raised him," the interpreter said. "I understand he's a very amateurish flier; he may not have turned on his receiver."

"Do you know the wave lengths to Hanoi and other Vietminh bases?" Hugh asked.

"Oh yes, or at least their assigned wave lengths. The pilot assigned to you knows them and he speaks excellent French. Your plane is waiting and the pilot will know the last plotted position of Carss's plane."

"Let's get in the air then," North said. He saluted the beribboned generals and accompanied Genung and the interpreter as they led the way to a ship waiting on the apron.

It was a powerful job—no jet, but one of the most advanced propeller planes put into the air before the jets had

217

taken over. North told himself it certainly should be fast enough to catch Carss's private plane regardless of the head start Bracht's kidnaper had.

And what would he do when they overtook Carss? Time enough to decide that when the question had to be answered.

Hugh North climbed into the rear cockpit of the plane as its engine roared. The helmeted pilot turned in his narrow place and thrust a brown hand over his shoulder to take Hugh's grip. As North adjusted his helmet with its built-in earphones and throat mike, the pilot spoke over the intercom in French.

"I am Lieutenant Lemang. Our target is reported flying in circles near Nang Rong. That is not far from the south branch of the Menag. Observers say he appears lost. What order, sir?"

"Let's sight the plane, Lieutenant," North answered. "We can decide what to do then."

The pilot nodded, opened his throttle, and gave his engine a minimum warm-up before he began taxiing off the apron. North tipped a salute to General Genung, then was hurled back in his seat by the plane's momentum as it thundered into motion. Through his earphones North caught the jabber of conflicting wave lengths, all speaking in Asiatic tongues, before a stronger voice bellowed something in Thai. At the end of the message, sent from the Don Muang tower, Lemang translated in French.

"Our plane is over Burram on the railroad north of Nang Rong. If he follows the railroad east he will soon come to the Cambodian border."

While he was speaking the young Thai lieutenant whipped his plane into the air, went over on a wing, and then straightened. North, peering down at the ground that streamed beneath, knew the pilot had given his ship full throttle on the take-off and turn. This boy was a hot pilot.

They had been in the air only ten minutes or so when the earphones jarred with a stream of Siamese. Lemang reported to North. "Now he's over Sisaket, east of Burram on the railroad."

"Can we catch him before he makes the frontier?"

218

"Difficult to tell."

"Call your commanding officer and ask him to query Cambodia and Laos points about putting up planes to turn him back. Not to attack him, you understand, but to turn him back."

"I'll try, sir." The pilot talked to Don Muang, and North heard the reply although he could not understand it. Lemang translated again. "Both those countries have limited air power, sir," he said, almost apologetically. "They will send up a plane or two to patrol the border, but if our man has any luck he can evade them. Our best chance is to catch him ourselves before he reaches Cambodia or Laos."

"When we sight our man can you tune me in on him and let me try to talk to him?" Hugh asked.

Lemang nodded and the plane roared on. Under them, the country changed from flat plains with wandering streams to thick timber growth, moderately high hills, a scarcity of clearings, and no roads at all. Then North spotted the railroad, twisting snake-like through this jungle, stretching toward the east. They passed over a fair-sized town with an airport set in the wilderness.

"Sisaket," Lemang said, "and there's our man. We'll go on his wave length in a minute, Colonel."

Squinting ahead, Hugh made out the speck that was Carss's plane. As he fixed his eyes upon it the speck grew to a dot and then took on the shape of an aircraft, so fast was the military plane coming up on it.

"We'll catch him well before the border," Lemang reported. "He's been following the railroad, making all the turns, while we've flown a straight course. I'm putting you on transmitter now, sir. *Allez.*"

The frying-pan crackle was shut out of his earphones and the colonel spoke into his throat mike. "Carss! Anton Carss! Antiaircraft guns and military aircraft will shoot you down if you try to cross the border. Repeat. You will be shot down if you cross the border a few miles ahead. You don't stand a chance, Carss. Turn back. *Répondez.*"

Lieutenant Lemang caught the French change-over and switched North's earphones to receive. There was no response,

219

only the crackle of static and the faint, unintelligible chatter of interfering wave lengths. Three times North repeated his message as the military plane gained on Carss's ship and three times there was no reply from the fugitive aircraft.

"Put me on Hanoi's wave length," North ordered as his plane came up on Carss's tail.

"You're on," Lemang said tersely after an adjustment.

He was indeed on; through North's earphones came the strong signals of a voice yelling in thick German. But was it German? North listened and tensed. That was Russian and it was Carss who was talking.

The colonel knew only a smattering of Russian, not enough to understand what Carss was saying but enough to positively identify the language. By now Lemang's pursuit plane was alongside Carss's cabin plane and North could see the director-producer shouting into a hand mike, his swarthy face twisted with rage and fear. Beyond Carss slumped a figure that must be Hans Bracht. Hugh could make out the second man's head drooping against his chest. The report had been that Bracht had appeared doped at the airfield; now he was unconscious. Or dead.

Carss stopped talking to Hanoi. There was a wait of a few seconds and Hanoi did not reply. Hugh spoke into his microphone. "Carss, you've had it. You've got one chance to stay alive. Turn back to Sisaket and land there. Otherwise you'll be blown out of the air by ground fire and military aircraft. I mean it, Carss. They're waiting for you in Cambodia if you get that far. They're waiting for you in Laos. You can't make Vietminh territory without crossing one or the other. Your Russian friends can't help you, Carss. Turn back."

He waited and his earphones came alive. By this time the faster military plane had shot ahead and above Carss's lumbering ship, and it was as though the Red agent were screaming after them.

"You lie," the director yelled. "You'll never kill Bracht to get me—you know you won't. Oh yes, he's alive—just doped a little. Kill me and you kill him. I'm going through. Don't try to stop me."

220

North said: "Maybe I wouldn't kill you both, but the people up ahead don't know who you're carrying, Carss. To them you're just an unidentified aircraft violating their sky."

Lemang put his ship over and they whizzed back over Carss's plane with what seemed to Hugh to be only inches to spare. Looking back, North saw the Red's ship wobble frantically as it was caught in the downdraft. Carss howled obscenities.

North spoke to the pilot in rapid French over the intercom. "Lieutenant, ask Don Muang to contact Cambodia very quickly. Ask Cambodia to have their nearest antiaircraft batteries send up a couple of rounds, blind. Maybe our friend will see them."

Lemang nodded and switched wave lengths to speak to Bangkok. The reply was terse and emphatic. The lieutenant in the forward seat half turned to grin at Hugh and nod, and the G-2 agent blessed SEATO that bound these little countries so closely together in a pact of mutual co-operation, no questions asked, in any emergency.

Unbidden, Lemang rammed his plane at Carss's again, this time thundering straight at the side of the cabin plane. Hugh's teeth clenched and his breath caught in his throat as they hurtled closer, closer to the fugitive ship. Then, at the last split second, young Lemang pulled up and roared over Carss's back. Again the slower ship fluttered desperately in the backwash.

Now Lemang winged over and came around to fly straight at Carss, head on. Again the hair rose at the back of North's neck. This was a grim version of the teen-agers' reckless game of chicken, played seven or eight thousand feet up and with an inexperienced pilot at the controls of the other ship. Should Carss panic entirely and make one misstep there would be the biggest fireball in the Siamese sky that the jungles below had ever witnessed.

Looking over Lemang's shoulder, Hugh could see Carss at the wheel of his plane, his face wrenched by his terrible fear. He seemed frozen to the controls and so did Lemang as the two ships roared at each other. Another ten seconds, five, and— But then Carss wrenched at the wheel and brought his

221

plane over dangerously tight on one wing as Lemang skimmed past his tail by a hairbreadth.

Without Hugh's order, Lemang switched the colonel's receiver back onto the Hanoi wave length. Carss was screaming his split-voiced terror.

"For Christ's sake, do you want to kill yourself? Nobody wins if we all go down!"

"You've lost already, Carss," Hugh flung back. "Tell your boss in Hanoi you did your worst and you still flunked out. How are they going to like it in Moscow when they hear the story? If you'd played it right you could have made it seem as though Bracht defected to communism, but this way —why, hell, man, every country in this part of the world is listening in on what's going on! You're not going to get through, but even if you did there'd be a stink that would carry up to the UN, and how would your bosses like that?"

He went onto receiving. ". . . damn your soul to hell! I've got nothing to lose anyway. I'm going through."

"Ahead, to your left, *mon colonel*," Lemang said rapidly. North veered his eyes in time to see a black puffball, another, a third, dot the sky far ahead of them. He spoke to Carss as the Thai aircraft did another wingover and headed back at the director.

"Look ahead, Carss," he ordered. "See those bursts? They're just warning shots, but they prove they're waiting for you in Cambodia. Do you want to try for Laos? Have you got enough gas left to get there? Even if you have, they'll give you the same reception—gunfire that'll rip you apart."

"If I've lost I've got to die anyway," Carss said, and now he had lost his screech; in its place was a whine. "I might as well take Bracht with me."

"But to be shot down, Carss!" Hugh cried. "The fire! The drop, down and down! Out of control! The flames around you and your ship going down, spinning! To die by fire is a terrible thing, Carss! Ever seen anybody who's been burned to death? Their bodies are black with great split places and—"

He saw Carss's mouth shouting words into his mike as

the faster plane shot past the cabin job. He went over to receiving in time to hear Carss yell: "Gimme a break! If I turn back what will you do for me?"

"I won't have anything to do with it," Hugh North replied. "That will be up to Thailand. I know what you'd get in the United States, but Thailand might give you a better deal. Land Bracht safely and you won't have his death to answer for. A lot of the pressure will be off when you surrender Bracht safely."

By now the military plane was some five miles away from Carss's ship. It was an eerie sensation to Hugh, talking to a man as though at gunpoint, trying to convince him to surrender, when both he and Carss were crisscrossing the sky thousands of feet above the earth, sometimes brushing wing tips, sometimes so far apart that North had trouble finding the other ship in the haze, and yet the Red agent's voice muttered now in his ear, so close.

"Wallen and his goddamn interfering—he ruined everything."

Lemang whirled his aircraft over and started back at Carss. The director-producer saw the pursuit plane plummet down at him, and the swarthy Red agent's nerve cracked at last.

"All right, all right!" he howled. "I quit. I give up. Keep that wild man off me—I can't fly a plane that well. He'll kill us all."

Before North could give a signal to the young pilot Lemang gave the other plane a brushing swoop and peeled off. As he turned for a repeat, North spoke rapidly over the intercom.

"That will be enough, my friend. Our man says he will go back."

Lemang nodded delightedly and turned toward Sisaket. "We'll let him land and perhaps he will make a run for it," the lieutenant told the colonel. "It has been a long time since I have fired my wing guns and they need clearing."

"Clear them if he runs or makes a move to harm the person in the plane with him," Hugh said crisply, "but don't shoot him otherwise."

223

Anton Carss, however, made no attempt to escape at Sisa-ket. While Lemang wheeled his plane in a wide circle over-head, the Red agent brought his plane in for a rough landing, bounced across the field, and plunged the nose of his ship into a tangle of bamboo thicket at the far end of the runway. The Thai pilot swooped low over the grounded plane, zoomed, and came back.

Carss was out of the plane by that time. Hugh North saw the pudgy director take a few staggering steps and then collapse to the ground in a lump. Hans Bracht remained inside the plane.

"Down—*vite!*" North said sharply.

Lemang brought in the pursuit plane with a fishtailing swoop, touched smoothly, and raced across the field to within twenty-five feet of Carss's aircraft. The wheels of the military plane had barely stopped turning when Hugh had his helmet off, the canopy back, and was over the side, run-ning toward Carss with his gun in his hand.

Carss turned a greenish-gray face up toward the colonel as Hugh reached him. The director tried to sneer, but it was a sad attempt and short-lived. Anton Carss's last shred of control vanished as he blubbered: "It was such a good plan but it all went wrong—*it all went wrong!*"

"They have a way of doing that for people like you," North said. "Maybe that's our biggest hope—that Somebody or Something sees to it that they do go wrong."

CHAPTER **8**

"WILL be sorry to see you leave Thailand, Colonel North," Captain Pokh said wistfully. "Most excitement since the war. Now you go, everything back to ho-hum. But I guess you glad to take doctor home, hey?"

"Very glad," Hugh ´ said heartily, "especially since he's going home under a small army of security guards."

The little captain cast a glance at the connecting door between Room 437 and 439. "How he taking it?" he asked in a low voice. "How does he like finding out his wife no good, playing Carss's game?"

"He's taking it very well, considering," Hugh replied. "Of course it was a shock, but—well, Tao Muong was long on beauty but short on brains, a movie-struck girl, and if Bracht can forgive her as he has I guess we all can. Perhaps she didn't actually realize what she was doing, making those tapes for Carss that nearly landed her husband in Communist hands."

"So she not kidnaped at all in beginning, hey?"

"No. According to that part of Carss's full confession—"

"How he do all this talking, Colonel?" Pokh interrupted. "Thought Red agents die with sealed lips."

"Carss is in a terrific bind," North explained. "He messed up one of Moscow's most important plots after convincing the Reds that his plan was foolproof. The Commies don't like agents who fall down on the job. Carss's life wouldn't be worth a tical if he was turned loose tomorrow. His only hope is that your government will give him a prison sentence instead of the rope or the firing squad, and toward

225

that end he's telling everything he knows, hoping his information will be worth a stay of execution."

"He don't know Thai prisons very well," Pokh said grimly. "He seems strange agent for Reds to choose for this job."

"Carss *says* the Reds have members of his family as hostages and they forced him to work for communism in Hollywood. He *says* he's always hated communism."

"You believe this?" Pokh asked.

"No," North said briefly. "But getting back to Tao Muong, Carss says she set the whole thing in motion herself. First she wrote to John Wallen, her movie idol, sending her picture and asking him to get her into the movies, offering to do anything. Wallen showed the letter to Carss, his director, as a joke. You see, Wallen didn't know who Tao Muong Bracht was, but Carss did; he knew a lot about Hans Bracht, as did every Commie agent in the United States, naturally."

"And Carss told her to come to Hollywood?"

"No, he sent her a letter on studio stationery and signed Wallen's name, offering her Hollywood with a fence around it and enclosing a plane ticket. He was careful to say that if she had any *relatives* who objected to her having a screen career she could forget the whole deal. He knew she'd never give up this chance and he had a hunch she'd run away from Bracht, being sure Bracht wouldn't say yes. The hunch paid off. Tao Muong ran away to Hollywood."

Captain Pokh nodded. "What happen then?"

"Carss met her plane, explained Wallen was on the set, took her to his home, and made his proposal. Tao Muong knew he was a great director and she listened. Carss told her that if she wanted to be a second Marilyn Monroe she'd have to make these tapes he'd rehearse her in. Never mind what the tapes were for, did she want to be a star or not? She decided she did. She made the tapes."

"But don't Carss take big chance? What if Tao Muong say no and tell police?"

North said grimly, "Tao Muong was doomed the minute she walked into Carss's house. If she refused to make the

226

tapes, she died. And when she agreed and made the tapes, she died."

Captain Pokh clucked his tongue and shook his head dolefully. "Too bad," he murmured. "Poor Dr. Bracht."

North nodded silently and went on with his packing. Beyond the connecting door came sounds of Hans Bracht, similarly engaged. The great man had borne the shock of his experience, his heart-rending discovery of Tao Muong's death and her role in this plot, with remarkable fortitude. Now, although his face still was rigid with grief and disillusionment, he seemed to North to be putting everything behind him but the need to get back to Project Galaxy, and that was as it should be.

"How John Wallen mixed up in this so he killed too?" Pokh asked.

"Wallen had a side line of blackmail," North explained. "Somehow, personally or through a fellow snoop, he found out that Tao Muong was at Carss's house. He investigated and found it was true; he even managed to see Muong alone and talk to her, found out who she really was. You see, Wallen was Muong's hero; she thought he had brought her out to Hollywood and naturally she would spill everything to him. Wallen was confused, but he knew this would make good blackmail material. But when he went back to get more dope on Carss, Tao Muong wasn't there. The tapes were finished and she was gone. Carss has told us where the body's buried, incidentally. Down near La Jolla.

"Wallen lay low, waiting for the chance to put the big bite on Carss. When he found out that a supposed G-man was in Bangkok, interested in something connected with Hans Bracht—Ross told him that, you know—Wallen figured it was time to move. He went to Carss and told him what he knew, asked for money plus the starring role over Lita to keep quiet. Carss told him to go to hell, and when Wallen threatened to lower the boom—talk—he knew he had to kill Jack. Which he did, the first chance he got after that party."

"With Misser Ross's knife."

"Yes, he used that convenient balcony to steal that."

227

The colonel walked to the bureau to lift out a pile of shirts. "You see, Carss had to put up with Wallen, as dangerous as he was, until the company reached Bangkok. To have disposed of Wallen before that would have upset the *Tiger, Tiger!* production plans and Carss had everything set on a certain time schedule. That's why Carss tarried in Hong Kong until Bracht arrived. His schedule, of course, was ruined and when it was kicked over Carss's best laid schemes gang a-gley."

"Pardon, pliss? What is this gang a-gley? Has to do with Miss Hollberg, perhaps?"

"No, she and Chu Hoong were just side issues that kept interfering with this case."

"Carss killed Marchet, certainly?"

"Yes, poor Marchet was doing just what I thought, hanging around Wallen's suite in the belief Bracht was staying there, waiting to make a touch. At least Carss said that when he came out of Wallen's bedroom after knifing Jack there was Marchet in the living room. He'd seen it all, or Carss thought he had, anyway. Marchet escaped, but the Frenchman didn't know which way to turn. He hated the police because they might shut off his drugs. He distrusted me because he thought I was an agent for some international anti-drug agency. He didn't know who to go to, so he went to his room after wandering around, and Carss trailed him there. You know the rest."

He snapped one suitcase shut and started loading a Valpack.

"What about Lex Ross's cut face? That true story he tells?"

"Oh yes. Carss was trying to throw suspicion on anybody handy; he was beginning to feel the strain. That's what made me look him over closely. Why would a director who said he was so worried about his picture voluntarily sic me on one of his own stars? Carss had had Lita go to Lex's room and stage that scratching incident as soon as he got back to his suite from killing Marchet. You see, he'd taken a couple of scratches himself climbing out of that window, but the cuts were on his shoulders where we couldn't see

228

them. Carss wanted Lex's scratch where it could be seen easily, so off went Lita to do the job."

Pokh's eyebrows expressed his amazement. "How Carss get Lita to do that?"

"God knows, I don't," North admitted. "He had a great hold over Lita, more than we realized. He says she just did everything he told her to unquestioningly. Anyway, he cooked his goose with me when he told me to ask Lex about the scratched face, a scratch Lex might have gotten from Marchet's broken window. How did Carss know about Marchet's window unless he'd been there?"

Pokh nodded admiringly. "Who is this Walter Wells I overhear you speak to Carss about?" he asked.

"At one time, when he was mixed up with a society pinko group years ago, it was Lex Ross. Later, after Ross left the Commies, the Reds gave the same Party name to Anton Carss. It's a new trick of theirs; when a comrade deserts they give his Party name to another agent in the same field. Then, if the real agent is traced by his Party name, the trail sometimes leads to the reformed comrade and he has one hell of a job clearing himself, delaying the chase after the real agent."

"A little mixed up," Pokh said dubiously.

"It takes some figuring," North acknowledged. "It damned near threw me off completely. Ross had told me he once had been a Commie known as Walter Wells. When I queried Washington they told me Walter Wells was still a dangerous active agent. For a while I thought Ross was the Red running this show."

"Speaking of Ross, he is in clear altogether, hey?"

"Entirely—and a damned brave patriot in his interfering way."

North buckled a strap on the Valpack and moved it from the bed to the floor near the door. "Maybe Ross did more than he'll get credit for. When Carss saw Ross masquerading as Bracht it bothered him. How was he going to be sure he got the right man? So he decided to speed up his schedule. His original plan was to smuggle Bracht out of Bangkok to Sara Kaeo in a packing case on one of the trucks

229

or maybe a railroad car. At Sara Kaeo he had a Commie pilot ready to fly Bracht to Hanoi. He knew Bracht would co-operate in hopes of getting Tao Muong back. What he didn't know was that Bracht was getting more and more sensible. He was starting to co-operate with me, beginning to realize that this whole kidnaping deal was probably a trap to get him.

"Back to Carss; after he sent me to Ross he used Muong's final tape to phone Bracht and have her voice tell the doctor to do what Carss said, ask no questions, and they'd be together before another day had passed. He went to Bracht's room—your plain-clothes man had been slugged by an Imperial porter whom we have, by the way—and when the doctor put up an argument Carss slugged *him* and gave him a needle.

"We don't know yet how Carss got Bracht out of the hotel to the car that took him to the private airport, but he did it somehow. The rest, the chase and Carss's final crackup, I've told you."

Pokh's brown eyes glistened. "How I would have loved to be with you. How exciting."

"It was exciting, all right, a little bit too. I hope my next assignment doesn't have a disguise artist, a jewel smuggler, and a dope ring mixed up in it."

"Speak of dope"—the little captain laughed—"Aloysius Robinson has talked so much he has everybody at headquarters tired of listening to him. Big international dope ring all busted, like you say." He lost his grin. "But already black market in Dragon's Tooth Elixir because of expected shortage. That is bad."

The colonel yawned, stretched, and started to build two drinks. "What are you people going to do with Mary Hollberg?" he asked.

"Oh, nothing." Pokh chuckled. "Is like she say, we got no proof of nothing. She going out on plane to Karachi this evening, happy like bride."

"Fine." North nodded. He handed the little Siamese his drink and raised it in a toast. "Thanks for everything you

230

did, Captain Pokh," he said. "I doubt I'll ever forget my Bangkok teammate."

"I never forget you, either!" Pokh beamed. He sipped, then grinned over the rim of his glass.

"One little thing," he continued. "General Genung very upset when I talk with him a minute ago. Big rebuke made to government about noisy Bangkok, all the time shooting, running about, during sleeping hours at hotel. Gentleman says he going to complain to his government about it, sure thing."

"Salenkov?"

"Salenkov." Pokh nodded. "Russian textile commissar turns out to be only Russian textile commissar after all."

"And am I glad we had him," Colonel Hugh North said. "He's the only one who stuck to the script."

STIRRING STORIES OF
GREAT PEOPLE

▶ **ABRAHAM LINCOLN, by Lord Charnwood**

"The most complete interpretation of Lincoln as yet produced..."—*The American Historical Review.* Order C-51 (35¢).

▶ **ANNE FRANK: THE DIARY OF A YOUNG GIRL**

A deeply moving story of adolescence that has become a
classic of our time. Order C-317 (35¢).

▶ **THE AUTOBIOGRAPHY OF BENJAMIN FRANKLIN**

One of the masterpieces of American letters. Order
W-218 (45¢).

▶ **BARUCH: MY OWN STORY**

The fascinating autobiography of Bernard M. Baruch, millionaire, counselor to Presidents, international statesman.
Order GC-52 (50¢).

▶ **THE DOCTORS MAYO, by Helen Clapesattle**

An extraordinary book about three idealistic doctors and how
they built the world-famous Mayo Clinic. Order GC-30 (50¢).

▶ **LOVE IS ETERNAL, by Irving Stone**

The deeply moving love story of Mary Todd and Abraham
Lincoln. Order GC-32 (50¢).

www.ingramcontent.com/pod-product-compliance
Lightning Source LLC
Chambersburg PA
CBHW050514260626
47157CB00004B/1324